THE BLURRED LANDS

IAN W. SAINSBURY

for my sister, Ruth

Copyright © 2018 by Ian W. Sainsbury

All rights reserved.

No part of this book may be reproduced in any form or by any electronic or mechanical means, including information storage and retrieval systems, without written permission from the author, except for the use of brief quotations in a book review.

ONE

John Aviemore could make a coin disappear or reveal the word in someone's mind because he cheated. John knew the coin was in his other hand, or the word someone had glanced at in a book was the only one he had allowed them to read.

Those who watched John perform magic believed they were witnessing the impossible. Like a filmmaker or a writer, he chose what his audience would and wouldn't see. If someone had told him reality worked in a similar way, he would have laughed.

The first of May was when everything unravelled. May Day. A celebration of spring. Green shoots, new life, fresh starts.

John was unmoved by all of it. For the past three years, he had barely acknowledged spring. Last year, it was only when he'd noticed the leaves on the crabapple tree had turned yellow and red that John realised summer had come and gone.

Winter had been easier to accept. Black nights, bleak mornings, overcoats and scarves.

John poured his tea. In the garden, blue tits and finches squabbled over the hanging seeds. He turned his chair to face the interior of the house where some shadows could still be found.

It was three years to the day since Sarah's death.

Three years. He was fifty-one years old, a father and a widower. His son, Harry, was in Los Angeles, trying to run a business, negotiate a divorce, and maintain a relationship with his twelve-year-old daughter. John was glad his son lived so far away although the thought made him feel guilty.

John had the day to himself. He'd lived the past one thousand and ninety-five days, as the bereavement counsellor had advised, one at a time. As if there were another option. He had neither repressed his grief, nor allowed it to prevent him functioning. He had got up in the morning and gone to bed at night. He had continued to invent, and perform, magic tricks. He had eaten healthily.

Over the course of the past thirty-six months, he had cried twice. John had never been one for crying. Even when he'd put his hand flat onto the hot iron at the age of three, he had only sucked his cheeks in and stared at the blistering flesh rather than wailing. John wasn't proud of his lack of emotional display. He wasn't trying to be strong, or 'refusing to engage with his loss', as Sarah's sister had suggested. He just wasn't much of a crier.

Today would be difficult. Twenty-three years of marriage had left their mark. His life was shaped by the years he had spent with Sarah.

John planned to spend the day in town, visiting places that meant something to him and Sarah. Waterloo Road, the theatre near Harrow, Tate Modern.

The day was warm enough not to bother with a jacket.

John waited until after nine, when the trains would be less busy, and walked to Wimbledon station.

His phone buzzed in his pocket. He considered not answering, but it was work.

"John, good morning, I know this is last minute but..."

He let Marco talk. A show, tonight, at the Charleston. They'd asked if John was available. Five times his usual fee. John was ready to say no, then he thought of the empty house.

"Yes, Marco, I'll be there."

If there was a moment when the whole episode began, it was then, when John Aviemore decided he'd rather be working than sitting in a slowly darkening sitting room on the anniversary of his wife's death.

TWO

The Charleston was John's regular gig. On Thursday evenings, he performed close-up magic to hotel and restaurant guests in the bar before and after their meals. Other magicians table-hopped, but John liked to have more control over his performing area. Once he had shown guests one minor miracle, they were invited to his private table and treated to ten minutes of magic. Such was John's reputation that Thursdays were now the hotel restaurant's busiest nights.

Marco called John over when he saw him in the doorway.

"John, thank you for doing this. We need to speak about these people, mm? Come, come."

In the manager's office, Marco perched on the edge of the desk. A small man with a waxed moustache, dressed, as always, in an immaculately tailored three-piece suit, his customary smile was absent. John looked up at the framed photograph of room 112. When Marco had taken over, room 112 hadn't been slept in for years. A small but persistent leak had caused a big brown stain on one wall. The previous owners had tried to repair it three times before giving up. Marco had taken a different approach. He had renamed it the Hemingway Suite and claimed the famous author had stayed there, leaving behind an unpaid bill and a bourbon stain on the wall. 112 now had a waiting list and commanded a higher price than any other room.

"I don't have anything to show you," said John. He was accustomed to starting the evening in Marco's office because the hotelier loved to see John's new tricks first.

Marco waved his hand in the air and shook his head. "These people, this party, mm, the ones who asked for you. They are a little unusual."

Marco tried a smile, but it was a half-hearted effort. "I am embarrassed, John. I am not sure what I want to say to you."

John waited. Marco shrugged and continued. "They, er, they are, well..."

His voice faded, and he looked embarrassed.

"What is it?" said John.

"Oh, nothing, nothing. I am ashamed I feel this way. I thought I had left such nonsense behind."

John waited for Marco to go on.

"I grew up in a small Sicilian village. My grandmother was a very superstitious woman."

Marco's expression darkened, then—as if remembering where he was—he laughed and waved his hand dismissively. "What am I saying? I'm sorry, John, I don't know why I am behaving this way. They are odd, yes, but so what? I iron my socks, who am I to talk, mm? I am sure you will amaze them as you do all our guests. Come."

Marco led John along the corridor to the Bloomsbury

Suite. "Look in on me when you're finished, John. Have a good show."

The hotelier knocked on the door. After a short pause, a voice answered, too quietly for John to hear the words.

Marco stepped back from the door. John turned the handle and walked in.

THREE

The room was much darker than John had expected. None of the lights were on, and the only illumination came from six black candles in holders near the centre of the long table.

Lack of light made some tricks impossible. John began to review which elements of his routine he should disregard and which he should add. As he did this, he stepped further into the room and adopted what Sarah called his sorcerer's smile. She had claimed it was this smile that made her fall for him. John had admitted to many hours in front of a mirror getting it right.

"Too confident, and it's seen as a challenge. Too shy, and it's an invitation to be ignored. Get it right, and it says, this is going to be amazing. Relax, you're in safe hands."

"That's a lot from one smile. How did you get the idea?"

"Doctor Who," admitted John.

He walked to the end of the long table and placed his briefcase in front of him. John was six feet tall, his dark hair flecked with white. His suit was an anonymous black, and he wore a white shirt without a tie. John had the strong hands of a craftsman, and he linked his long fingers together while he spoke.

"Hello. My name is John Aviemore, and I'm here to show you some magic. Three promises before I begin."

The pause after this remark was intentional. It established his control of the room and made anyone filling the short silence look rude.

"One: I will not embarrass or offend anybody. Two: I will lie and cheat. Three: I will show you something impossible, and four—"

He left another pause and waited. When someone pointed out that he had said *three* promises, he could deliver the line, "Didn't I say I would lie and cheat?" The icebreaking laugh that followed would allow him to finish with, "Promise number four is that you will be entertained."

On this occasion, his pause was met with silence.

Four people sat at a table large enough to accommodate ten. In the furthest corners of the room, where the flickering light of the candles couldn't reach, others watched, but in the gloom, he couldn't make out their features.

Ignoring the half-hidden figures at the back of the suite, John concentrated on the two couples at the table. On his left was a woman in a red dress. Her auburn hair was long and loose, covering her bare shoulders. The neckline of the dress plunged nearly to her midriff, and John was careful to keep his eyes on her face. She was beautiful, her skin as white as if she had never seen the sun, her lips pale but full. Her eyes were dark, their colour impossible to determine.

The man to her left was slender, and dressed in a white silk shirt unbuttoned to show as much skin as his companion. His head was shaved smooth, his eyes deep-set and fixed on John.

Their companions were more conservatively dressed.

The man wore an olive greatcoat, but it must have been tailor-made for him. He was head and shoulders taller than anyone John had ever seen. His straggly hair was unbrushed and hung halfway down his broad back. His beard was similarly generous. His partner was so much his opposite, it almost seemed a joke. The size of a ten-year-old child, her fine, night-black hair was crowned with a gold circlet. Her nose was snub, her lips thin, and the skin on her neck translucent. John fancied he could see the blood moving through the veins beneath. Her dress was a sleeveless green slip.

John began his first effect, allowing the familiar rhythm of speech, misdirection, and manipulation to calm his nerves. He had played to every kind of audience, from coldly dismissive to wildly enthusiastic. He'd never had a reception like this, though. The silence, the attention on his face rather than his hands. The shadowy figures at the back of the room.

"In times gone by," he began, "magicians, or conjurors, were considered to be con-artists, thieves, or, worse still, devil-worshippers. To be fair—"

John took a cigarette paper from a packet and crumpled it between his finger and thumb—"that description was, mostly, accurate. Conjurors were little better than beggars, using their art to extract a few coins from their audience. If the tips weren't good enough, there was always an accomplice working the crowd, picking their pockets, cutting the drawstrings of purses and stealing their contents."

John took a small, ornate Japanese fan from his back pocket and, tossing the crumpled paper into the air began to wave it expertly, keeping the paper floating a few inches above.

"However," he continued, "occasionally, a magician

would prove to be neither a petty criminal or a practitioner of the dark arts. Such a conjuror might be noticed by the court of a king or queen and rise to a position of prominence."

John had timed his patter perfectly. The cigarette paper had filled with air and now resembled an egg. As it should, since John had substituted the skin of a boiled egg for the paper, which he had concealed in the fold of skin between his thumb and forefinger. The next few actions took place in under five seconds, and John's every move was decisive and forceful, in direct contrast to his soft-spoken delivery.

"The magician just had to impress—"

His right hand snapped the fan closed, and at the exact moment of the snap, his left hand came up with a real egg, seeming to grab the inflated egg skin out of the air.

"—the right people."

Tossing the fan into his briefcase along with the egg skin, John leaned across the table and swept up the tiny woman's empty water glass. With a well-practised motion he cracked the egg into the glass. The traditional conclusion of the effect was the appearance of a raw egg, but John had added his own touch. A miniature bird, as colourful as a parrot, whirred upwards out of the glass and took to the air in a blur of red, blue, and green. It hovered in front of him like a hummingbird. He slid a net from his right-hand jacket pocket. The clockwork mechanism gave him between five and seven seconds, and John looked for the moment when the bird's beak dipped. He brought the net forward when he saw it, and the bird dropped into it. He pulled the lever on the handle with his forefinger, and swapped the bird for a handful of colourful glitter, which showered the table when he punched his fist into the net, his hand concealing the bird.

The cloud of glitter dropped to the table, looking more magical than ever in the candlelight.

The Egg Of Paradise had been John's opening effect for five years. It was so elegant, and the finale so beautiful, that it had brought guests back to the Charleston, dragging friends along after them, begging to "see that thing with the bird."

It was a guaranteed crowd pleaser. Or it had been. Not tonight, not for the party in the Bloomsbury Suite. After a few seconds of silence, they applauded awkwardly, as if it were a custom they were unused to.

John had an urge to bolt for the door, leaving his briefcase and his professional reputation behind. Then he remembered Sarah. After one of his first gigs as a professional magician, he had sat on the end of the bed, waiting to tell her how scared he'd been, and that he wasn't good enough. She had rolled over, murmuring, "I'm so proud of you." He had decided to give it another month. That had been over a quarter of a century ago.

Tonight, he stood his ground. He continued his act with steady hands, his voice firm and his smile in place, despite the instinct to run.

The show was shorter than usual, but John put that down to the lack of response from his audience.

There was something wrong in this room, and John's instincts told him he was in danger. Not violent, bone-breaking danger; something less tangible but just as serious. He kept his mind on what he was doing, ignoring his rising heart rate. He was going to stay in control. He always stayed in control.

John skipped his sponge ball routine and hurried through his version of Cards Across. His small audience's reaction continued to be off-puttingly unpredictable..

When he borrowed a bread roll to use as an impromptu floating ball, he noticed all their food was untouched, their cutlery still clean. Wine had been poured, but left untasted. Instead, each couple passed a flask between them and sipped from that.

John finished with a floating ten-pound note, changing it into a fifty as he plucked it from the air. By this time, he was ready for their lack of response. He bowed anyway.

"I hope you enjoy the rest of your evening." John's voice sounded distant to his own ears. The sense of danger was stronger. He swallowed, scooping props into his briefcase. They were just odd people, that was all. No law against it. He clicked the case shut with shaking fingers. Would he be able to make himself walk the ten feet between the table and the door? Or would he run?

He looked up as the observers at the back moved, strange creatures emerging from the gloom like a nightmare. A face with too many teeth smiled at John, revealing a second set behind the first. Another figure unfolded as it approached, each step adding to its height until it had to stoop under the ceiling. A monstrous worm insinuated itself under the far end of the table, sliding towards him.

Decision made, John ran for the door.

The woman to his right scooped something from her lap and threw it into his face. John shut his eyes as a black cloud of fine dark powder hit his skin.

Everything stopped.

FOUR

John woke up in his own bed, scrabbled for the light and looked at the clock. It was six forty-five. Somehow, he had finished the show and returned home with no recollection of how he'd managed it.

On top of the dresser was a pile of cash. He'd been paid, then. Which meant he'd been to see Marco. No memory of that either.

John had never been much of a drinker. Even in the weeks after Sarah's death, he had avoided the numbing effects of alcohol, preferring to confront the pain head-on. His grief rolled itself into a razor-spined ball that waited for him everywhere. He sliced his hand on it as he opened the curtains, it slid its sharp points into his lower back when he sat down to work. At night, it unfurled itself inside his skull. While he slept, it was awake, thinking of new methods of torture.

Only once had he attempted to subdue it with a bottle of vodka. He had blacked out, and, rolling on his side to vomit onto the kitchen tiles at five in the morning, he'd found the sharpest kitchen knife in his hand with no memory of how it had got there. After that, he'd stopped drinking for a few months, and he and the spiky ball of grief had come to an accommodation. He acknowledged its constant presence, and it occasionally withdrew its poisonous spines.

But last night, he'd blacked out again. This time, there had been no alcohol involved.

Then there had been the dream. It had begun when the small woman had thrown dust into his face and ended when he woke up at home.

John pushed himself upright, remembering the sights, sounds, and smells of the dream.

He was underwater. No, he was standing upright, but his senses were distorted. He could see the long table in the Bloomsbury Suite, the black candles, the untouched food and the four figures watching him. All sound was muffled, and ripples passed across his field of vision.

He couldn't turn his head, couldn't move his eyes, couldn't even blink. His vision faded.

Soon there was only darkness, and silence.

His thoughts slowed and became confused. He remembered the monstrous creatures that had moved across the room towards him. He knew they must have reached him by now. John was helpless, but he felt no fear. His energy had been sapped, leaving him on the brink of unconsciousness.

Then, at that moment between wakefulness and sleep, balanced perfectly on the tightrope between the two, John found a third option.

He stepped out of his body, seeing himself from outside.

The candles had been extinguished, but he saw the whole room clearly.

The creatures from the shadows moved around him, examining him. Some exuded the threat of violence, others were fearful. None were able to get closer than three feet away from John. If they tried, they gasped or howled with pain.

The nearest beast was the snake-like shape he had seen slide under the table. John couldn't comprehend what he was looking at; if he focused on it, he found himself staring at an old stain on the carpet instead.

There was no such problem with the towering origami creature whose protruding black eyes stared down at him from the ceiling. Its limbs were no thicker than pipe cleaners, its carapace dull metal. A dark, jagged mouth dribbled thick mucus, which hung from its twitching face in long strands, before detaching and dropping.

The creature with too many teeth had stopped short of John and was straining towards him as if held back by an invisible lead. It stood as tall as John's waist and wore old-fashioned blue-striped pyjamas, but this was no child. It was muscled like a pit bull terrier with a similarly truncated neck. The eyes staring from its stubbled face were so red they appeared to be full of blood. The thick head kept jerking forward, and John couldn't take his eyes away from the sight of that mouth opening, widening until it reached the sides of the thing's face, the two layers of teeth within biting and jabbering, grinding and clacking.

John saw bare-breasted women, coarse hair covering muscular legs that ended in cloven hooves. There were obese twins, naked and hairless, laughing and pointing. An old woman sat in one corner, looking incongruous in a tartan skirt, white blouse and pastel pink cardigan, until John looked at her knitting, which glistened as the needles moved. The bag at her feet said WOOL on it in a cartoon font. It was full of entrails.

A man in a brown suit was moving in slow motion,

using a stick. His features were hidden under a wide-brimmed hat and, now that John looked closer, the face beneath was in motion, every pore of his skin wriggling and spasming. Closer still, and John saw it wasn't a man at all, but a colony of ants, millions of them working together to produce this person-shaped illusion, the face always unclear as insects scuttled across it, forming part of an ear, then a cheek, the nose, the corner of a mouth, and the neck before disappearing under the shirt collar.

With an effort, John wrenched his attention away from the bizarre set of creatures examining his body and moved closer to his audience. They were arguing.

"She might be right," said the giant, his massive chest lending his voice a commanding resonance. "He might have power of sorts."

"Impossible. But he is well-protected," said the man opposite. He was tall and broad but looked like a child up against the giant. "Surely she cannot believe a human male could ever—"

He was interrupted by one of the giant's enormous fists banging the table in front of him. Every glass smashed, and the untouched food flew off the plates. John caught movement out of the corner of his eye as the snake-like creature slid under the table in search of scraps.

The tiny woman spoke. "What Astarte believes is no concern of yours. I would advise against questioning her wishes."

The red-haired woman shook her head at that. "Our concern is that Astarte has been too long in the cage. Her powers are waning. She failed once. What has changed?"

The giant was on his feet in an instant, his features purple with rage. "SILENCE!" The sound was an express train roar that filled the Bloomsbury Suite. The creatures around John yelped and scurried back to the shadows, the man opposite pushed his chair back from the table. The woman who had provoked the outburst stayed where she was, facing the fury with no outward show of fear. John saw the woman's leg tremble under the table.

The huge man spoke into the silence. "If you speak of Astarte, you will speak of her with respect, or I will—"

"You will what, dear?" *His tiny, dark-haired companion was looking up at him coolly.* "We all seek the same prize. Sit down."

To John's surprise, the giant looked at the diminutive woman, nodded, and sat down.

None of what they said made any sense. John lost track of the conversation although he was sometimes the subject of their discussion. Reality had become slippery, and he was finding it hard to remain focused on what was happening.

The smaller woman looked at him. For a moment, John was certain she could see his second body, his astral body. Even as he remembered the word astral, *John dismissed it. For a man who made his living creating the illusion of magic, he had no time for crystals, tarot cards and spirit animals. Even in a dream, any hint of new age mumbo jumbo irritated him.*

The woman was still looking at the place where his astral body eavesdropped on the four of them. Her eyes narrowed for a moment, then she turned to the rest of her party.

"He carries the blood. She has found a way of using him."

The giant nodded, his massive fingers combing through his beard. "The Warden spoke of this. As did his father."

The man in the silk shirt seemed bored. "Don't tell me we are to give credence to the Wardens? They are so corrupted, they might as well be human themselves. Their theory is laughable."

"Perhaps," said the dark-haired woman. "But Astarte wants him, so perhaps not."

"The line continues," said the woman opposite her. "His son has a daughter."

The giant sighed, a long, low sound like an autumn wind through a pile of dead leaves.

"Enough talk," he said. "We must make sure he enters the Blurred Lands again."

The other man shrugged. "Very well. I hope she is right this time. Our hand might be seen in this if the Adept or the Warden look for it."

The giant shook his head. John could have sworn he saw living creatures scurry about in that scraggly beard and thick hair.

The small woman responded. "Don't forget the curse: proof, if you needed it, of Astarte's power. And the Warden is distracted by the imminent death of his Adept. I will ensure the human reaches the Lands."

If there was more discussion among this bizarre group, John didn't hear it. His vision was dimming, and the surrounding sounds were becoming muffled and indistinct.

Finally, there was only silence, darkness and a sensation of floating.

John realised his eyes were tightly shut. With an effort, he opened them and saw a familiar ceiling, the lampshade over his head one that he and Sarah had found in an antique market in Camden Lock a decade earlier.

Hallucinations, paranoia. Oh God, was it happening again?

FIVE

Room 38
Fir Trees Care Home
Elstree, London

Evie, my darling great-granddaughter,

If you're reading this, then I am dead. I can't tell you what a thrill it is to write those words. I feel like a character in a Victorian bodice ripper. You don't know what I'm talking about, do you? This is the most important letter of my life, but I'm already straying from the point. Sorry.

As I'm writing this, you're twelve years old. Twelve-and-a-half as I'm sure you'd insist on pointing out. Depending on when, precisely, I breathe my last, you might read this while you're still a child.

So I need to get your attention. Set out my stall.

I know your dreams.

Before you think your great-granny has lost her mind, read on...

When you were small, I planted a dream in your sweet little head. I gave it enough charm (and I don't mean that in the sense you imagine) to make it adhere, and enough power to ensure it would recur. In fact, I may have gone a little over the top. I wouldn't be surprised if you still dream it now.

You're walking in a forest. (You might have thought of it as a fairytale forest, growing up as you did in Los Angeles, which is not renowned for its wooded groves.) You don't know the names of the trees, but there are oak, ash, elm, poplar, plane, horse chestnut, and pine among them. You are surprised, perhaps a little frightened, by the size of the leaves and twigs around you. They are so large that you struggle to fight your way through them. Then you discover you can fly, rise above them, and head for the sky. But you don't fly like most people do in dreams, you fly with pulsing beats of your tiny wings, brown blurs at the edges of your vision. You know you are a bird now, and you rejoice in your freedom, seeking your sisters in the treetops. You see many birds on branches, singing out to you as you pass, and you answer them with your happiest song.

You keep flying up because you can hear the most beautiful birdsong imaginable. Clear, trilling notes full of the sheer joy of being alive reach you from somewhere in the uppermost branches of the forest. When you get to the top branch of the tallest tree, you see a single bird waiting for you; a tiny, insignificant brown bird, its beak wide open, singing. You land alongside her and listen to that wonderful song, which tells you many secrets. Then, too quickly, the song is over. The bird looks right at you, and you know this wise little creature loves you. She opens her beak one last time and, quite distinctly, says your name. *Evie.*

Right. I imagine the above has, as the young people

probably don't say any more, freaked you out. How was it possible for me to create a dream?

I will answer that question, and many others. I have arranged to have these letters sent on to you when I die. Read them carefully.

I do not have the luxury of time. I no longer believe there is much chance of my being alive when you need me. We were supposed to meet again, you and I, next year. No power on Earth could have prevented that meeting. Unfortunately, the virus eating my mind did not originate on Earth. And so, you may learn of our family secret before you are mature. This, let me be perfectly clear, is very dangerous. But it is far less dangerous than the alternative.

Doubtless, you will find it odd being addressed thus by a dead woman you have probably forgotten. You will have to become accustomed to the odd, the weird, and the unbelievable.

I shall have a nap, then resume. Naps are something else I need to tell you about. They are important, and they're not just for old ladies.

Oh, just in case you didn't realise, I was the bird who sang your name, Evie.

Mae.

SIX

John walked the mile from Waterloo to Bonneville's, expecting the fresh air to diminish the effect of the Bloomsbury Suite show and the dream. He navigated the London streets as if he still hadn't quite woken up, his mind going over the previous night.

He called Marco on the way.

"Ciao John, great job last night. They were very happy with you. Very drunk, too. I hope they didn't give you too much of a hard time."

John stopped in an alleyway and put his hand on the brick wall as he spoke. "Marco, did you see me before I left?"

"Yes, to pick up your fee. You weren't drinking too, were you? Did they share the champagne? They got through a case and a half. More money than sense, mm?"

"But what about what you said in the office? About them being odd. What did you mean?"

Marco didn't answer immediately and, when he did, his tone was concerned. "I just told you they were a bunch of rich, drunk brokers. Nothing odd about that. Listen, John, are you okay?"

John leaned up against the wall. He said something about his hearing giving him problems, made an excuse and ended the call.

At the door of the magic shop, he stood outside, his thoughts straying to the dark-haired woman who had thrown dust into his face.

When had he blacked out? When did the evening at the Charleston Hotel stop and the dream begin? Marco had no reason to lie to him. Was it all in his head?

"Dreaming your life away, my boy?"

"Augustus," said John, and stepped forward to embrace the old man.

"Come on in, John," said Augustus Bonneville, "and tell me all about it."

Bonneville's had stood in the same small side street just off The Strand since the golden days of magic, when David Devant and Nevil Maskelyne ran their own theatre dedicated to the art.

The ten-year-old John Aviemore had purchased his first set of cups and balls from Augustus. The old man had demonstrated the ancient trick with such grace and beauty that John had decided, there and then, to become a magician. In a rare moment where he overcame his natural shyness, he had announced his intention. His father had smiled and said nothing, but the old man—and he had seemed just as old back then to John—had given a tiny nod of approval.

"I am going through what I can only describe as a Lapsang Souchong obsession," said Augustus, as he waved John through to the rear of the shop. As always, John slowed down as he passed through the Aladdin's cave of Bonneville's, its shelves stacked high with mysterious boxes, floor-to-ceiling glass cabinets full of playing cards, coins, linking rings, floating balls, appearing canes, dove pans, and faded old boxes.

"Anything new?" said John as he followed Augustus. The older man laughed dutifully. Amateur and professional magicians alike were magpies in disposition, ignoring the hundreds, or thousands of tricks they already owned in favour of pursuing the newest, shiniest effect on the market.

"Perhaps, perhaps. Have I shown you the one when you pick a card at random, and I divine its identity?"

John shook his head, chuckling. Just being around Augustus made him feel better.

This morning, John wasn't there to discuss tricks or gossip about the latest attempt to get magic back on television. He wanted Augustus to help him make sense of the previous evening.

Stravinsky's Rite Of Spring, one of the old man's favourites, was playing in the small back room. Augustus limped over to turn it down. One night, very late, after a few cognacs, Augustus had said something strikingly odd about Stravinsky. "I miss real music, but Stravinsky gets closer than most. He must have visited the Lands or lived close by." When John had asked what he meant, the only reply had been a soft snore. There was a beautiful hand-carved recorder on a shelf, but John had never heard Augustus play it.

Augustus poured the tea and sat opposite John.

Augustus Bonneville was five-foot-five in his platform shoes. If he were to flatten the white hair that surrounded his skull like a cloud, that would be reduced to five-foot-two. His thin face was heavily lined, and his eyebrows were magnificent. He looked like a man who knew things ordinary people didn't. He looked like a real magician.

And yet, when he stepped outside the shop, his hair

pulled under a cloth cap, he could be as anonymous as the next person hurrying along the pavement.

"You're not here to talk business, are you?" Augustus put a china cup full of dark, pungent liquid in front of John. If Augustus was currently drinking Lapsang Souchong, everyone who visited Bonneville's would be expected to do the same. John took an experimental sip, and concluded that, if it were an acquired taste, he didn't plan acquiring it.

Augustus brought his own cup over and sat down. He made two trips because his right arm was withered and useless, a result of the same explosion that caused his limp. Augustus had no memory of the accident.

"No, Augustus, I'm not. I'm—" John was unsure where to start his description of last night. Marco's odd behaviour? The strange audience, who neither ate nor drank? The shadowy creatures at the back of the room?

He would tell Augustus everything and see what he made of it. He sipped some tea, regretted it, and cleared his throat. Perhaps he'd start with the easy stuff.

"Marco booked me for a corporate gig at the Charleston. Really well paid. I wasn't going to do it, because, well..."

"Three years since Sarah died," said Augustus. He didn't follow up with an expression of sympathy. He didn't have to. John had been thirteen when his father had died, and the old magic shop proprietor had been the only steady male presence in his life ever since.

"Yes."

He had fallen silent, so he tried another sip of tea. It was now cold as well as disgusting.

"Tell me about the show," said Augustus.

John described Marco's odd pep-talk before the gig, the uncharacteristic nervousness of the hotel manager. Then he moved on to the occupants of the suite. That was when the morning became as strange as the night before.

"There were two couples," he said. "Brokers, I think. They were celebrating some big trade they'd made."

He stopped. What was he saying? That was the same story Marco had given him. He visualised the room from the evening before. The table, the black candles, the provocative red-haired woman and her sensuous companion, the giant and the elfin woman by his side.

"Typical crowd, really. Young, loud, trying hard to impress each other."

John stopped again. He tried to choose the right words in his mind before saying them. He repeated to himself, *one of them was a giant, one of them was a giant.*

"One of them was really drunk," he said, the words and sentences forming of their own accord. "The champagne had been flowing for a while by the time I got there, and it was hard to get their attention. I went through the motions, didn't give it my best. I was glad to get paid and go home."

Augustus was looking at him sharply. "John. You know I'm always delighted to see you, but did you really come all the way here to tell me that?"

No, thought John.

"Yes," he said aloud.

"Oh," said Augustus. "Well, I'm sure you were the consummate professional, and they got their money's worth. Now then, I have news of my own."

John smiled, despite wanting to jump and scream that he had lost control of his mind, that he was saying things he didn't intend to say. Apparently, it only happened when he tried to talk about last night's performance and dream. He tested his theory.

"Marco said something about superstition before I went

into the room. He was scared of something." It seemed he could speak freely of events that had occurred just before he entered the Bloomsbury Suite.

Augustus still had that sharp look. "And yet it was just some drunk city types? Nothing out of the ordinary?"

John tried one last time, determined to tell Augustus the truth. The creatures, the dust in his face, the seamless transition to the strangest dream of his life. The way he'd been able to leave his own body.

"Nope. Nothing at all," he said. "What's your news?"

"I'm going away," said Augustus. "An old friend needs me. I was going to pop by tonight, but you've saved me a trip. I might be gone a week or two."

John felt a mild twinge of panic. Augustus had never gone away for so long.

"I don't suppose you've reconsidered your stand on mobile phones?"

"The devil's work," said Augustus. "I'll have my post forwarded. Write to me here if you need anything." He stepped forward and shook John's hand. "Take care of yourself, my boy." He paused, as if tempted to add something, then shook his head. He placed his other hand on top of John's. His skin was, as always, cold.

"Take care," he said again.

On the walk back to Waterloo, John spent the first twenty minutes going over what had just happened. He might be able to persuade himself that last night had been some sort of fluke - a break in consciousness and a vivid dream brought on by overwork, and his grief on the third anniversary of Sarah's death. He didn't believe it, but at a pinch, he might accept it as an explanation. But that couldn't explain the past hour. He was wide awake on a cool May morning in London, and he'd just had a conversation with his oldest friend during which his lips moved and said words without his consent. Which meant what, exactly? He was having another breakdown after all this time? Either that or fantastical beings from some dark fairytale had cast a spell on him.

John wasn't keen on either diagnosis. He would think about it later. Maybe see a doctor. He knew that's what his son would advise. But, as he couldn't even say the words to describe what had happened to him, he didn't see how medical expertise would be of any help.

Maybe a change of scene. A holiday.

By the time he opened his front door, he had decided a city break might do him good. Berlin had a magic shop he'd never got around to visiting.

He scooped up the junk mail on the mat and took it through to the kitchen, dropping it on the table. Then he saw it. Underneath a flyer for the church fete, a heavy cream envelope, and his name written in fountain pen across it.

John knew the handwriting. Burning the woman's letters three decades earlier hadn't destroyed the memory of how she wrote his name. Back then, seeing *John Aviemore* written in her hand had made his chest hurt. It was hurting now, but for very different reasons.

He had to sit down before trying to open it and, when he did, his fingers trembled. He slid the letter out, opened it, and began to read.

SEVEN

The contents of the letter made no sense to John at first. He forced himself to slow down and start again.

He looked at the envelope.

Looking at that familiar writing three decades on, he felt that old knot in his gut. He was twenty again, believing himself to be in love. What he had really been experiencing was lust, of course, but lust in such an intense, unfiltered, form that it was as distinct from his previous fumbling relationships as heroin was from a sip of shandy.

The knot in his gut shifted like a coiling snake.

He was momentarily angry with himself. First, this inability to speak of his experience in the Bloomsbury Suite. Now, an adolescent reaction to a lover whom he hadn't seen for thirty years.

The single piece of headed notepaper was typed, and signed by the same name printed at the top right, a Tobias Hackleworth. Mr Hackleworth was writing from the firm of Stinder Hackleworth regarding the estate of one Ashleigh Zanash. Mr Aviemore was requested to attend their offices at his convenience to discuss a significant bequest.

The address was only a few miles away across town.

Without thinking too hard about what he was doing, John called a taxi, picked up the letter and his keys, and went outside. Four minutes later, he was in the back of a cab, reading the letter for the third time and trying to stop his hands shaking.

Ash was dead.

The offices of Stinder Hackleworth were on the third floor of a tall, narrow building that hunched out over the cobbled street below. Tiny lead-lined windows dotted its half-timbered facade, and a multitude of house martins' nests crammed into its eaves. This accounted for the strip of cobbles in front of the building turned white by bird shit.

John checked above before skipping across the danger zone and up the three stone steps.

There was no buzzer. John pulled the brass handle hanging in front of the black door. He heard no corresponding bell from within, and he pulled it again. Still nothing. According to the sign, the first floor was occupied by Fishermust, a cartographer, the second by Boddinbrokes Bookbinders. The floor above the solicitors was referred to as The Empty Room, and someone had gone to the trouble of engraving a brass plaque to announce it. A larger sign stated, in black letters on white, Noone House.

Was that *noon* or *no one?*

An imposing black door on such an old building might be expected to open with a long, loud creak. Instead, it swung inwards smoothly and silently. John stepped inside. The ground floor was laid out like an old-fashioned hotel lobby. A huge oak desk dominated the space, sitting in the middle of the room. The black and white diamond flooring looked original, the white of each tile now a faded parchment yellow, and the whole surface covered with dust. A curved staircase with dark wooden balustrades swept up in a clockwise spiral to the floors above.

Four doors led off from the lobby. The closest, on John's left, was open, and music came from within, although it was music of a kind John had never heard before. It was rhythmical, but the beat shifted constantly, making it hard to follow. The melody rose and fell, sometimes going so high he could no longer hear it. At those moments, embarrassingly, he felt the beginnings of an erection.

The music stopped abruptly as a young man slammed the door shut. He looked at John's groin and smiled.

"Music to screw to," he said, and laughed, too loudly. He was unshaven with curly dark hair. Even John knew the navy shell-suit the man wore was twenty years out of fashion. The jacket was unzipped to reveal a vest which may once have been white. The man took a packet of cigarettes out of his pocket and lit one.

"Sign in," he said, pointing at the desk. An enormous old ledger sat there, open at the halfway point. A fountain pen lay across its pages. John picked it up and wrote his name, along with the fact that he was visiting the firm of Stinder Hackleworth. He looked at the fifteen or so entries above his own. They were all out of focus. He squinted and rubbed the bridge of his nose, but it didn't help. His own name was legible, but he couldn't make sense of the others.

The young man leaned against the bannister, taking long drags on his cigarette.

"You know that's illegal in the workplace?" said John, wondering if this man had just wandered in off the street.

"Fuck off," said the man, without any particular malice.

He pointed the cigarette upwards. "Third floor, first door, knock three times."

John walked towards the staircase, trying not to appear intimidated.

Only the presence of a grandfather clock differentiated the second floor from the first. On the third, in place of the clock, there was a long-dead yucca plant.

John raised his hand to knock, then hesitated.

—*Knock three times?*—

John knocked four times, taking a childish satisfaction in his tiny rebellion.

The door opened, and John walked in. He looked down at the black and white tiles, then across to the staircase, the desk, and the open ledger. He was back in the lobby. The unshaven young man took the half-smoked cigarette from between his lips and blew smoke in John's face.

John took a few deep breaths and, like a child in a dream, pinched himself hard on the arm.

The man smirked. "Three times, pal."

John focused his attention on the staircase, ignoring the shell-suit. What he thought had just happened couldn't have happened. He breathed in through his nose and out through his mouth.

On the third floor, he knocked twice.

"We can do this all day," said the young man in the lobby as John passed him for the third time. "But what would be the point, eh?"

John climbed the stairs again, his mind racing to find a rational explanation. If he was having a breakdown, here was further evidence of its progress. And yet, he had never heard of symptoms like these.

This time, when he reached the third floor, he knocked three times.

"Enter." It was a woman's voice, shrill and imperious.

EIGHT

The Stinder Hackleworth office was lit by oil lamps. Although the door was large and imposing, the room behind it shared similar dimensions with a cabin on a cross-channel ferry.

The lamps might be expected to provide ample illumination for so small a space, but, in fact, the opposite was true. Each one gave off a sickly yellow glow that struggled to stretch further than six inches from its source.

Towers of paper further reduced the room's usable floor space, with stacks of yellowing legal documents and folders standing as high as John's chest. He edged forwards into the gloom. There was a desk under a dirt-encrusted window at the end of the room. Behind that desk was a heap of discarded clothing.

"Yes?"

The voice came from behind him. John jumped. The owner of the voice was a little under five feet, but a few inches of her height came from grey hair modelled into a hairstyle he'd only seen in films from the nineteen-sixties. It was a beehive. It looked like an iron oven glove.

"I'm here to see Mr Hackleworth," said John. The beehive did not respond. "Mr Hackleworth?" he repeated, taking out the envelope. "I have a letter."

"What?" she shouted.

"A letter," repeated John, holding it towards her.

"No post," she barked. Her hair moved a fraction of a second after her head. The effect was hypnotic.

"I'm not delivering a letter," he said. "You wrote to me. Mr Hackleworth wrote to me. About a bequest."

She snatched the letter from his hand and inspected the envelope.

"Yes," she screamed.

"Is Mr Hackleworth available?"

The beehive jerked one gloved hand to the side and extended her finger towards the desk.

"There."

After delivering this last volley, she scurried away. When she disappeared behind one of the stacks of papers, her footsteps ceased immediately. She didn't appear on the other side of the stack. John listened, but he couldn't even hear her breathing.

"Mr Aviemore, I presume? Tobias Hackleworth, solicitor, lawyer, barrister, judge, jury, executioner. You know the drill, I'm sure. Good, good, good. Please, take a seat."

A face smiled benignly from the top of the pile of clothes behind the desk.

"Do sit down. I don't shake hands, no, I don't. Forgive my fashion sense, it's just that I feel the cold somewhat. Ironic, for a man of my size, but there it is, there it is."

John realised that the pile of clothes was, in fact, being worn by the fattest man he'd ever seen. The bald face seemed disconnected from the body beneath because his chins and neck were concealed by at least five scarves.

Now that John was closer to the desk, he wondered how Tobias Hackleworth had manoeuvred his bulk behind it. More to the point, how would he get out again? Maybe Hackleworth would eat the desk when it was time to go home.

John found a low stool and perched on it. The seating arrangement reminded him of parent-teacher nights.

"Good of you to come in, Mr Aviemore. We've been wanting to have a look at you, haven't we? see what the fuss is all about, all the palaver, the hullabaloo and suchlike."

Hackleworth leaned forward to get a better view of his visitor. The wooden desk scraped an inch nearer as the enormous belly pressed up against it. When the solicitor snorted, it shot forward and would have knocked John off the stool had he not sprung to his feet.

"Oops a daisy, a dandelion, a buttercup. Apologies, regret and all the rest, I wouldn't be surprised. I shall lean back, Mr Aviemore, please, please, resume your seatedness forthwith. We were hoping to see you at Noone House, and here you are, how marvellous."

John sat down. So it was pronounced *noon* then. At least he'd solved one tiny mystery.

When Hackleworth's stomach hit the desk, John saw that the items of clothing making up his eccentric outfit—hoodies, baby-grows, dungarees—were sewn together with twine.

John pushed back against his growing anxiety. Whatever was happening, whatever was going on with his mind, he just had to make it through the next few minutes. He would find out what had happened to Ash. Then he'd go home and decide what to do about the possible recurrence of a mental illness he'd put behind him in his twenties.

"Mr Hackleworth, I'm here about the bequest." John

swallowed. He hadn't said her name aloud for over thirty years. Names had power. "From Ashleigh Zanash."

Hackleworth's towering bulk shifted to one side and, for an alarming moment, John feared he would lose his balance and fall. At the last second, his hand shot out and grabbed a handle on the wall. John hadn't noticed the handle before. It was heavy brass, blackened by time and oily residue from the lamps.

Hackleworth pulled the handle, revealing a deep drawer. John looked up at the window and saw, dimly, the early afternoon sun above the rooftops. The drawer was emerging from an outside wall. Which was impossible. It was stuffed with files.

"Now, let me see, Zanash, Zanash. Z. Inconsiderate, very inconsiderate picking a name beginning with Z. Suppose she thought she was being clever, or funny. Joke's on you, Miss Zanash, because you're dead, dead, deceased and gone, six feet under and that's that. Right then, A...B...C...D...E..."

As he spoke, Hackleworth pulled the drawer further into the tiny room. It slid out of the wall, past the desk, missed the stacks of paper and continued on its way. In the half-light, John could no longer see the door, but, as the rich voice pronounced, "M...N...," John knew the drawer must have reached the far wall. And yet it continued to emerge.

"Zebulon. Too far. Let me see, where are you? Slippery minx, this one, but we all knew that, did we not? We did, we did, and that's a fact. Here we are."

Hackleworth removed a fat file and dropped it onto the desk. With a practised, powerful flick of his wrist, he pulled the drawer back. It reversed its journey in a blur of speed. When it reached the end of its trajectory, there was a loud bang and a ricochet of dust from the wall.

"Zanash, Ashleigh, late of this parish, born, yes, undoubtedly, or, perhaps more accurately, emerged, certainly, once upon a time; lived her life, since no one else volunteered to do it for her, was cruel, kind, loving, hateful, predictably unpredictable that one, oh yes, yes, indeed. Rumours, speculation, tittle-tattle, all the usual. Not one to be pinned down, hung up, or—dare I say it? I do, I do—beholden to reality, if it didn't suit her, and it rarely did, did it?...here we are, here it is, all is well."

He withdrew an envelope from the back of the file and placed it on the desk.

"Well, Mr Aviemore, there it is, the worldly goods. Could she be said to do any worldly good? I would, in the spirit of charity, want to say yes, yes, and yes, but it would be a falsehood, a travesty, an untruth. So, unhappily, I must say no, if pressed, or—possibly—if unpressed. Still, one never likes to lose a client, even if, well.." He stared up at the ceiling, then back at the envelope on the desk.

John picked it up. "How did she die?"

The mound of clothes moved. It might have been a shrug.

"Nothing is immutable, is it, is it? She of all folk proved that. But here we are, nonetheless. The immutable has been muted, quieted, silenced forever. As to how, I'm afraid I have no answer. Illness, old age, at the point of a poisonous dagger? Who can say? But she remembered you, John Aviemore, yes she did. If I could ask you to sign this, if you please, and all is done, done and dusted, dust to dust, Ashleigh's ashes."

John looked up at Hackleworth's smiling face. There was no antipathy in his bland features.

The document was cryptic, but John had learned to translate the opaque language of the law after Sarah's death.

He was signing to acknowledge the receipt of the bequest, which he could claim by going to the address at the bottom of the paper.

He stared at the address in shock as he realised what the document meant.

The address was familiar to him. He had spent the most intense, unforgettable summer of his life there.

And he'd been mistaken about having to go to the address to claim the bequest. The address *was* the bequest.

Ash had left him the cottage.

NINE

Evie,

I saw them again in my dreams last night. A writhing dark mass of tiny insects, that's what they look like. At least, that's how my mind interprets the attackers. They have been waging war against me for nearly thirty years, and now, they smell victory. Three decades is a heartbeat to their mistress. Still, for all her power, she couldn't take John. My son John, your grandfather. Gosh, I must seem unspeakably ancient to you. I can't tell you how proud I am of your grandfather. I never knew how hard it would be, not telling him who we are. But we share our secrets only with life partners, and with our female successors. That rule has kept us safe for centuries.

I'm getting ahead of myself again. And I'm rambling. I don't know how much of my mental fogginess is due to the natural ravages of old age, and how much is the result of the curse beginning its final assault.

I'm buying a precious few minutes every day to write these letters. A few minutes of clarity. The price is a more rapid crumbling of my remaining defences. If I can finish telling you what you need to know, it will be a price worth paying.

When I was a little older than you, I found out who my mother really was. It happened shortly after my monthly cycle first began. I was fourteen.

We lived in Surbiton in the nineteen-fifties. Father was a bank clerk. Mother cooked, cleaned, looked after my brother Michael and me, and wore pearls in the daytime.

My dreams were the first sign that something was happening. Night after night, I woke up with my hair sticking to my face, my bedclothes twisted around me, as images from my dreams floated away like soap bubbles. I was no prude, Evie, but I was shocked by my nocturnal imaginings. They were awfully disturbing, and there was no one I could talk to.

I certainly didn't consider approaching my mother. I would never have guessed she was the only person I could truly confide in. Until I had a daughter of my own, of course. Sadly, that has been my cross to bear. After your grandfather was born, I was unable to have any more children. It was a cruel blow. I was so excited when John and Sarah announced they were expecting. Terrible to admit, but I was crushed when the baby was a boy. I know I'm speaking of your father, but I will not lie to you about how I felt. Naturally, I came to love Harry in the way only grandparents can. When he found a girlfriend—far too young— and sprung his news upon us, I think he expected me to be angry. His face was a picture when I squealed with excitement. And when you were born—a girl—I cried for a week. Finally, a girl. All would be well.

But I see I have digressed. Back to my mother, silhouetted by the landing light outside my bedroom in nineteen-fifties suburbia.

"Get dressed, Mae," she said. "There's something I need to show you."

This was a time before children questioned their parents. I did as I was told. Downstairs, we both swaddled ourselves in coats, scarves, gloves, and hats. It was midwinter.

The wooded area she took me to was a ten-minute walk away. It overlooked the Thames. If you climbed one of the oaks, you could see Hampton Court Palace Golf Club. When mother led me between the trees, the only sound was the brittle crunch of our wellingtons breaking through the crust of the snow.

Mother stopped in front of an old oak, its frosted branches hanging low. My breath clouded in front of me.

"I was nearly sixteen when it began," she said. "I thought it would be the same with you. I haven't prepared. Perhaps one can never prepare for this."

Her voice was different. It wasn't just the way a voice changes when reflected off ice and snow. I knew not to interrupt. Questions would come later.

She removed her glove, reached out, and touched the bark.

"The roots of this oak spread as deep and as broad as the branches above. We see the trunk, the branches and the leaves. But a hidden world sustains them. Without that world, they cannot exist. Do you understand?"

My voice sounded shrill and weak compared to hers. "Yes," I answered. "I think so."

She turned then, and smiled. Her face had changed. She was still my mother, but... it's hard to explain. Imagine looking at your own mother and seeing not only her, but a line of female ancestors reflected in her face.

Mother spoke again, her voice still full of power.

"Mae, it's time you learned who, and what, you are. My own mother took me away to teach me. We spent hours every night on the border of the Blurred Lands. She woke me before I had rested sufficiently so that I could more easily enter the Between. We don't have that luxury. London is dangerous now, and I cannot leave. You must learn here."

Evie, if you're bewildered by this, imagine how I felt. My mother had always kept her own counsel. A little withdrawn, but not cold. Now I saw the whole woman, and it was simultaneously the most frightened, and the most excited, I'd ever been. I saw the past and the future in her. We members of the Three come as close as humans can to experiencing time like the noones.

Ah, the noones. You need to know about them, too. And the Wardens. So much to tell you. I cannot write much more today. Let me leave you with an image that often returns to me in dreams.

Mother sang a low, soft, note, full of hidden harmonies. It was not a beautiful sound, nor was it ugly. But the breath caught in my throat, and my mind stilled.

She lifted her arms, and a shadow passed between us and the moon.

It was a tawny owl. As I watched it glide, another owl passed overhead, then another. They settled on the branches of the oak. At ground level, another movement attracted my attention. Three foxes were sitting there, one cleaning its paws. A few feet from them, but paying the other animals no attention, two badgers had ambled into position. Other creatures followed until, within a minute of my mother's summoning, she was at the centre of a circle whose perimeter was made up of dozens of nocturnal animals. The moonlight flickered as it fell onto the scene, and I looked up. A thousand moths flew above and, beyond them, a cloud of bats drew spirals.

"Mae," said my mother. "The world doesn't quite work the way you think it does."

Well. The only possible response to that was an expression that hadn't yet been coined, more's the pity.

No shit.

TEN

When his stomach growled at ten o'clock the next morning, John realised he hadn't eaten since lunchtime the previous day. He peeled a banana and ate it in front of the computer. Despite two hours of searching before bed and another hour after breakfast, John had turned up no information about Ashleigh Zanash. The name had returned no results. He tried alternative spellings, used Ash instead of Ashleigh, but eventually conceded defeat.

He also searched for Stinder Hackleworth and wasn't surprised to find nothing about them either. If their office was anything to go by, they didn't even own a typewriter, let alone a computer. Noone House also drew a blank.

John considered the little he knew. At the age of twenty, he and Ashleigh Zanash had embarked upon a brief affair. A fling. A passionate, unforgettable fling, but a fling nonetheless. He remembered the exact shade of her green eyes, so dark, they sometimes seemed black. He remembered the way her copper-tinged fair hair fell across her face. He remembered how he'd been aroused by Ash before he'd even spoken to her - she'd come up behind him and, on tiptoe, her breasts pushed lightly against his back, said, "If I asked you to come home with me, would you do it?"

And, of course, he remembered the sex, of which there had been a great deal. The various encounters had blurred into each other and faded over the years into a melange of fingers struggling with buttons, sweat-slick skin, and the sound she'd made as she pulled him into her.

What he couldn't recall was anything useful, such as what she did for a living, any friends she might have had, which part of the country she came from, whether she owned or rented the cottage.

His memory shied away from their final encounter, the night he broke up with her.

Over the course of five weeks, thirty-two years ago, Ash and John had spent seven nights together. They had never seen each other since.

Why would she leave him the cottage? The bequest made no sense. They were nothing to each other now. Nothing.

John shook his head, spotting the signs that he was trying to deceive himself. The way he'd been utterly consumed by their relationship still frightened him if he was honest. And—even if it had not been the underlying cause—it had been the catalyst for his breakdown.

He turned off the computer. He needed to talk to another human being, not lose himself in disturbing memories.

A year ago, Augustus had installed an answerphone in Bonneville's, so John was treated to an acerbic and mischievous message.

"This is Augustus Bonneville. I have more important things to do than answering the telephone, such as reading, drinking tea, and thinking. If this is an emergency, for goodness sake, call someone else. I'm hopeless in a crisis. By all means, leave a message. I occasionally remember to listen to them."

If Augustus wasn't answering the phone at ten thirty on a Saturday morning, it meant the shop was closed.

"Shit."

John was a pragmatic man. He enjoyed breaking problems down into manageable chunks before taking a methodical approach to solving them. But this wasn't trying to get a sliver of magnet into a toothpick for a vanish, or finding a way to make a pound coin float. All the logic in the world couldn't help him work out how a filing cabinet could pull its contents from thin air, or how knocking four times on a door could transport him from the third floor of a building to the lobby below. As for the creatures in the Charleston, and the fact he couldn't speak of them... how was he supposed to explain that? And now, the bequest from Ash. What was it that came in threes? Good things? Bad things? Buses?

He picked up a picture taken at Harry's wedding in Los Angeles. Sarah was laughing, her head thrown back, and John's expression was one of surprised devotion. He remembered that expression.

He was struggling to keep his attention focused on anything.

Breathe. Just breathe.

The cottage would be worth some money. A detached property just outside Bristol with a wood on its doorstep? He didn't even need to go there. He could put it all in the hands of an estate agent.

That was one reason not to go. But there was another reason. A reason he was avoiding thinking about.

He hadn't been back to Bristol since his breakdown.

Suddenly decisive, he shut down the computer.

A walk on the common, lunch and a pint in the pub, maybe the cinema in the afternoon. That would clear his mind. Tomorrow, he could call the estate agent and put the sale in motion. That just left his disturbed mental state to deal with.

As John picked up his keys, he heard quick, light footsteps coming up the path. He opened the door as the doorbell rang.

A woman in tight jeans and a sleeveless T-shirt, her long blonde hair tied back, jumped and took her finger off the bell.

"Helen."

"John." Helen stepped forward and hugged him. "Coming to see me?"

"No, no, er, just off for a walk."

John realised how he must look. He had slept badly and hadn't shaved for two days. He patted his unbrushed hair flat. "Sorry," he said. "Three years since Sarah..."

Helen interrupted, smiling. "Of course, of course, that's why I'm here. Three years. I wanted to see how you were holding up."

As if aware that the smile was wrong, Helen scowled, then frowned, before settling on a neutral expression. She and her partner Fiona had been friends with John and Sarah since they'd moved in eight years ago. Helen was twenty years younger than John, but looked younger still. She and Fiona jogged together most mornings before six, and he had rarely seen them eat anything other than salad and grilled vegetables. As Sarah had told the pair of them one night at dinner, if it weren't for the fact that they were happy to come over and get shit-faced with their neighbours now and then, they'd be insufferable.

"I'm, I'm..." John didn't know what he was, so he stopped speaking.

"You need someone to talk to," said Helen. John was surprised at her directness. Although Helen was a GP, John had always avoided the subject of his health with her. They were friends, not doctor and patient. But, after Sarah's death, Helen had offered her help, insisting he could call her day or night. It was time he took her up on the offer. If she recommended a specialist, he would see one. His dread of mental health practitioners was not only illogical, but embarrassing for someone who prided himself on being rational.

"Yes," John admitted, "you're probably right." He thought of the events of the past two days. "In fact, you're definitely right. I need you."

"Oh," she said, "you're too late, I'm afraid. I'm spoken for. And I'm gay. Double whammy."

Helen had always teased John and Sarah that were she ever to consider experimenting with heterosexuality, she'd give John a go. Sarah had found it hilarious. John too. Maybe she was trying to put him at ease, but her flirting jarred today.

"Yes," he said. "I seem to have missed the boat somewhat."

"Somewhat?" she said.

She tilted her head. "You're really not all right, are you? Come on, let's have a coffee."

She started walking while she spoke, and John followed.

"Fiona's at work despite the fact we both took the week off. A big case, apparently. Why the law should be more important than yoga, circuit training, watching old films, and having sex is a mystery, but there you go. She needs to sort out her priorities."

She turned left at the end of the path. John stopped in confusion. Helen's house was the other direction.

"Oh," she said, "I'm in the middle of cleaning. Floor's wet. Let's chill at the coffee shop and admire the yummy mummies."

"Lead on." Helen took his arm. Since when had she ever done any cleaning? Helen had often held forth on the fact that anyone earning over a certain amount was morally required to hire a cleaner in order to stimulate the local economy.

In the coffee shop, on the comfy settees and with a large mug of tea in front of him, John relaxed a little. Helen was an excellent doctor. She would know how to help.

"Right, Mr Aviemore," she said, stirring another sugar into her latte. For someone so committed to a healthy lifestyle, five sugars seemed excessive, as did the massive slab of flapjack she devoured in a few quick bites. "What's up?"

John looked around the coffee shop. It was half-full, and the speakers dotted around the ceiling played music at a volume loud enough to blend individual conversations into a homogeneous murmur.

"I'm going to tell you what happened on Tuesday night, but there's a problem," he began.

"What kind of problem?"

He explained how he'd been unable to talk to Augustus. "It wasn't that I didn't want to. It was more like my own brain was sabotaging me. Every time I opened my mouth to describe the evening, I said something different. Things got even weirder yesterday when I went to the solicitors."

"Right," she said, her manner now serious. "The disconnect between what you intend to say and what you actually say is rare, but I've read about it."

John put down the mug. "You have?"

"It can happen when recalling traumatic events the brain wants to suppress. Would you describe the events of that evening as traumatic?"

"Yes," he said.

"And yesterday? Was that traumatic too?"

"No. Just bizarre."

"Good. Start with yesterday. Then we'll talk about Tuesday night."

"Fine." John hesitated. Helen might not be so keen on inviting him over for dinner parties after hearing about magic doors, enchanted filing cabinets, and music that caused erections.

She leaned over and put a hand on his.

"Whatever you tell me is in confidence, John. I'm unshockable, and it will not affect our friendship. I know the prevailing wisdom is that men are better at compartmentalism than women, but when I file away something in a mental box, it stays there. Take your time."

He told her about the letter and the visit to Stinder Hackleworth, leaving nothing out. When he reached the part about knocking on the door and ending up back outside, she showed no more surprise than she had when he'd described the building.

John waited for her to respond. A waiter came over with more coffee, tea, and a second flapjack for Helen. After he left, she leaned forward.

"Don't stop. Now that you've told me something you think I might not believe, carry on. Tell me about Tuesday evening. Don't think about it, just talk. Start when you first arrived at the hotel. Did you go to the restaurant? To the toilet? Straight to the room where you were going to perform?"

He told her about going to Marco's office, and the

manager's uncharacteristic nervousness. He described following him to the Bloomsbury Suite, the doors opening, the black candles. Then he talked about the audience. This time, there was no breakdown of communication between his brain and his mouth. Liberated, he almost gabbled as he described the red-haired woman and her bald companion. He told her about the enormous man opposite and his tiny female partner, who'd thrown dust in his face. Then he spoke about the impossible creatures emerging from the shadows, the dream that night, and the lack of certainty about when the evening ended, and the dream began.

He told her everything.

By this time, Helen was on her third latte. She sipped it, the froth clinging to her upper lip. When John pointed it out, she licked it off suggestively without breaking eye contact. It was every bit as disconcerting as any of the creatures in his dream. Completely out of character, too. After the last few days, John could only conclude that he'd imagined it. What the hell was happening to him?

"Right", said Helen, all business now. Yes, he'd definitely imagined it. "First things first. What was the name of that firm of solicitors?" She picked up her phone.

"Stinder Hackleworth," he said, "but don't bother searching for them. They're not online."

"I have a better idea," said Helen, holding the phone to her ear. "Fiona, this is the love of your life. I'm so distraught by your absence I've taken a man out for coffee. Oh, no one you'd know. Oh, all right, it is John, smart arse. Ever heard of the solicitors Stinder Hackleworth? Oh, yeah, okay, I'll wait." Helen held the phone a few inches away from her ear. "She's asking the senior partner. He's two hundred years old, and he knows everyone. If he hasn't heard of them, they —hello? Right. Thank you. I'll see you later. I'll—what? Oh.

Yes, I suppose that might go some way to making up for your absence today. Bye, love."

Helen looked John in the eye. "No such solicitor. Still got that letter?"

John reached into his jacket pocket and pulled out the document. For a horrible moment, he thought it would have a different name on it, but there it was in ornate script at the top.

"Great," said Helen, then went back to her phone. "I'll call an Uber."

ELEVEN

The rain fell with a listless persistence that made Noone House look cold and uninviting. Its tiny windows stared out like the multiple eyes of a spider, each pupil dark and dead.

"Come on," said John, quickening his pace as he crossed the bird-shit border. As he got to the bottom of the steps, he stopped, looking up in puzzlement.

"What is it? This is the place, right?" Helen climbed the steps and stood at the black door.

"The plaques," said John.

"What plaques?"

"Exactly." He examined the space where the brass plaques had listed the companies with offices in Noone House. "There was a map-making firm and a bookbinder. Then Stinder Hackleworth. The top floor was..."

He pictured himself standing there the day before. "It was unoccupied, I think, but there was something weird about it."

John leaned forward and looked at the brickwork. There was no evidence of any holes where the plaques had been screwed in. Maybe they had been glued in place. The bricks were old and sooty.

"I don't understand," he said.

Helen moved to stand alongside him. "What did you say this place was called?"

"Noone House. Why?"

She didn't reply, so he straightened up and looked at her. She was pointing at the wooden sign. That, at least, was the same as John remembered. White-painted wood with black letters. But it didn't say Noone House. It said E Cattridge, Antiquarian Books.

As John shook his head in bemusement, the door opened, and a face peered out at them.

"We only open to the public every other Wednesday, except in the winter when it's Monday afternoons. If we're preparing for a book fair, it's the third Friday in the month."

The voice was high pitched and grating. A small face looked up at them, beneath a rigid mass of hair.

It was the beehive.

"Hello," he said. "I was here yesterday. I saw Mr Hackleworth."

"Not yesterday," she shrieked. "Closed all day. No Mr Battleworth here."

"Hackleworth," said John. "The solicitors upstairs. Stinder Hackleworth."

"No one upstairs," said the beehive.

Helen put a hand on John's elbow and squeezed before he could speak.

"Have you been here long?" she asked.

"Thirty-two seconds," came the prompt reply.

"Um, I mean,"—she looked back at the sign—"E Cattridge. The bookseller. Is that you?"

"Eric Cattridge was my grandfather. Father's name was Ernest."

"Eric and Ernie?" said Helen.

"No, Eric and Ernest," said the beehive.

"Oh. And you are?"

"Ermintrude Cattridge. Three generations of rare book sellers."

"Do you specialise in particular books?" asked John, looking at the woman directly, trying to elicit some sign she knew who he was.

"Yes," she said, staring back at him. There was no hint of recognition in her eyes.

"Mrs Cattridge," said Helen.

"Miss," the beehive corrected with a shriek.

"Miss Cattridge. My friend John visited a building yesterday, very close to here. He's convinced this is it. Could we take a quick look to set his mind at rest?"

Since the beehive was pretending not to know him, John expected her to refuse and slam the door in their faces. Instead, she took a step backwards.

"Follow me."

Helen raised her eyebrows at John and stepped over the threshold.

The lobby of the building shared the same dimensions but almost every detail was different. There was no desk, no ledger. The floor wasn't tiled, it was carpeted in a faded gold and red pattern. The walls were papered with a striped pattern familiar to anyone who had stayed in a hotel in the nineteen-sixties. The curved bannister still followed the staircase to the upper floors, but it was a light polished pine, not the dark wood John remembered.

The four doors leading off to other rooms were the same. They were all shut apart from the first on the left - the one from which the strangely arousing music had emerged. John could see most of the room. It was lined with books. They were all hardbacks, their titles indecipherable. The beehive glided across the carpet with surprising speed and closed the door.

"Alternate Wednesdays only."

Helen pointed upstairs. "May we have a look?"

"No one upstairs."

"Please?"

The beehive looked at her watch and folded her arms. "Be quick."

"Come on," whispered Helen, taking John's arm, "before she changes her mind."

The grandfather clock ticked on the second floor.

"That's the same," said John. His confidence returning, he led the way up to the third floor and the dead yucca plant. Without knocking, he pushed the door open.

The room was empty. Not only that, the bare floorboards were covered in a layer of dust broken up only by an occasional mouse or rat turd.

John walked through the room, coughing as his shoes flicked up small clouds of dust. It was empty. The window let in enough light to illuminate hundreds of cobwebs on the ceiling, and a cursory glance was enough to prove there was no drawer in the far wall. There was one major difference between the room he was standing in now and the room in which he'd first met the beehive and Tobias Hackleworth. It was double the size. Yesterday, three strides in any direction would have brought John to a wall or the door. This room was twenty feet from door to window and fifteen feet across.

He turned to Helen.

"I want to go now," he said.

Helen took him to the nearest pub. It was dark and warm inside, with booths along one wall. Narrow steps led down to a small table with two church pews as seats. That was where Helen steered John after she'd bought him a pint of stout with a large whisky as a chaser.

"Consider this a prescription," she said, as she put the glasses in front of him. "Drink. You'll feel better."

John did as he was told. Remarkably, despite the fact he was doubting his own sanity, Helen was right. Within five minutes, he felt better.

Helen sipped a gin and tonic. "I have a few questions," she said. "Answer honestly and quickly. Don't think too hard about it. You game?"

"Yes."

"Good. Let's start with the letter. Ashleigh, right?"

"Ash. Yes."

"You said you had a sexual relationship the summer after you finished university. Did you love her?"

John hesitated. Helen growled like an animal. John looked at her in shock, but she continued as if nothing had happened. "No hesitations. I told you not to think about it. Did you love her?"

"No."

"Infatuated with her?"

"Yes."

"To what extent?"

"To the extent that it became dangerous."

"How dangerous?"

"I had a breakdown afterwards. Spent some time in an institution."

"What condition were you suffering from?"

John paused again. It wasn't something he liked to talk about. Helen's nails scratched along the table top. He didn't remember her nails being so long.

"Psychosis brought on by stress. It was temporary. The depression lasted longer."

"Any episodes since requiring hospitalisation?"

"No, none."

"Not even minor episodes?"

"No."

"Good. Are you still mourning Sarah?"

"Yes."

"Did you receive the letter from the solicitor before or after your performance at the Charleston?"

"After."

"Did you start thinking about Ash when you received it?"

"Yes."

"About the sex - and your feelings for her?"

"I suppose so, yes."

"It was the day after the anniversary of Sarah's death. Did these thoughts about Ash make you feel guilty?"

"A little. I put them out of my mind."

"Hmm."

Helen sat back and closed her eyes. John thought about saying something, but she immediately held up a finger to stop him.

"Did Ash ever take you anywhere other than the cottage?"

"We walked in the woods once."

"Did you have sex then?

"I don't see what that has to do—"

Helen hissed between her teeth. It was such an odd, unexpected reaction, that John, who had been staring into his pint, looked up in surprise. For a moment her features looked like they belonged to someone else, but a second later, her face was calm, her eyes still closed. She opened them as he was looking and smiled.

"Nearly done. What are you planning to do with the cottage?"

"Sell it."

"Are you going over there?"

"No. I can handle everything from here. I forgot about Ash for thirty years, I don't want to dredge it all up now."

"I understand, John. You want my professional opinion, right?"

"Yes. Or you can refer me to a specialist, I suppose."

"No need."

John looked at her.

"You trust me. That's why you came to me."

"Yes, I trust you."

"You did the right thing. I almost went into psychiatry rather than general practise. I still keep up with all the latest research. What you're describing is a textbook example of an aftershock."

"A what?"

"A severe episode of mental illness is like an earthquake. You can experience aftershocks months, years, even decades later. Your dream occurred three years to the day after the worst experience of your life. It's clearly triggered a mild relapse of the psychosis. The letter has made it worse."

"Oh." John wasn't sure what to say. The word *psychosis* wasn't something he'd ever wanted to hear again, even when modified by the word *mild*. He remembered the Bristol hospital, his mother asleep in the chair next to his bed. Terrified she was losing him. He couldn't reassure her. He was terrified he was losing himself.

"Will it pass?" he managed, after a few deliberately slow swallows of beer. "How worried should I be?"

"There's no need to worry at all if you're willing to take my advice. It'll take a few weeks to turn things around, I expect, then you'll be right as rain. But I'm not sure you're going to like it."

John took his time answering. His throat was tight and his head hurt. The idea of another breakdown terrified him. The loss of control, the helplessness, the peculiar horror of being institutionalised.

"Look, Helen, if you can help me, I'll do whatever you say."

He drained the rest of his beer and put both his hands palm-down on the table. "What do I need to do?"

"CBT," said Helen, pushing his whisky towards him. "Cognitive Behavioural Therapy. Over a ninety-five percent success rate in curing the kind of condition you're suffering from. Drink up."

"I've heard of CBT. If you're scared of spiders, you have to handle them. If you're scared of the dark, you spend a few minutes every day in a dark room. Wait. What do you expect me to do? Ash is dead."

"CBT means facing your fear head-on. In this case, although you ended the relationship with Ash, she—or, rather, your idea of her—still has a hold over you. She's a ghost in the machine, messing with your mind decades after your relationship. You need to exorcise her."

There was a gleam in Helen's eyes, an unfamiliar twist to her lips. John had never seen her so serious.

"How?" he asked.

"Stay in that cottage. Your decision to sell the property without even visiting it shows how strongly you associate it with your psychosis. Go there, break its hold over you, break *her* hold over you."

John drank the whisky. He remembered following Ash along the path to the cottage that first night, knowing what was about to happen, his heart clenched tight with something as close to fear as it was desire. He should have trusted that instinct.

"Can't you just prescribe Prozac?"

Helen looked him in the eye. "Is that what you want? It's up to you. I've given you an informed opinion, which you are free to ignore, despite the serious risk in doing so. It has to be your decision, John. I can't make it for you. What are you going to do?"

The subtle lighting in the pub darkened as if someone had twisted a dimmer switch. John was aware of a movement behind Helen. Behind the bar was a mirror and, reflected in it, the giant from the Bloomsbury Suite looked back at him, his tangled hair scraping the ceiling, a pint of beer looking like a shot glass in his gnarled fist. John blinked and looked away from the mirror to where the giant was standing. There was no one there.

Helen, seeing his face, looked over her shoulder, then back, her eyes fixed on his as she waited for his answer. The air itself seemed tight, a balloon skin stretched thin to the point just before it burst.

John made his decision. In the end, it boiled down to the fact that he was scared and angry. Scared of what memories might surface at the cottage, and angry at the fragility of his own mind. He wasn't twenty anymore, callow and untested. He'd seen a child brought into the world, lost his mother to dementia, and had to stand by while cancer inexorably chewed his wife's life away from the inside out. He would not be intimidated by the ghost of a woman who should have just been a fling.

"You're right," he said. "I'll go."

The clink of glasses resumed, and someone laughed at the bar.

"Good decision," said Helen. When she picked up her glass, he noticed her hand was shaking.

TWELVE

John arrived at the cottage exactly a week after receiving the letter. A call to his manager cancelling his gigs for a month, a message on Bonneville's answerphone to let Augustus know where he was. As far as Harry was concerned, it was a short holiday near Bristol. He didn't tell his son he owned the cottage. John had never spoken of his stay in hospital, and as uninhibited sex sessions with a girl he'd known before Harry's mother had never been a topic of family discussion, he felt no need to mention it now.

Mid-afternoon, he picked up the keys from the estate agent, who handed over a heavy piece of ironmongery from a cabinet full of modern keys.

A fifteen-minute drive and he was parking in the layby on the edge of Leigh Woods. Back in the eighties it had been a muddy verge, but since then, it had been widened and covered in gravel, with space for three cars. A public footpath followed the periphery of the field opposite, and the flies around the bin next to the gate suggested it was popular with dog walkers.

John opened the boot and pulled out a heavy canvas bag

and a rucksack. He'd brought enough clothes for a week, some old sheets, paint pots and brushes. If he was going to confront his demons, he'd get some decorating done at the same time. The last bag contained a kettle and enough provisions for the first night.

He walked along the road from the end of the layby towards the big oak on the corner.

The footpath past the oak was as overgrown as it had been thirty years ago. It was nothing like as well-used as the one favoured by the dog walkers, but the odd cigarette butt and some discarded beer cans marked the edges as it led into the woods. Twenty yards in, and the path turned to the left. Straight ahead, a high iron gate, rusting and blackened with age, blocked John's progress. A metal postbox on a wooden stake had been hand-painted with flaking letters: *Sally Cottage*.

John put his hand on the gate, twisted the iron ring to lift the bar out of the latch, and pushed. It swung open. He didn't move for a moment, just stared ahead.

Built of stone in the mid-nineteenth century on the site of an earlier, simpler dwelling, Sally Cottage was like a child's drawing in its dimensions. It was north facing, made of grey stone, with a slate roof and a single chimney rising above the east end. The four small symmetrical windows, those on the ground floor on either side of the door, the others above them, had wooden shutters in a style common on the continent, but unusual in Britain.

John stepped up to the door and fought with the key in the lock before it opened with a deep clunk.

Thirty years earlier, the living room had been carpeted, but it had since been stripped back to uneven, dirty floorboards. On the right was a big stone fireplace, blackened with the scars of a million flames. An old, sagging sofa faced the fire. Great chunks of plaster were missing from the ceiling, and long cracks radiated from the solitary light fitting. John recalled a much warmer, softer light. With a twitch of surprise, he remembered that Ash had lit the cottage with oil lamps like the ones he had seen in the offices of Stinder Hackleworth. The ambience back then had been almost erotic, the subtle dance of lamplight lending a romantic glow to the living room. Although, John admitted to himself, pretty much everything associated with Ashleigh Zanash had been erotically charged.

He pulled at the torn wallpaper. There was more paper below, cream in colour and textured. John didn't remember that. The room had been painted a dark colour in his time, red or purple, with gilt-framed paintings hanging on every wall. Now the paintings were gone, as was any trace of the room where Ash had first undressed him, her eyes full of hungry desire.

He dropped his bags onto the least dirty patch of floor and ducked under the low archway that led into the galley kitchen. The oven looked new, the hob unmarked. A fridge freezer hummed in the corner.

Back in the living room, he hung the big iron key on a nail that looked like it had been there since the cottage was built. He walked up the stairs. John had spent most of his time in Sally Cottage in the master bedroom. He'd rather get his first look at it while there was still daylight.

The door was open. Enough sunlight made it through the tree canopy outside to illuminate the room, but the gentle waving of branches in the breeze filled the space with moving shadows. John flicked on the overhead light and they vanished.

The bedroom was large, and it was dominated by the enormous bed in the middle. Space-wise, it would have made more sense to have pushed it into a corner, or against a wall. But the bed's position, like the bed itself, was a statement. It was a stage, waiting for the players.

It was made of iron, heavy and intricately wrought. The headboard rose six feet from the mattress, and was fashioned in two pieces later welded together, giving it the appearance of a pair of gates. The design of the headboard took the form of branches growing from an unseen tree, the trunk of which—if the maker's vision were followed through—would be underneath the bedroom, its iron roots plunging into the foundations of the cottage.

It was the same bed where John had lost his virginity in the summer of his final year of university. The same bed where he'd been introduced to many sexual acts he'd previously only imagined, and a few his imagination failed to predict.

An old dresser stood by the window. There was no other furniture.

It made perfect sense for the bed to still be here, John told himself. It probably weighed as much as a small car. Why would anyone move it? Even so, his pulse was racing.

He supposed Helen would have advised him to sleep in that bed, but there was a limit to what John would do in the interest of cognitive behavioural therapy.

He would sleep on the sofa.

THIRTEEN

Evie,

And so we come to the rub. The reason I'm writing to you.

Magic. It's a word that has gone in and out of fashion. The word itself became the common English term for those who practised the supernatural arts back in the fifteenth century. Delve further, and you'll find similar words in old French. Further still, via Latin, back to the ancient Greek - magikē. Witches, wizards, shamans, warlocks, mages, conjurors, sorcerers, enchanters, necromancers.

A very long time ago, the Wardens and the Three decided it was easier to keep things simple, etymologically speaking. We practise the art of magic, so we are mages, or magicians. The greatest practitioners on Earth are known as Adepts. There are three Adepts on Earth as I write. When I die, there will be two. Until you are ready to step up, Evie, which I hope will be very soon after my death.

No magic can prevent death. Humans are mortal. If we did not die, we would not be human, we would be something else.

The curse that is killing me came from a god of the fourth realm. I know that means nothing to you now, but trust me, it's about as bad as it gets. Some curses can be deflected, weakened, or undone. Not this one. I've fought it for decades, but I am tired now.

I do not know how long I have before I can no longer rely on my memory. Weeks, perhaps. It might be days. Just in case I have less time than I think, please don't forget the address at the top of my first letter. John, your grandfather, knows where it is.

I wish I could be there with you to pass on this knowledge. I have already emphasised the importance of secrecy to the Three. I have never met another Adept from our own realm. This simple precaution means no enemy can ever discover the identity of the other Adepts if they should capture one of us. I only know that the other families live on different continents. We only communicate through our Wardens.

Our realm, our universe, is the most fecund, when it comes to magic. It's the youngest realm, too. Some of the oldest realms are in decline. Mu has not been heard from for centuries. Shambhala fell silent after the gods' war. Over eons, realms are born, and realms die, just like everything else.

Back to magic, then. Yes, magic. You've read those boy wizard books, I'm sure, seen some films. You probably say movies, I imagine. Tales about people with strange powers have been around ever since the first cave dwellers needed a story to go along with the pictures on the walls.

The stories reflect the hidden reality. Magic was once a common part of what it meant to be human. Monsters roamed the earth, dragons circled the tops of unclimbable mountains. It's hard to separate myth from truth, although the older I get, the less convinced I am that there's any point in trying. Mother said little about our origins during our nightly walks to the woods. She knew I would understand when I became an Adept. You and I don't have that luxury.

Here is the little I can tell you about our earliest history. You'll have to forgive the broad strokes.

Once upon a time, there were seven realms in which all living beings existed, and everyone could move around them as easily as you or I might take a trip on a bus. In those days, humans could communicate with animals, trees, and plants; even talk to the wind and the rain.

Of the other six realms, five are now unreachable from our own world to all but an Adept. But those who dwell there are not completely out of reach. They can still access the Blurred Lands, as can we, where our realities overlap. Two realms have chosen not to exercise their right to do so since the Accord. We don't know who, or what, lives there. Of the other four, only the closest realm, Da Luan, can be visited by humans. Any human can enter the Blurred Lands, but if they get through to Da Luan and spend a night there—or eat and drink anything—they cannot return. The other two realms whose inhabitants might occasionally be encountered in the Lands are Erebus and Tartarus. Erebus once gave us mythical creatures. Tartarus was the home of the beings who became our greatest threat.

This is so difficult, Evie! Much of this will be incomprehensible until you take your place among the Three. But if, as I suspect, Astarte is planning to shatter the Accord, this realm will need you before you are ready, and every piece of knowledge I can impart may help. Please, child, bear with me.

Right. Right. I am going to break a rule. My gut tells me

you may need a clincher. Even after discovering that I planted a dream in your head.

To avoid you dismissing me as your crazy great-grandmother, I will skip a month's worth of one-to-one lessons and give you a word of power. It doesn't matter a jot if you believe me or not. The word will work either way. I need you to do this so you know I'm telling you the truth, and that all of this is real.

Make sure you're alone when you sing. Yes, sing. The word itself is an empty vessel. You must fill it with intent. Music is as old as magic, and as mysterious.

Find a place with trees. Sing the word. Pick one note, and very, very gently, let it sound. Have you ever made a wine glass hum by running your finger along the rim? It's a little like that. Let it come through you rather than from you.

When you have sung, wait. An animal or bird will come to you if you have spoken well. If you touch a tree, it will speak to you, but that is a conversation I would advise leaving until you are good and ready. Their wisdom can overwhelm the unprepared.

Every animal and every plant, every living being, when summoned by a word of power speaks with the voice of their *duen*, the spirit of a species. What I mean is, if you talk to a mouse, she will not tell you about her quest to feed her family, or her keenness to avoid predators. When she speaks, you will know what it is to be her. This may change your perspective and your opinions. There's a good reason I'm a vegetarian.

My first conversation was with a dunnock, or hedge sparrow, and I still feel a great affinity with that bird. Remember your dream? The bird who said your name was a dunnock. I hope your own experience is as gentle and as life-changing.

I will end here, for now. Come back to this letter when you have sung your word. Remember, make sure you're alone. Night time is best.

Go, sing your word. Read more when you have tested your mad great-grandmother's claims.

The word is *orvaelae*.

FOURTEEN

John finished his quick tour of the cottage and went downstairs. He was back where he'd had his first love affair. Back in the place where he'd nearly lost his mind. He found a broom in the cupboard under the stairs and spent an hour with a tea towel over his mouth and nose brushing clouds of dust towards the open door.

After a simple supper of French bread, cheese, salad and a mug of wine, he lay down on the sofa, staring at the flaking paint on the ceiling as the last of the light leached away.

It was 8:30. Too early to sleep, but he abandoned his attempt at reading the magic magazines he'd brought after realising he was taking nothing in. He had stopped at one glass of wine, but even that made him thick-headed and weary. His thoughts kept returning to those seven nights with Ash, thirty-two years ago. They had undoubtedly been intense, but he was a different person now. It was more than half his life ago, and he had spent twenty-five of those intervening years with Sarah, being as inexorably changed by her, as she had been by him. He looked back on the boy of his university years and hardly recognised him.

The shutters were wide open, and the red warmth of the sinking sun filtered through the green penumbra of the trees outside, giving the patterns on the ceiling a strange, blood-purple hue. Minute by minute, the shadows gathered, and John's eyes closed.

The first sign that he was dreaming was the sensation of floating. His surroundings were neither light nor dark. He saw colours that can only be seen in dreams, colours with no names, shifting like petrol in a rain-filled gutter.

There was no sense of time passing. John's thoughts lost coherence and dissolved into nothing.

He was standing outside his mother's room in Fir Trees, a care home that specialised in the treatment of dementia. The walls were an inoffensive pale yellow. Little effort had been made to soften the institutional atmosphere.

John had often stood outside the door of room thirty-eight, wishing he had made more of the conversations with his mother before her illness took hold. In Fir Trees, she rarely spoke.

Now, in his dream, he waited in the corridor outside her room, breathing in disinfectant and tea. There was the same stomach ache, the usual rising of bile in his throat, as he prepared himself to get through an hour with the frail, confused shred of a woman who had once been his mother.

"Come in, John. I had the kitchen bring me a pot of Earl Grey, and they've even rustled up some fruitcake."

Part of John knew he was dreaming, but nothing could prevent the swell of hope and love that lurched within him at her strong, happy voice. He took a step forward.

Immediately, he was lying on the bed, propped up against three thick pillows. His mother was standing with her back to him in front of the window, looking out across the lawn to the line of trees that gave the care home its name.

"I'm sorry this is happening, John," she said without turning. Rather than her usual shapeless nightgown, she wore a navy suit and a white blouse. "Thousands of years of balance, and now this. John, if we'd known, if we had suspected she would try to come for you again, I would have trained you to face it, even though there's so little a man can do. But she doesn't hold every card."

Mae Aviemore turned from the window and looked at her son. While her face had been averted, John had been convinced she was young again. Her voice had the rich, warm, tone he remembered from when he was a child. But when she looked at him, he saw the face of an eighty-one-year-old woman, the skin lined and sun-damaged, her hair wispy and dry.

John tried to speak, but his lips barely moved.

"You can hear me, can't you, John? Nod if you can."

With an effort, he dipped his head forwards.

"Good. I wasn't sure this would work. It gives me some hope. Oh, my son, I would do anything, I would trade places with you if I could. No one ever thought she would risk the balance like this. She's insane. She would tear a hole in the universe for a whiff of power. Gods."

On that disconcerting note, she stopped talking and smoothed down her dress, a gesture John remembered well. It was usually followed by a telling off. But her tone was very different in this dream. This was the mother John had always wanted, the mother who loved him, not the mother he had known, always careful to keep her distance, fearful of something she never revealed.

She sat on the end of the bed. How many times had he

done the same, talking to her but getting no response? Had it been like this for her - hearing him but unable to respond?

"John, time works differently here. Reality is malleable and unreliable. I hoped the responsibility I carry would never touch you. That changed when she took you."

He stared at her, trying to drink in the only complete sentences she had spoken in years while ignoring the fact that none of them made sense.

"I would fight for you if I could, John, but I am lost. Lost to you, lost to myself. This fragment is all I have, and it will not survive long."

His mother squeezed his hand. John lacked the energy to respond.

"First, the little I can tell you about her. She wishes you harm. You must not forget that. When she first caught you, she wanted to dominate you. Ultimately, if she could not break your will completely, she planned to control you. If she had succeeded, the damage she would have caused might have... well. No one knows for sure, but it is obvious her confinement has not led to rehabilitation. Your strength, which must have surprised her, was enough to push her away. She thought you would crumble. You did not. You hurt her, John, and she lashed out. She underestimated you. She won't do that again."

He sat up and looked around. He was tired, but some of his strength had returned. The bed was gone, and he was lying on a cart pulled by a placid chestnut horse. They were following a track through the trees. The dappled sunlight struggled to reach them through the dense branches above. John thought of the cottage ceiling.

A movement near his elbow startled him, and he flinched. Looking down, he saw a field mouse staring back at him with caviar-black eyes. It spoke with his mother's voice.

"She knows I'm here. Dammit!"

Something jumped onto the back of the cart and streaked towards John's face. He held up his arm. A brown and white shape landed on his chest, then raced away. The mouse dropped from the cart and ran towards the trees. A brown and white cat was gaining on it. As the mouse reached the undergrowth and vanished, the cat pulled up short, its tail flicking from side to side.

John sat back against the straw. A hedge sparrow was perched there. This time, he wasn't surprised to hear his mother's voice.

"My time is short. You are in the Blurred Lands, John. You're protected to some extent, and you may even have a little power. But you can never access that power if you deny its existence. Let go of your certainties. There is no solid ground. Once you can embrace that, this world will reveal its secrets to you. I—"

Her words were cut off as a sparrowhawk plummeted out of the green sky, snapped open her wings at the last moment and snatched the smaller bird. John followed her flight as she circled then dived again. Landing at the back of the cart, the sparrowhawk looked directly at him, her sharp curved beak closed, her fierce yellow eyes wild and arrogant, one powerful talon pinning her prey to the wooden planks. She didn't speak. The tiny bird was still moving, its beak opening and closing, its head straining to turn towards John.

"Mother?"

At that, the sparrowhawk lowered its head and, with three brisk stabs, pierced the breast of its prey and crushed its heart. When she looked at John again, the beak was smeared with blood.

He woke up.

FIFTEEN

For half a minute, John was disorientated.

He lay in the dark, eyes open, thinking about his mother. He pushed himself up on his elbows, reconstructing his surroundings as he reached out for the glass of water he'd left by his side. It wasn't there. John patted the floorboards then waved his hand a few inches to each side. Still nothing. He waited for his eyes to adjust to the darkness.

The night-filled room refused to resolve itself into recognisable shapes. He had left the torch near the sofa. Reaching out for it, his fingertips brushed the floorboards, but the torch had gone.

Upstairs, almost directly above his head, he heard a sound as if someone had turned over in their sleep.

Fully awake and alert now, John held his breath and listened. Nothing.

Just when he'd convinced himself that he'd imagined it, and was on the point of going back to sleep, he heard it again. The creak of bedsprings.

He sat up. Feeling his way along the sofa, John realised

why he hadn't been able to locate his glass of water or the torch. During the night, he must have shifted position, moving closer to the kitchen. Shuffling back up to the other end of the sofa, he found the torch, and the glass of water beside it.

He let out the breath he was holding, annoyed by how spooked he was. He drank some water and turned on the torch. The light emerged slowly, the beam pushing into the darkness as if it were encountering resistance.

He swept the light around the cottage living room. His phone was on the floor. He thumbed on the power. 03:46am. Battery at eighteen percent. He'd have to charge it soon.

At the bottom of the stairs, he flicked the switch for the landing light. It didn't surprise him when nothing happened.

John whistled a jaunty tune as he ascended. He was going to check out the mysterious sound. At quarter to four in the morning. With a torch that was behaving like a prop from a horror film, leaving monochrome shadows where he needed harsh, all-revealing light.

On the landing he went straight ahead, stood in the doorway of the bathroom and pulled the light cord. Nothing.

He stepped inside and swept the torch around the small space. Toilet, sink and a bath, his toothbrush in a glass on the windowsill.

The spare bedroom contained a single bed and a cheap desk.

The bathroom and the spare room were empty. Which left the bedroom.

Back out on the landing, he put the flat of his hand on

the bedroom door and pushed it open. It was the last thing he wanted to do, but he wouldn't let irrational fear stop him.

Inside, to prove to himself that he wasn't afraid, he shut the door, although his hand shook as he did it.

He half-expected the torch to turn itself off. When it didn't, he shone its weak light into every corner of the room. It was exactly as John had left it. Just the old dresser and the hideous iron bed. Nothing else. The cottage was hundreds of years old. It would make noises at night as ancient timbers expanded and contracted.

He was dry-mouthed and breathing too fast.

John took a small step backwards. His muscles obeyed him, and he moved, causing the bare floorboards—rather than the deep carpet John remembered—to creak.

John had watched plenty of ghost and horror films because they gave him ideas for new tricks. He liked the mechanics. He admired the way a sharp script, directorial devices and musical flourishes could manipulate the viewer. If this was a film, a cat would burst out from under the bed, scare everyone stupid, and puncture the tension.

He waited for a moment, but no cat appeared. As the skin on his neck and shoulders prickled into goosebumps despite his lack of belief in the supernatural, he turned his back on the iron bed and took a step towards the door. At the moment his hand closed on the doorknob, he froze, almost dropping the torch.

There had been a sound behind him. So subtle, it might have been nothing at all, or just one of the myriad sounds an old house makes.

Only it wasn't.

John knew that sound although he hadn't heard it for over thirty years.

It was the tiny, wet, alluring sound of a lipsticked mouth parting into a smile.

Not just anyone's lips, though. Ash's lips.

He swung around, eyes wide, a grunt of fear escaping him.

No one was sitting on the bed, waiting. No one was smiling as she waited for her lover to join her. The room was empty, the vast iron bed facing him like a gravestone.

Ash is dead. She's dead.

John went downstairs without rushing, put his pillow at the other end of his bedding roll so he could see the staircase, and deliberately closed his eyes.

He left the light on.

SIXTEEN

It was difficult to recall the fear of the previous night while he had a strong cup of tea, a piece of toast layered with thick-cut marmalade, and the sun was warming his face.

John leaned on the gate at the end of the path and enjoyed the birdsong. No birds sang in the cottage garden, but they kept up an impressive chorus beyond its boundaries.

He put the empty mug on the gatepost and walked back out towards the car, mobile phone in hand. There was no signal until he was standing on the edge of the road near the layby. Two bars then appeared on the screen. He called Fir Trees. The dream had reminded him it was a week since he had checked on his mother. Not that it made any difference to Mae. She often called her carers John, Harry, or Graham, confusing them with her son, grandson or long-dead husband.

"Fir Trees, hello?"

The line was awful, crackling with static. John walked along the road as he spoke.

"Hello?"

More static.

"Hello? Hello?"

"Yes, Fir Trees, Claire speaking, how can I help you?"

"Ah, good. This is John Aviemore. My mother is staying with you, Mae Aviemore."

John still found the euphemistic language of the care home disconcerting. The patients were referred to as 'guests' who were 'staying' there, as if Fir Trees were a five-star holiday resort and spa, not a hospice. All guests would check out, but there would be no repeat bookings, no reviews on a travel website.

"Mr Av... wh... if... do you...?"

"I'm sorry? Can you hear me? I'm calling about my mother. Mrs Aviemore."

Then, much clearer, but muffled, as though someone was covering the phone—"Gary? Gary? Can you check Aviemore? I've only just started me shift. She wasn't the one last night, was she? Can you check? Mr Aviemore? Hello?"

"Yes, yes." John stopped walking. The reception was better in this spot, although he was standing in the middle of the road. John stood side-on, watching for traffic.

"My colleague is just checking for me. Did someone call you?"

"No. No. Why? Has something happened?" He remembered the sparrowhawk's yellow eyes and crimson beak.

"I don't know. I only just arrived."

John's phone emitted a low beep, and he took it away from his ear. Battery life four percent.

"Look, my phone is about to die. Can you get someone to call me back?"

"Yes, Mr Aviemore. It'll probably be my manager. She'll call you."

Why the manager?

"What's happened?"

A tractor came round the corner, and John stepped onto the verge. The line stopped crackling and—combined with the roar of the tractor—he struggled to make out what she was saying.

"Hello? Hello? I'm sorry, I didn't get any of that. Can you say it again? Hello?"

He looked at his phone. The screen was blank.

"Shit."

John had come prepared for his stay at Sally Cottage. Rather than bring his notes and magic books, he would make a start on redecorating the place. After the events of the previous night, he decided to start with the bedroom. Just because he didn't believe in the supernatural didn't mean he didn't fear it; that was a redundant instinct baked into his DNA. But he wouldn't let it affect him.

John fetched the last tins of paint from the car. There were no dog walkers today.

He remembered the first time he had walked back to this layby. That first dawn, he'd left Ash face down, naked, in a tangle of sheets. He'd heard the expression 'taken my virginity' before, but never understood it until Ash had led him upstairs. She took his virginity with wild delight, reaching her orgasm as quickly as he did, with a cry of victory more suited to a field of battle.

He had left that morning feeling as if something were pulling him back to her, something more powerful, and more strange, than young lust. It grew in intensity every time he left her until the last evening in the woods. Invisible hands fastened onto his shirt that night and tried to force him back as he stumbled away in shock. From somewhere, he had found the strength to keep walking, then running, not daring to stop even when he reached his bike, but continuing until he collapsed on the outskirts of Bristol.

John opened the car, sat in the driver's seat, and turned the key in the ignition.

What if Helen's wrong? What if, by confronting my memories, I feed them, I give them the power to break me again?

The weeks after his collapse were lost to him. The few memories that survived were enough to make him want to drive away, and to keep driving. He thought of it now. He had opened his eyes in the hospital room, looked at his hands, the bed, the walls, the window, and, finally, at the pale face of his mother, and had not known what any of those things were. And he, John Aviemore, was not present. He was gone, lost in the featureless white plain of dreams.

John stared out of the windscreen at the trees, then turned off the engine and got out of the car.

He thought of what Helen had told him.

If I leave, this place will always have power over me.

He lifted the large paint cans and trudged back to the cottage.

Painting walls was a job John had always enjoyed. He had the kind of mind that thrives on introspection, and ideas often came to him when he was performing a repetitive task that required little mental input. Decorating was ideal.

John wore old jeans and a T-shirt from a 1983 David Bowie tour.

He started with the cottage bedroom, defiantly heaping

paint tins, old sheets, cloths, brushes, and sponges onto the monstrous iron bed. He had genuinely been afraid the previous night. If Helen's cognitive behavioural therapy was going to work, he needed to confront that fear head-on. Of course, the smell of wet paint meant he wouldn't be able to sleep in the bedroom, but John was certain that wasn't a factor in his decision. Well, reasonably certain.

He opened the shutters and the window, letting as much light and air as possible into the room.

It took an hour to clean the walls. There was no wallpaper to strip. The current choice of paint was a dark pink that reminded John of his blood-tinged spit in the sink at the dentist's.

When the sheets were tucked up to the edge of the skirting board, he made a start, concentrating first on the corners with a two-inch brush. As the morning wore on, he moved on to a bigger brush.

Even the ache in his arms, increasing his discomfort as the hours passed, gave him pleasure. He didn't do manual work often, but on the rare occasions he needed to, he liked going to bed feeling physically tired. Sleep came more quickly. Like many with a sedentary lifestyle, John took regular exercise, jogging on Wimbledon Common three times a week. The way his biceps were burning prompted him to think about buying weights. Or to start doing more digging in the garden.

John's mind drifted from thought to connected thought, his consciousness soon reaching the point where fresh ideas or insights often came to him. Instead, a memory, clear and sharp, emerged. It was from his time in the psychiatric hospital. Instinctively, he flinched away from it, as he might twitch the wheel of a car to avoid flattening a rabbit.

John put the brush down. He had made tea, and he took

a sip now, grimacing when he realised it had gone cold. He thought again about Helen's advice. Perhaps he should allow the painful memory to resurface. He looked at the bed, then at the trees swaying outside. Dust motes surfed the block of yellow light that poured through the open window.

He picked up the brush again. As the pink disappeared under the magnolia, he turned his thoughts to the memory.

He was trudging through a white landscape. The world was full of snow, but he wasn't cold. He didn't need to open his eyes because he could see without them. There were stars above him. Darker shapes sometimes loomed into view as he walked, but faded before he got close.

He heard his mother's voice. She was arguing with someone. Not just one person. There were other voices. One was female.

"You are wrong. It is not your choice to make, Mae. It is far too important for that. We must all agree and I, for one, do not." The voice softened a little. "At least wait until we gather the Three. In a few days, we can—"

"In a few days, he'll be dead. I will not wait." John had never heard such passion from his mother.

"He's stronger than anyone anticipated, Mae." This was the male voice. "He should have died. He has talent, this boy. If he had been allowed some training, he would have known what he was up against."

"Your time in this realm has turned your mind soft, Warden." The female voice was honey-toned, measured, and authoritative. "The Accord still holds because of the Three. Would you have us try something new? Do you have no regard for the laws that have protected billions of lives?"

"I would not have us crippled by blind adherence to the

law. There is no heir to the line. Astarte follows no rules, and she will exploit our weaknesses."

The unknown female again. "He is male. What possible motive can Astarte have for cursing a male?"

That male voice was thoughtful. "Her relationship with time is unpredictable inside the cage. Perhaps she has discovered something we have not foreseen."

"Explain why she would waste her time on a man."

"Species change over millennia. In my opinion, it may be possible—"

"Your opinion is of no interest, Warden. We have seen what has happened here. There is nothing we can do." The voice softened for the first time. "I am sorry, Mae."

His mother spoke again. Her voice was shaking, and her words were so charged with passionate intent that John drifted closer to the surface.

"You're wrong. There is something we can do. Something I can do."

John knew he was still in Bristol; that he had been moved from the local hospital. He didn't know exactly where he was, only that it was quieter than the first hospital although he sometimes heard crying from other rooms.

"Mae, you cannot. An Adept cannot put her family before her respons—"

"Don't you dare lecture me about responsibilities. You have no idea what the word means. He is my son. My son!"

Silence then, that stretched for half a minute. When his mother spoke again, she was calm, but resolute. "I will do this with, or without, your consent. I will not lose him. I am strong enough to contain it."

"You do not know that. You cannot know that. And if you are wrong, you weaken us all. It may have been Astarte's intention all along, using him to get to you. You will let your

son go, Mae, and your line will end with you. We will begin the search for the next Adept."

"No," said his mother. "John will not survive another day. He may be able to repair the damage, but only if I remove it now. I will not wait."

"You will do what is right for—" the voice vanished mid-sentence, as if someone had flicked a switch. His mother spoke to the man and came closer, but John was already sinking deeper into the whiteness. He listened to his heartbeat, slow and solemn, like the chime of a distant church clock.

As if from a great distance, the male voice spoke again. "I suspected it the first time his father brought him to me. The boy could have wielded power, Mae. The old law should not blind us to the facts. Do what you can for him. I will stand by you."

John stared at the wall of the cottage bedroom. He had finished the first coat.

The memory, now that he had allowed himself to experience it, had revealed a surprising detail. He had recognised the male voice. There could be no mistake. He'd never known the owner of that voice was so close to his mother. As far as John knew, they had only met on a couple of social occasions. And yet he had come all the way to Bristol when John had suffered his breakdown.

The male voice had belonged to Augustus Bonneville.

SEVENTEEN

Evie,

If you did as I asked, I imagine I have your undivided attention now. I have opened your eyes, and you cannot unsee what has been revealed. For centuries, the concept of a hidden world has been bandied about by occult gurus. Some even published books claiming to have visited new dimensions. Ninety-nine percent of it was appalling tosh. They had no more visited the Blurred Lands than I have been to Belgium. Nothing against Belgium, I'm sure it's delightful.

There was one author whom, I suspect, had glimpsed a noone. She wrote a series of articles detailing sightings of fairies in the New Forest over the centuries. She never finished her work. The report I read said she spent a night alone in the forest. When she came out, she didn't write—or speak—another word for the rest of her life. The impact on a twenty-first century human of an encounter with a being from another realm cannot be overestimated. Here, there be dragons. Possibly real dragons if the rumours are true.

One day, you will be an Adept. You will assume my role

as one of the Three. Not immediately after my death, as you are not yet mature, but soon enough. The Wardens will get twitchy while our realm relies on only two protectors.

Back to your pre-history lesson. Now, that's a lazy phrase. How can anything be pre-history?

Magic was once commonplace in our realm. All women can draw upon it to some degree, but there were always those who had a talent for it, and that talent ran in the family. As you now know.

I'm afraid I can offer you no detailed description of what, precisely, magic is. I suppose if we got the best scientific minds on the case, we would know more, and understand why so few can harness its power. But as magic use in our own realm has, since the Accord, been kept secret, it's unlikely it will ever be properly studied.

What I can do, is explain the little I know.

The language of magic, and humans' fascination with it, goes back as far as the beginning of recorded history. Why do we talk about a spell of weather? Because, in ancient times, spells often influenced the weather. A hurricane might be diverted from a town, a landslide held back until those in its path could get to safety. Unfortunately, over time, the deployment of magic led to conflict.

All use of power has consequences. Conjuring a rain storm for thirsty crops might save a village from a hungry winter, but nothing can arise from nothing. For the rain to fall on those particular fields, it had not to fall elsewhere. Perhaps a nearby village went hungry that year. What if they saw the rain-fat clouds ignore the wind and answer another call? It may have made them angry enough to decide the theft of their rain was an act of war. Such a conclusion gave them justification to take up arms against the rain-thieves, to burn their village, and take their harvest.

Whether the magical creatures and gods came before the conflicts that ravaged our realm, no one can say. But come they did, from the other six realms, the powerful, and the power-hungry. They whispered hate into the ears of those who were ready to listen. Skirmishes escalated into battles and battles turned into wars. The pattern of violence and death suffered by those who have the most to lose on behalf of those with all the power was set. And we humans still follow it.

We called them gods because that was how they were perceived, but they are not gods. Does incredible power turn a lusting, petty, vengeful, mad creature into a god? No. But they were feared and worshipped as such. The seven realms, particularly where they overlapped Earth, became a giant board game for these creatures, and the ordinary inhabitants of the realms their pieces. Millions died.

It was a human woman who stopped it. Her name, heavy with connotations in many traditions, was Eve. I was pleased when I heard what they called you, Evie. Such an auspicious name.

When you become an Adept, you will learn more of this history. I will stick to that which is most important. The practical instructions I need to give you are crucial, but I cannot leave you ignorant of what you might have to face.

One god remains, but she is imprisoned. Her name is Astarte. Even caged, she is dangerous. Stay away from her, Evie. I underestimated her once. Do not make the same mistake.

One last revelation for now, one that shocked and thrilled me back in the nineteen-fifties. If feminism was even a word back then, I hadn't heard it. When my mother told me that, behind all the posturing, noise, and self-importance of the men whom I assumed to be in control of everything, it was women who held it all together, I laughed in disbelief. Maybe it won't be as shocking to you. I hope not. It seems that society is finally moving towards parity between the sexes.

Until then, remember this. Only women can access magic, only women can use Earth's true power. It's a dark, fierce, raw natural magic that keeps a balance between the realms, and there's not a man on this planet who can touch it.

EIGHTEEN

By the time John looked at his watch, it was already mid-afternoon. He picked up the dirty brushes before giving the bedroom an appraising look.

The first coat had covered the dark pink, but the result was a colour that even the posh paint companies had yet to name - a kind of sickly, fleshy hue.

"Slapped Arse," said John aloud, trying to think of a name for the unattractive shade he had created. It would need another coat. He tried to think of other names, partly to take his mind off the way the room had changed in ways that had nothing to do with his decorating.

The atmosphere had thickened as it had the previous night. There was a smell, foul and sweet at the same time. His skin was crawling again.

"Untreated Rash," he said, as if coming up with daft paint colour names would dispel his gathering unease. "Fetid Blancmange. Pink Porridge."

It worked. The goosebumps disappeared, the room was just a room again.

"Shaved Ball Sack," he said, and went downstairs.

John cleaned the brushes in the sink and put them on the back doorstep to dry. He had planned to break for lunch, but it was now past three o'clock, and he wanted to get out of the cottage, and breathe fresh air.

He made himself a sandwich and filled up a water bottle. The phone had no signal, no messages. The battery, despite being plugged in for hours, was back at eighteen percent. He swore at it and stuffed it into his pocket. He should get some reception at the edge of the woods.

From inside the cottage, it had looked like a beautiful spring day, but the atmosphere in the woods was that of a baking hot afternoon. Everything was still, with not a breath of wind to stir the air. The only sound, as he trudged between the trees, was his own chewing as he ate the sandwich.

After walking for minutes, he stopped. Something wasn't right. He had looked up Leigh Woods online before making the trip from London. It was a well-maintained National Trust site. He should have found the footpath running east to west through the woods by now. The river Avon was his destination. Not only to get mobile phone reception, but, according to the website, a great view of Clifton Suspension Bridge to the south, perhaps the most iconic landmark in Bristol.

He took a swig of water, then checked the compass on his phone. Turning northeast, John set off again. There was no way he could miss the river. Once he reached it, he'd find the path. There would be signs and, probably, other walkers.

That was odd, John admitted. Not only had he not seen another person, he was yet to find any evidence of their presence. No rubbish, for a start. Although Sally Cottage was the only dwelling inside the woods' perimeter, the affluent, unimaginatively named village of Leigh Woods lay less than half a mile to the south. Posh houses meant posh teenagers, and teenagers should have meant condoms, drug paraphernalia, and empty vodka bottles in the woods. But there was nothing. Not even the only fruit found in all seasons - a hanging bag of dog shit.

As he walked, John found a path of sorts, although he doubted it was the one the National Trust had shown on its map. There should be a broad avenue with benches at regular intervals. This was a rough, narrow track, which never took a straightforward route towards the river when there was an opportunity for it to dart off to one side, loop between some trees and a bramble patch, then head off back towards the river.

John heard the Avon before he saw it, the tranquil dull rumble of a wide river. He quickened his pace at the sound. The water was a rich green-brown—Deep Snot, John christened it, still thinking of paint colours. The river was fast flowing, heading for the Bristol Channel and the Celtic Sea.

After the preternatural stillness of Leigh Woods, John was glad to be in the open. He took out his phone to check for messages. The battery was dead.

"Bugger it." He looked to the south and frowned. Where the hell was the bridge?

It was three-forty-five. John guessed he had been walking for just over half an hour. It had taken him longer than he thought to reach the river, but he couldn't believe he had strayed so far that he was out of sight of the famous landmark.

He put the water on his left and started walking. The river curved to the east ahead of him. With every step he took, he expected to see the bridge come into view, but it didn't happen. He kept his eyes fixed ahead and tried not to panic. He was walking along the bank of the Avon river, which was spanned by a large suspension bridge. Hard to miss. Any time now, it would come into view. Any time.

After twenty minutes, he stopped again, took a long drink from his water bottle, and looked at the woods on his right. Leigh Woods' longest edge ran along the river, but it was less than a mile long. Even if he had got so lost as to exit the woods at their northernmost tip, he should still have passed the bridge, or at least seen it within ten minutes. The entire woods were only about three-quarters of a mile square, so how he had spent nearly an hour in there was also a mystery.

So. No bridge. There was no avoiding it now. If this was connected to John's mental health, he had never heard of a condition that removed famous landmarks from the minds of those who suffered from it.

There was another, bigger, problem John had been trying to avoid acknowledging.

Reluctantly, he turned, putting the woods at his back. He looked across the water to the ridge beyond and up to what lay beyond it.

Or, rather, what didn't lay beyond it.

Bristol had disappeared.

NINETEEN

As he headed back to the cottage, John compared his state of mind with what he remembered from the time of his illness. If Helen's advice was sound, it was important not to allow events to overwhelm him, however bizarre they might be.

He was following a different path back to the cottage, but it was as twisting and narrow as the one he had found earlier. When he came to a small clearing, he sat down with his back against an old oak. He was breathing faster than normal, but his hands were steady. His thoughts, as he examined them, were disturbed but not panicked.

He remembered little of that night out here in the woods, but he had a clear memory of his own mental chaos. It wasn't a memory he cared to evoke.

He considered the situation logically. Either a city of nearly half a million people had vanished, or his mind was not accurately interpreting reality.

John sighed. Bridges and cities were not in the habit of disappearing. However, psychosis sufferers sometimes reported hearing voices or experiencing hallucinations.

Therefore, he had not seen what he thought he had seen. Clifton Suspension Bridge still spanned the Avon Gorge, and Bristol still existed beyond it.

The lack of other people was a more difficult conundrum, but if he could accept that his mind had erased a bridge and a city, John would have to accept it could erase any human beings he had encountered.

His conclusions were bleak, and frightening, but there was one crucial difference between the experience of the younger John and what was happening now. Despite the fact that he was displaying symptoms of mental stress, John's moment-to-moment experience of his own mind was calm and rational. From the morning spent painting, to his over-long walk this afternoon, there were no gaps in his memory. He was dealing with the situation in a way that suggested no loss of control. This was very different to the behaviour he had exhibited as a student.

He thought back to that last night with Ash, approaching the memory with all the caution he might need if he were defusing a bomb. There were large gaps in his memory from that period. What remained were isolated moments that surfaced from time to time, particularly after waking from bad dreams.

For the first time since he had left hospital as a damaged twenty-year-old, he allowed some of the scattered images and sensations from that night to arise, and—as dispassionately as possible—he examined them for similarities with what was happening to him now.

He had been running for what seemed like hours. His lungs burned with every desperate breath he drew, propelling his exhausted body forwards. Fog had drifted in from the Bristol Channel, and he couldn't see more than a few yards in any direction. He looked down at his bare feet. They were filthy, swollen, and bleeding. He slowed, then dropped to his knees on the hard pavement. How far from the woods was he? Far enough? How could he ever be far enough to escape what was coming after him?

He whimpered, a pathetic, thin, desperate sound like a dying animal. His elbows scraped along the tarmac as he crawled forwards, the skin a mixture of tiny stones and his own bloodied, torn flesh.

A shape loomed out of the fog, towering over him. He tried to scream, but wheezed instead, tasting his own blood in his mouth. He spat it out and fell onto his side as another shape loomed into view, followed by a third.

"Son? Son? Can you hear me?"

The words meant nothing. He tried to raise his hands in defence, but his body didn't respond. He was twitching like a landed fish, terrified of the attack he thought was coming.

"What a mess." A different voice. "Stark bloody naked. Look at the bloody state of him. See his eyes? He's on something. Bloody students."

"Have a heart, Graham, look at the poor bastard. We need to get him to a hospital. 'Ere, Benny, fetch me jacket from the cab. Graham, go and knock on the nearest door. Call an ambulance, will you?"

Two of the shapes vanished, but the third came closer. John tried to scramble away, but only managed to take the skin off his palms pushing backwards in panic.

"Settle down, son, settle down. No one's gonna hurt you. You'll be all right. My name's Rob."

Something in those words made sense, and, for a moment, he dared to hope he might have put enough distance between him and the horror behind him. His eyes flicked to the shape now squatting beside him. A beard. Black hair. Human.

"You're in Clifton. The hospital's not far away. I'll stay with you until the ambulance gets here. Oh, cheers, Benny."

He had began to hope that he might, for the time being, be safe, when the bearded man took something from the other shape that came out of the fog.

"Just going to cover you up, son. You're shivering."

Out of the sky, an evil, dark creature unfolded its wings and dived, blotting out what little light there was as it dropped towards its victim.

John tried again to scream, but he had no strength left. He passed out.

That had been the only memory John had allowed himself to revisit for more than a few seconds in the thirty years since the Clifton bin men had found him, naked, covered in mud, grass and twigs, his body bruised and bloodied, his mind already shutting down.

The other memories were far worse. Knowing they were the memories of a broken mind was no help when they arose in the grey half-dawn, when John would wake, sweating and gasping, next to Sarah. He didn't lie to his wife, but he could never bring himself to describe the monsters his diseased brain had conjured to haunt him. Instead, he told her they were dreams about the hospital. Mental health care was less enlightened in the mid-eighties. Sarah had no difficulty in believing the experience would still give him nightmares.

Helen had encouraged him to face his fears. These were among the worst. He had never allowed himself to dwell on the shadowy images that had given him decades of nightmares.

Now, with his back pressed up against the reassuringly solid tree trunk, he did just that. He thought back to the last night he'd spent with Ash. It had begun, as usual, with sex.

Every night he'd spent with her had been a combination of sex, fitful sleep, and short conversations that led to more sex. That final night, he had been determined to talk to her, rather than give in to their usual overpowering lust. Right up to the moment he saw her, he was unaware he was deceiving himself.

They'd ended up in the woods that night. It was the only time they'd left the cottage together. Closing the back gate behind him was John's last clear memory of that night. The rest came in disjointed images.

There'd been a fire burning in a clearing and, by its flickering light, he and Ash had screwed like animals, tearing each other's clothes off without even a semblance of foreplay. He had seen movement in the trees once, as if they were being watched, but Ash had pulled him back towards her.

Then...

He woke. It was much later. He had done what he had come to do - spoken to Ash. Told her he was leaving. He didn't ask her to go with him. He knew, without knowing how, that it was impossible. And he promised himself he would never come back. If he did so, he feared he would be lost, consumed, his last shred of self-will taken from him. He needed to prove he could walk away from this. Whatever was happening between him and Ash wasn't healthy. Although he couldn't have explained why, he had been afraid to tell her, scared of how she might react. To his great relief, she had taken the news calmly, asked him to hold her one last time. They had fallen asleep on the soft earth.

Now the moon was higher. The fire was still burning, and in the yellow and reds of its light, John saw Ash, kneeling, her back towards him. Both of her hands were in the fire itself, the flames going up to her elbows. She didn't flinch, and her skin wasn't burning. He tried to get up, but his head and limbs were heavy. He told himself he was dreaming, but knew he was not. Ash was speaking or chanting. Her voice thickened the air, each word adding weight to the one before. This strange song was not without purpose, he realised. She was making something.

That was the first image John could bring to mind from that night. He was both pleased and scared by how much detail he could evoke. Pleased because he was still rational. Scared because he didn't want to recall the horrors that had triggered his illness.

John stood up, brushing soil from the back of his trousers. He scanned the clearing, then froze. The west gable of the cottage was visible through the trees. He was only yards away. Yet he was sure the cottage hadn't been there when he had first sat down.

He set off towards it. When a suspension bridge and an entire city had vanished, the appearance of a small stone cottage was no big deal.

The evening was already darkening when John opened the back door. He looked at his watch. Eight o'clock He had been out all day. He checked his phone. No signal, battery at eighteen percent again. He made a mental note to buy a new handset.

He left by the front door, heading for the layby and the wisp of phone signal it offered. There would be voicemails, particularly the one from the manager at Fir Trees. Like many children of those in the final stages of dementia, John had long since said goodbye to his mother. The occasional moments of lucidity these days were illusory. She wasn't responding to him, she was playing back a memory, like a needle falling at random on the vinyl beneath. Had he been a religious man, he would have prayed for her death. It wasn't that she was suffering - she was no longer there to suffer. It was John who suffered, holding the hand of a ghost who could never say the words he wanted to hear.

He thought of his dream the night before. He couldn't recall many details, but he remembered his mother speaking to him. It had been an important conversation, and an intimate one, the sort of chat they had never had in reality. Mae was of the generation that had seen child-rearing as a subject for which there were rules. She had treated cooking the same way, boiling vegetables until they drooped from the fork, and looking askance at suspicious foreign innovations such as garlic. She didn't mistreat her son, but, as he grew up, he suspected his birth had come as a disappointment. He had been shocked one long Sunday afternoon when, aged seven, he had overheard his mother crying. Standing outside her bedroom door, he listened to his father's murmurs of awkward consolation as she wept, raging at her inability to produce another child.

Why? thought John. She struggled to show him much affection. Why would she want another child?

Something in his dream had suggested an answer, or at least the beginnings of one, but John couldn't bring to mind anything helpful. All he remembered was that she had been warning him.

When, after three hundred yards, he still couldn't hear traffic, or see the streetlights through the trees, he stopped.

He pulled his phone out of his pocket. No signal.

It was getting darker more quickly than he expected. The sun wasn't due to set for another forty-five minutes.

It was 8:40pm, but he was sure he hadn't been walking

for even five minutes. His phone showed the same time. How had he lost over half an hour?

John looked over his shoulder, and his mouth went dry. He couldn't be seeing what he thought he was seeing. He turned, slowly. Three feet away, there was a wooden stake with a metal postbox on top.

Sally Cottage. *No junk mail, no free newspapers, no unsolicited callers.*

Next to the stake, the high iron gate. Just behind it, the cottage. But he had been walking away from it towards the road.

He turned and ran.

His breath quickly became hard to regulate, and his legs complained at being asked to do anything more strenuous than jogging. The last time he had run through these woods, John had been twenty. He felt every one of those thirty-one extra years as he gasped his way along the path.

When the panic faded, he slowed to a walk again, ashamed at his own reaction. Whatever was happening, the rational, methodical, patient mindset he had developed as an adult was what he needed now, not the knee-jerk terror of a teenager in a horror film.

The sun withdrew its last yellow-orange tendrils, and darkness rolled in behind it. As John's eyes struggled to adjust to the rapid change of light, he caught sight of something man-made ahead and quickened his pace. When he got closer, he put his hands on his knees and stared in disbelief.

He was looking at a gate. Next to it was a metal postbox. Sally Cottage.

Shaking his head, and taking long, slow breaths, he opened the gate. In the semi-darkness, the cottage looked sinister and withdrawn, its windows like eyes, its door a gaping mouth.

He moved forward, acknowledging his fear, but overriding it. He visualised himself reaching the door, turning the handle and walking in.

As his hand reached out for the door handle, the light changed, a glow illuminating the small garden.

He stepped backwards and looked up. The light was on in Ash's bedroom. The master bedroom, he corrected himself, not Ash's bedroom.

As he looked up, shadows flitted across the window as if someone were moving around.

John went inside.

TWENTY

Closing the door behind him, John stood for a moment, listening. The cottage was silent. The bedroom above, even back when it was carpeted, had been a soundstage of creaks and groans from the old floorboards. Now, stripped back to floorboards, curtains gone and all soft furnishings removed, every sound echoed around the cottage.

Silence. Or, rather, the usual array of tiny noises from inside and out. John took a few steps of his own, and the floor creaked below his feet. He stopped and listened again. Still nothing, but the glow from above spilled onto the landing. The light hadn't been on when he'd first seen the cottage from the gate. He knew the most likely reason was faulty wiring. Yes. It must be faulty wiring.

His watch, and phone, now agreed that it was 11:17pm. Another two-and-a-half hours lost in the last ten minutes.

With a show of bravado he didn't feel, he squared his shoulders, turned, and crossed the room to the stairs. The light was stronger now, and the flickering was not that of a faulty bulb, but something passing in front of it.

John gripped the bannister. He found he was watching his actions at a remove as if through the lens of a camera. He wondered if this was how the brave gathered their courage, by acting as if they were observing someone else. As he climbed the stairs, he knew that if this were a movie, the score would now introduce an ominous wash of low strings, discordant and unnerving.

At the top of the staircase, he forced himself to drop his distancing tactics. The door to the bedroom was half open. Now he was closer, he could hear muffled sounds. Music. There was something familiar about it, a rhythmic pulse filtered of any frequencies that made it recognisable.

He put his hand on the door, leaned forward, and pushed it wide open.

The instant his foot touched the floor, the sound changed into the chorus of Don't You Want Me, by The Human League. It was loud, but other sounds were louder. Laughing and shouted conversations sprung up around him.

The room had changed. It was at least double the size. The light came from a single standard lamp in the corner. He was standing on a carpet. On the far side of the room was a staircase. People occupied every step, some in earnest conversations, some kissing in the desperate way only the young or drunk do, others waiting to get to the bathroom.

John had walked into a party. Not just any party. He looked to his left and saw, through a serving hatch in the wall, a big kitchen. Every surface was covered in bottles, some empty and others full. The full ones were being passed through the hatch to a cluster of eager girls who handed them round and drank straight from the bottle.

Blue Nun, thought John. *Yegods.*

He walked to the serving hatch and someone passed

him some beers. Then he was pushing through a mass of dancing bodies, holding three bottles over his head. He hadn't decided to do it, but he had lost all agency. His body was no longer his own to control.

Another John was in charge now. John knew him well because it was his twenty-year-old self. He remembered this party, he remembered this song, and he remembered the next ten minutes.

This was his friend Simon Hodge's house in Clifton. Or, rather, Simon's parents' house. They were in Spain and had left their student son in charge of a six-bedroom home and an extensive wine cellar. Simon, John remembered as he reached the knot of bobbing figures around the record player, died in a car crash the year after graduating.

It was 1986, and he was minutes away from seeing Ash for the first time.

"Johnny! You're the man!"

Chris grabbed two of the bottles, handing one to Alison. They were all English students. Alison was the brightest of the three. Chris was loud and funny, his puppy-like energy so unlike Alison's quiet intensity it was inevitable they would end up together. John was the third wheel, but he didn't feel awkward. Well, no more than usual. He and Alison shared shyness, a love of Blake's poetry, and a worldview which gravitated towards the pessimistic. Chris had announced he and John would be friends the first day of freshers' week, and it had been easy to go along with him. John knew, when they parted company the following year, Chris would promise to stay in touch but wouldn't, and that was fine.

"Cheers!"

They drank, the cold beer tasteless but refreshing.

John knew he should, as Chris put it, be 'scoping the room for birds'. John had sworn he would speak to a girl tonight. As plans go, it had seemed simple and unambitious while he'd been rolling up his jacket sleeves and putting borrowed mousse in his hair. Now he was in a room full of women, it was impossible. John could only speak coherently to a woman he found attractive if one of two conditions were met:

1) they were on the other end of a phone, or
2) he was very drunk.

At twenty years old, John was still a virgin.

Two burly, rugby-playing lads had commandeered the record player. The sleeve on the top of the pile was Two Tribes by Frankie Goes To Hollywood. John was, by his own admission, a terrible dancer, which was another obstacle to his romantic ambitions. He tried to avoid it whenever possible, but there was something about the groovy pomposity of Two Tribes that made him want to move his body around. Unfortunately, he did this in a jerky, uncontrolled way guaranteed to amuse anyone far enough away not to be hit by one of his flailing limbs.

He took another sip of beer, concluding that he wasn't anywhere near drunk enough to make a fool of himself. Then the DJ tag team dropped the needle, the orchestral opening began, and he found his fingers twitching against the cold bottle. Before he knew it, his head was bobbing in anticipation of the guitar riff.

Chris looked at him. He had witnessed John's dancing skills on previous occasions.

"Mate," he said, an urgent note of caution in his voice, "you're not thinking what I think you're thinking, are you? Tell me you're not. No, no, no, John... MATE!"

Too late. Handing Alison his beer, John made his way into the mass of bodies in the centre of the room. He was bouncing on his toes as he went, and the nearest knot of girls parted to let him through, exchanging glances and giggling.

John shut his eyes. His shoulders moved, then his elbows shot out as if he was being puppeteered by someone having a seizure. The first line of the song was coming up, and he took a lungful of air, ready to sing along.

At the point when the lyric kicked in, he opened his eyes for a second, the bodies between him and the door parted, and he saw her.

She was wearing... something, John assumed, otherwise she would have provoked more of a reaction from those nearer to the door. But he didn't notice any clothes. That wasn't to say she was naked, just that—had you pinned him down the next day and asked him to describe her, which is precisely what Chris did—John would not have been able to recall any details about her clothing. Her face, though, was another matter. He was sure he stared at it for ten minutes straight, but when he found himself standing inches away from her, Frankie still hadn't finished the first chorus.

If there was a part of the brain dedicated to lust, that part had gone from zero to a hundred percent in milliseconds and had told the rest of his cerebrum to take the night off.

She had long auburn hair, thick, braided, a few strands falling across her face. Dark-green eyes. A strong face, direct, uncompromising.

John had always been adamant he didn't have a 'type' when it came to women. To his friends, he claimed he would be delighted with anyone intelligent, awake, and facing in his direction. In private, however, his fantasies had gravitated towards an unfashionable Rubens-esque ideal. If the rest of his prefrontal cortex had still been allowed a say, John might have thought, *hang on... pre-Raphaelite face, body by Rubens - you're not worried that this woman looks pretty much exactly what you imagine when your hands are down your pants?*

John took his eyes off her for a moment as someone banged on the window. When he looked back, the woman had gone.

He blinked in confusion, looking from left to right. She wasn't there.

"No," he whispered, only now noticing his erection and moving his hands to cover the evidence of his straining jeans.

He turned his head to scan the rest of the room, despite knowing there was no way she could have got past him unnoticed.

That was when she'd come up behind him and, standing on tiptoe, her breasts pushed against his back, said, "If I asked you to come home with me, would you do it?"

The resumption of activity in his jeans made him gasp, and he didn't answer immediately. Just tipsy enough to be brave, and unbelievably horny, he put one hand behind him. Her fingers interlaced with his, then she traced her thumbnail across his palm, and he moaned.

Did I just moan? he thought, but out loud, he said, "Yes."

The moment after John said "yes" to his fantasy woman at the party, the house, music, Chris, Alison, and another fifty drunk students vanished, along with Clifton itself.

The woman in front of him opened a high, iron gate. He

didn't even know her name. When should he ask her what her name was?

"Ash," she said, and he wondered if she could read his mind, before realising he had spoken out loud.

"Um, right, Ash. Um. Good." She stopped walking in front of the cottage door. There was a key in her hand. John was still confused about what she was wearing. He made an effort to pay attention to her clothes, but as soon as he did, he forgot why and imagined her naked. Why was she looking at him like that? Had she changed her mind?

"No, I haven't," she said. *Still speaking my thoughts out loud, then? Smooth.* He froze, wondering if he had said that out loud too. She gave no sign of having heard it, but she hadn't unlocked the door.

"Um..?" he said.

"Do you have a name? If not, I'm calling you Um."

"A name? Yes, yes, I do, yes."

Still looking at him.

Shit.

"John, John, it's John. John. That's my John. Name."

"Well, John, come in."

Another missing piece of time, and he was sitting on the biggest bed he had ever seen in his life, a Gothic nightmare made of iron. Ash was in the bathroom. He wasn't sure whether he should get undressed, or if that would be too forward. But Ash had taken him up to the bedroom, told him she wouldn't be long. And she'd kissed him before leaving the room, the kind of kiss that suggested a hunger he doubted he'd be able to satisfy, but was prepared to try very hard to do so. She wanted sex. With him. Tonight. Here. He was sure of it.

He'd already taken his jacket off and hung it on the back of a chair. Now he kicked off his trousers. He was keenly aware of how unsexy men were considered to look in socks, so he peeled them off. He pulled his T-shirt over his head. Leaning back, propped up on one elbow, he tried to assume the posture of a man of the world, whatever that was. He raised one eyebrow, thought of Roger Moore, and lowered it again.

If he was too awkward or over-keen, might Ash realise he was a virgin, and change her mind?

Perhaps he shouldn't have taken his clothes off. What if she wanted to seduce him, undress him? Panicked by the idea, he leapt off the bed and started to get dressed as fast as possible. When Ash opened the door of the bedroom, he had one leg in his trousers, a sock in each hand, and was attempting to squeeze his head through the arm of his T-shirt.

"Take those clothes off, John."

He pulled his head back out of the T-shirt, his hair sticking out in every direction.

John straightened up, dropping the socks and hitting the lantern above with the back of his head. It swung wildly, giving the unlikely scene an unreal quality.

Ash was naked. She was naked, and she was walking towards him. She was naked, and she was walking towards him, and she was pulling his trousers off, then his underpants. She was naked, and she was walking towards him, and she was in front of him, and she was pulling his trousers and his underpants down, and she was taking his hand and, while she leaned up to kiss him, she was putting it between her legs, and he knew then it was going to happen, and every part of his brain not involved with receiving, or giving, pleasure, shut down.

"Is this your first time?" Grammatically, that was a question, but the way she said it left John in no doubt that she knew the answer. She was breathing heavily, looking at him with such anticipation he couldn't believe she was looking at the same face he saw in the mirror every morning - bland, uninteresting, average. Then her long fingers found his penis, she pushed him back onto the bed, and he stopped thinking.

TWENTY-ONE

Evie,

If you have read this far, if you have sung a word of power, then you may be more frightened than excited now. You'd need to be unintelligent not to be frightened, and you struck me as a bright girl, even when you were tiny.

Your world, the world you lived in before you read this, is gone. Forever. There can be no bringing it back, but you must continue to live in it. The rules and expectations of society no longer apply to you, but it is essential that you behave as if they do.

We are no better than anyone else. That's an easy thing to say. You might even think you mean it when you say it. But, and you must never forget this, Evie, it's true. We are more powerful, but we are no better.

Soon, I will be dead. One day—a very long time in the future, I hope—you will die, too. But the power carried by our ancestors and descendants will continue. Have you ever waded into a shallow stream and made a dam with the stones you found there? You can change the course of the water for a while. But once you have gone, someone else can move stones and alter the course you constructed. Even if no one ever came, the force of the water would eventually dislodge your stones, and find its own course again. Magic is a stream, Evie. We do not know where it comes from, we only know where to find it. We can move some stones around, that's all. The stream continues long after we are back in the soil.

Evie, there will always be a temptation for women born into the Three to confuse the use of power with power itself. Once, hundreds of years ago, this led to open hostility in the Blurred Lands. The peace between Earth and the other realms hung in the balance. After a bloody and costly campaign, a rogue Adept was killed. That line of the Three was exiled, and the Wardens found another line to take their place. All power can be dangerous, but magic is the most insidious and dangerous of all. Never forget it. Look to your family, Evie. Remember who you are, think on your mortality, and use your power wisely.

Forgive the dire warnings, but I need to teach you something you mustn't try before you are ready. Promise me. If you are reading this before you reach maturity, before you... oh dammit, I'm going to have to stop being so old-fashioned. If you are reading this before you've started your periods, then you must promise me you will not try what I am about to describe. Our control over magic is linked to the cycle of life and death that takes place in our own bodies every month. What I have taught you so far can be learned by any female with a gift for magic and the right training. But what you will learn now is only possible for Adepts, or those training to be Adepts.

I'm deadly serious about this, Evie. What I'm about to

tell you opens the door to the seven realms. You must not open this door until you are ready. Promise? Good. Then I will tell you how to access the Between.

TWENTY-TWO

The green-filtered sunlight was already streaming through the window when John woke up. He was still dressed. And he wasn't on the sofa. He sat up on the iron bed. The walls were magnolia, the floorboards covered in sheets. The bare lightbulb hung above him.

He stumbled to the bathroom and washed, splashing cold water on his face.

Downstairs, he made tea and toast. The loaf of bread, which he knew he'd used the day before to make a sandwich, was unopened. The butter was untouched as was the marmalade. In the fridge, the milk was full, and the packet of cheese had all eight slices again.

He checked his phone. The battery was dead, despite being plugged in. He switched the plug off and on a few times. Nothing.

John took his tea outside, leaving the back door open while he stood on the wet grass in bare feet, watching the heat of the morning sun lift the dew.

He scratched his crotch. John had already given his genitals a good check upstairs. His whole body, in fact. He was still fifty-one, not twenty, and it was clear he hadn't indulged in a night of vigorous sexual intercourse. Nights like that left physical evidence, but he wasn't sore, and his balls didn't feel as if someone had used them for a table-tennis match.

It had just been a dream. A memory. Except it hadn't been that at all.

He heard distant birdsong. There was no sound of traffic from the nearby road and, despite a clear sky, there was no evidence of any planes, no contrails interrupting the solid blueness. John was certain that, if he were to open the back gate and walk, he would end up back where he started again. There was a low buzz of dread at the top of his spine where instincts evolved over millennia were telling him he was not just alone, he was more alone than any human ever.

This wasn't a—what had Helen called it?—an *aftershock* from his breakdown. This was really happening.

When he had walked into the cottage bedroom and found himself in 1986, it hadn't felt like a hallucination. The creatures he'd seen in the Bloomsbury Suite, the missing city and bridge - none of them were hallucinations. He could treat them as such, but that would be to deny the evidence of every one of his senses, plus his continuing capacity for logical reasoning.

He had been there. In Clifton. With Chris and Alison at the party where he'd met Ash. The party where, afterwards, his best friends had insisted he'd left alone, without saying goodbye.

He had relived the evening in exactly the same level of detail as when it had happened. Not only externally although that had been convincing enough. Until the previous night, ninety-nine percent of the details of that evening had long since dissolved, leaving a handful of individual moments he could bring to mind. But now, having lived it all again, he could remember everyone who was there, what they were wearing, what they were drinking. He could remember Alison brushing fluff off Chris's shoulder. And the fact that everything reeked of cigarette smoke.

There were enough details to persuade him that what he had experienced was more than a hallucination. But it was the interior experience that clinched it. Every thought, however banal, that had passed through John Aviemore's mind on that night in 1986 had been present to him once again, without exception. He had been a passive witness to his younger self's stream of consciousness.

While he had carried the beers across the room to Chris and Alison, the label in the back of his T-shirt had rubbed against his neck. This physical sensation led to a trivial train of thought. And yet he had relived it without omitting a single detail.

He had a spot on his neck which was already tender, and the label wasn't helping. He wondered if he should go to the kitchen, try to find a pair of scissors, try to cut it out. That would mean asking someone to do it for him. Maybe a girl. That might work. He'd been near the kitchen just now for the beers, and there were three possible candidates. One was too pretty, he'd clam up if he asked her. She was wearing a short skirt. Her friend was cute, but she was already drunk, swaying. That left the girl with the glasses and the Alice band. She had been uncorking bottles with a lick of speed that suggested she was well-practised. John remembered then that she waitressed in a Clifton restaurant. What was her name? Kara? Tara? Clara? Shit. She was in a few of his lectures. He couldn't ask her to cut the label out in case he got her name wrong. And what if she said no? They'd laugh, and he'd have to laugh too, although his cheeks would go bright red, because that's what they did in every awkward situation, which was a bad bit of biology. What was the evolutionary advantage of blushing when you'd made a prat of yourself?

Half of John had wanted to slap his younger self and tell him to get his head out of his own arse. The other half wanted to give him a hug and tell him everything would all be all right.

Putting his half-finished cup of tea on the windowsill, John walked out of the back gate into Leigh Woods. His brain was aching like an overused muscle. He needed some simple physical exercise.

Five minutes into his walk, and he was already more relaxed. Despite suspecting he was experiencing something so far beyond common experience that there wasn't even a name for it, John found that breathing air freshened by trees on a sunny morning made him—if not happy—then, at least, calm. The soft earth gave a little under his feet with each step.

He thought about Sarah. Her presence arose naturally, as they had enjoyed woodland walks on hundreds of occasions during their marriage. Even if it was only Wimbledon Common on a Sunday evening, hand-in-hand among the joggers and dog walkers, they had shared an impulse to get close to the natural world. Sarah knew the names of many of the plants and trees. John was happy to listen and learn from her. Later, over supper in one of the nearby pubs, they would discuss the week ahead, maybe talk about how Harry and Evie were doing, then get home for a video call and catch up with them.

John knew why Sarah was on his mind now. He couldn't stop himself feeling a strong residual sense of guilt over what had happened last night. It hadn't been a dream or a memory; it had been a second-by-second replay. He couldn't change anything. The only difference from the original experience had been his own presence as an observer in his own younger mind and body. Which meant he had been just as excited, just as horny, just as desperate to explore her body as he had been at the time. His dream, memory, replay—whatever the hell it was—of the three times they'd had sex that first night had been vivid and visceral. Hence the guilt, and the deliberate reconnection with Sarah.

But what was there to feel bad about? The encounter had taken place years before he and Sarah had met, so there was no betrayal. The logic of this didn't prevent the twist of regret, anger, and guilt in his gut.

John walked for an hour. He tried to head north, but every time he checked the position of the sun, he found he had strayed from his route somehow. There was no sign of the edge of the woods.

When he came out of the trees into a small clearing, his mood was darkening, and he was increasingly aware of how afraid he was. He was trapped, his dead ex-lover might be haunting him, and he had no idea how to escape. It made no difference if this was all in his mind or real.

He was so wrapped up in his own thoughts that he didn't realise he wasn't alone until the music started.

TWENTY-THREE

Years ago, by the look of it, an elm had been split by lightning, and half of it had fallen into the clearing where John was now standing. The trunk had long since been claimed by ivy and moss, the death of the tree providing an opportunity for new life to flourish.

Perched on the toppled trunk was what John at first imagined to be a child. He was thin, his profile drawn and angular, his eyes shut as he blew into a wooden instrument, producing a plaintive, eerie sound.

John didn't want to move, half-believing that if he did so, this vision would prove to be a trick of the light. The boy was wearing a brown tunic, knotted around his middle with twine. His feet were bare. He blew again, shaking his head, dissatisfied with the sound.

As John watched with fascination, the boy rubbed one dirty thumb along the edge of the wooden whistle, and a thin strip of wood peeled away and fell to the ground below. John squinted, looking for a knife, but there was nothing to see. The boy raised the instrument to his lips again. This time, the sound was clearer. Nodding to himself, the child played a simple melody of three notes played over and over. After repeating the phrase four times, the boy took a breath and resumed. The melody was the same, but as he continued, the air itself rippled like a heat haze around him.

John, standing as still as possible, held his breath when an enormous rabbit hopped into the clearing, heading towards the boy. No, John realised, not a rabbit, but a hare. He had never seen one so close. It was sleek, muscular, and wild; black eyes fixed ahead, long ears twitching.

With an impressive leap, it joined the boy on the fallen tree, watching him as he played his tune. The boy's eyes were half-shut, and he nodded along with the music. After the hare sat beside him, the melody changed, slowing and lowering in pitch.

A few seconds after the new melody began, John blinked in surprise. He had almost fallen asleep on his feet. When he looked back at the boy, he saw that the hare's head had dropped, and it had stretched out on the trunk, breathing slowly; relaxed, eyes closed.

The boy stopped playing, but the atmosphere created by his tune still lent a soporific ambience to the sunlit clearing. Turning to the sleeping hare, the child stroked its sleek fur, then slipped one hand underneath its head. It didn't stir. With a dextrous movement, the boy jerked the animal's head up and to the side, cleanly breaking its neck with a crack that dissipated the effects of the music. Using only his hands, he began skinning his prey.

John couldn't quite reconcile the beauty of the music and the savagery of the act. When he got over the initial shock, he acknowledged that the killing had been instant and, probably, painless. The boy's actions had looked respectful. Didn't the Native Americans thank the spirit of the animal they killed for food?

Once his bloody work was done, the boy turned, without fear, and looked at John.

"Are you hungry?" he said. "There's enough for both of us."

Once that face was turned towards him, John could see that his initial assumption was wrong. This was no child. The grey eyes were too knowing, the language too sophisticated. A quick reassessment put the lad in his teens or even older although John had seen bigger preschoolers. Physically, he exhibited none of the common features of dwarfism, and when he jumped from the tree trunk and walked round to a small pile of branches, he moved with the lithe grace and confidence of an athlete.

"Well?" He stared at John with frank curiosity.

John smiled. "Er, no, no thank you. I've eaten. But, please, go ahead."

As John spoke, the expression on the boy's face changed from relaxed and at ease to tense and guarded. His disconcerting eyes narrowed in suspicion. He reached into the pocket of his tunic, and John flinched, expecting to see a weapon. It was the wooden whistle. The boy brought it to his lips with as much speed as if this were a shoot out. The melody that emerged was brighter, faster, and more complex, but again, featured a phrase that repeated over and over.

There was no change of atmosphere this time. The boy stopped playing. His mouth hung open with astonishment.

"You're no noone," he said. "What are you? You can't be what you seem to be. Can you?"

"I don't understand," said John. "What do you mean?"

The boy looked left and right, then shot a glance over his shoulder. His grip tightened on his recorder. For a moment, John was convinced he would bolt. Then he relaxed a little, put the instrument back in his pocket, and pointed at a spot on the ground between him and John, about six feet away from the fire.

Keeping his movements as slow and non-threatening as possible, John walked forward and sat where the boy had indicated.

"I'm not going to hurt you," said John, then wondered why he had bothered. However physically dominated the boy might be, someone who could whittle wood with their bare hands and enchant animals with music wouldn't be afraid of a tired, scared man in his early fifties.

The boy waved a hand at the piled branches while singing something under his breath. John watched him pick up the skinned hare, then looked back at the branches as they crackled and spat, flames licking around their leaves, sending smoke up towards the treetops.

The boy neatly gutted the animal and impaled it on a sharp stick before dropping it onto a spit made of two forked branches. As the flesh glistened, then darkened, he licked the blood from his fingers, staring at John all the while.

He cooked his food in silence, then ate, leaving the hare on the stick while he tore strips of flesh away with his teeth. The boy's initial offer to share with John had evidently been generous, because he was hungry enough to eat every last scrap himself, sucking the bones when he was done.

He fixed his gaze on John throughout, looking him up and down, sometimes staring at items of clothing with interest, spending a minute frowning at his boots. Eventually, he nodded.

"Human?" he said, as if it were the most natural question under the circumstances. John, taken aback by the implications of the question, was slow to reply.

"Yes... yes," he said. "Human. I'm human."

The boy nodded again, and John felt emboldened to ask the obvious.

"And you are...?"

"Noon." The boy pronounced the word as if doing so fully answered John's enquiry.

"Right," said John. "Noon. Wait." He thought of the building where he had encountered the solicitor, Hackleworth. "N, O, O, N, E?" He sketched the shape of the letters in the air in front of him.

"Yes," said the boy. "Noone."

As in Noone House. What the hell?

"I'm John. John Aviemore." When John held out his hand, the boy spat on his own then rubbed his palm briefly against John's. His skin was cold, despite the warmth of the day.

"Gaius," he said.

"Guy Uss?"

"Call me Gai. Well met, John Aviemore."

John couldn't help but smile at that. It was exactly the sort of thing Augustus might have said.

"How long?" said Gai.

"I'm sorry?"

"How long have you been here?"

"Two nights," said John. "I think."

"Hmm." Gai walked back to the fallen trunk and picked up a canvas knapsack from behind it. He reached in and pulled out a bottle, removing the cork with his teeth. He offered it to John, twirling the cork between his fingers with impressive dexterity.

John's inclination to demur was overruled by the friendliness he felt towards Gai. It was like meeting a distant relative.

He took the bottle and drank. The liquid was alcoholic,

and sweet. It was so light it was almost like drinking vapour. John gave the bottle back and watched as Gai drank.

"What is that? I've never tasted anything like it."

Gai re-corked the bottle.

"Mead," he said. "Good stuff, too, not the usual. Nicked it from Obe's personal stash." He held the bottle up towards the sun. "It's all I have to drink until I can get out of here."

"You too? You can't get out?"

"Seems that way. I got lost here last half-moon. Time works differently near the cage. Might be that I've been here twelve moons."

"Cage? What cage?"

"It's my fault. Too curious, even for a noone. We know not to get too close. There are warning charms all over this edge of the Lands. But, hey, I'm the most talented magician for a thousand moons, everyone knows that. And father gave me his blessing. Said I should explore the area." He looked rueful for a second, then smiled. "Anyway, now you're here, they can't say I'm reckless. You came to find me. Here I am, John Aviemore."

"I didn't come to find you, Gai. I was out walking, that's all. About this cage..."

"I don't understand what you mean. You walked here today, so you and I were meant to meet."

"No. It's just a coincidence."

"A what?"

Gai wouldn't answer John's questions until he'd explained the meaning of the word. When John had finished, he was still puzzled.

"How can two *incidences* that lead to a significant event occur without any connection?"

He demanded an example. Without knowing why, John told Gai a story he'd never told anyone before.

"A young woman was working at a design agency near Waterloo station. It was Tuesday, the third of July, nineteen-ninety. She knocked a cactus off a window sill. It was in a terracotta pot. Her elbow caught it as she was opening the window. Her office was three floors up, and she leaned out. A man was tying his shoelace below. She screamed a warning and, to her horror, the man looked up a split second before the cactus was about to hit him. She heard the pot smash as she sprinted across the office and ran downstairs. When she got to the door of the building, she was already crying. She knew there was no way the man could have avoided the falling pot plant. To her amazement, the man was standing in the doorway, unharmed. In his cupped hands was soil, pieces of terracotta, and a dented cactus. She was shaking and upset. He took her back inside and got her a glass of water. Three months later they were married. The cactus didn't survive."

"So? How is this a coincidence?"

John was lost in his own thoughts. "What? Oh, I'm sorry. It's just that I know everything about this story, and it's full of coincidences. I was the man. The woman was Sarah, my wife. She had swapped desks with a co-worker that morning because she wanted more natural light for a drawing she was working on. That meant she didn't know how stiff the window was, which meant her elbow caught the cactus which her co-worker denied even owning. I was on my way to a magic convention, and I was late, so was jogging along Waterloo Road. My lace came undone just as I was under the window. I heard a scream, the pot smashed on the pavement right next to me, so I scooped up what I could and took it to the door. All those unrelated incidents led to Sarah and I meeting for the first time. All coincidences."

Gai stared at him as if he were an idiot. "Not coincidences. The word means nothing, the concept is stupid."

John shrugged. "Some people take comfort in believing in fate - that things are 'meant to be,' the same way as people take comfort in religion. Not everyone is comfortable believing their lives are governed by chance."

"Your... wife. She is your life partner."

"Yes. She was. She died."

Gai offered no platitudes. "Then, if you had waited a few minutes to tie your shoe, someone else would have been her partner?"

"Well, we wouldn't have met that day. So, yes, it's probable we would have married other people."

Gai was looking at him intently. "And yet, what you said then was a lie. You believe you would have found each other somehow, am I right?"

John looked at the sky. The sun was already touching the tree tops to the west. He had left the cottage in the morning. He thought he'd been out for two hours, maximum. Apparently not.

Gai waited for his answer. John frowned.

"I want to believe it, yes. Because I loved her. But it would mean our freedom is an illusion, that our future is already written, and I can't believe that."

"Hmm." Gai offered him the bottle. "Noones do not have a word for 'coincidence'. Everything is connected. It is so obvious, we do not even have to state it. We do not believe anything, we just are. Bizarre concept, belief. I would like to know more about it."

The edges of the clearing were darkening now. There was something strange about it. Behind the tree trunk, instead of a line of trees, John could see the outline of a rectangle hanging in mid-air. As he looked at it, it became a window.

In confusion, John looked at Gai, who was shaking his head at him.

"You have been in the cage. She has you. You cannot leave unless she allows it. Even with your power, I doubt it can be done."

"Who? What cage? My power?" To John's left, the trees had vanished, replaced with a solid wall, painted white. There was an image on the wall, but he couldn't make it out. From all sides, carpet was growing like grass, fibres pushing up through the soil and replacing the forest floor.

"The spell I cast on you had no effect. You drank the mead and didn't pass out. You're a riddle, a conundrum, an impossibility. You have power. Which must be why I'm here. I can help you. Teach you. Otherwise, she will destroy you. She tried this before. Lured a clueless virgin into the cage, bound him to her with sex magic. Somehow, she failed. The kid got away." The noone winked. "He looked a lot like you, John Aviemore. Which means you've either aged badly recently, or, more likely, time is being distorted by the cage."

John stared at him in astonishment and tried to prioritise his thousand questions in order of importance. "What does she want?"

"What does any prisoner want? To escape."

A wooden desk was taking shape a few feet in front of where John was standing. He saw a bookshelf above it appear inch by inch, taking on more definition every second. The area around Gai was darkening.

"Who is Ash?" shouted John. "Who is she?"

"Astarte," said Gai. John looked blankly at him. "Ishtar. Ashtoreth."

"Am I supposed to know what that means? What am I dealing with here?"

"She needs you. You must find out why."

Gai was still there, but he was fading at the same rate that the room was appearing. John looked at the wall on his left. The image was clearer now. It was a poster, the top right corner hanging loose, revealing the blutack beneath. A drawing of a two-headed man looked back at him. Theatre Clwyd's 1980 production of The Hitchhiker's Guide To The Galaxy. The poster had been on John's bedroom wall during his second year at university. He looked at the jagged words, Don't Panic, and did the opposite.

Gai had gone. John shouted anyway.

"Is she a ghost? A demon? What?"

Gai's voice came to him as if he were at the far end of a long tunnel.

"Worse than either. She is a god."

TWENTY-FOUR

John's student accommodation in Bristol was on the top floor of a three-storey building divided into six flats. There was a communal kitchen and sitting room on the ground floor, and a bathroom on the second floor. In John's room, there was enough space for a bed, a desk and chair, a bookshelf and a sink. The other room on his floor was occupied by Chris and—more often than not—Alison.

He looked at the fold-up travel clock next to the single bed. 06:48. Perfect.

John smiled as he unfolded his legs from the narrow bed, which was three inches too short for him to stretch out in. He was thinking of the nights he had spent in the enormous double bed a few miles away in Leigh Woods.

John put on a striped dressing gown. His feet were in slippers. The slippers in question, which were fluffy, were at the top of a list of clothing items Chris had suggested he throw out if he ever hoped to get laid. John now wore them with pride.

There was a reason he liked to be up early these past few weeks. The post arrived just after six-thirty.

As he turned the corner of the last flight of stairs, he saw a pile of flyers and bills on the mat, but no letter. He bit back his disappointment.

After that first night, Ash had taken his address and promised she would write to him. His absolute confidence that she would, after the amazing night they had spent together, had taken a knock when he heard nothing for three days. After six days, he had become convinced that Ash had found his performance inadequate and embarrassing. He recorded a mix tape featuring the music of The Smiths and prepared himself for a self-indulgent weekend of misery. When the first letter arrived a week to the day after that first night, he revisited his re-evaluation and decided he was, in fact, a rather impressive lover for someone with so little experience, and a sensitive and attentive companion to boot.

Another letter had arrived a week after the first. Seven days had passed since then. John reminded himself that there was a second post in the early afternoon.

He made tea in the least stained mug, struggling to get the kettle under the tap without knocking over the tower of dirty dishes. There was no milk other than the unopened bottle at the back of the fridge, which had been there since he'd moved in. His housemates claimed it had been there a decade and had christened it Nigel. Someone had put a tiny hat and scarf on it. The liquid inside was grey. John drank his tea black.

At the foot of the staircase, he saw it, just the tiniest cream-coloured corner visible underneath a two-for-one pizza offer. With the toe of one furry slipper, he slid the other envelopes aside and saw his name and address, blue ink on the thick cream envelope. The looping handwriting made his heart beat faster.

Upstairs, he shut the bedroom door with his shoulder and leaned against it, as he carefully tore open the envelope. The heavy, old-fashioned stationery and the use of a fountain pen might have suggested a long romantic epistle, but Ash's letters were brief and unromantic. The latest was the tersest yet: *Tonight? A.*

John glanced at the clock again 07:12. Better get downstairs for that shower. He picked up his wash bag. When he opened the door, Ash was standing there.

John looked at the washbag, but it had become a bottle of wine.

He was standing outside Sally Cottage..

John handed Ash the bottle. The transition from his bedroom to the door of the cottage twelve hours later had been instant, but undramatic. John knew it had happened, but, following Ash—naked as usual—into her front room, his memory of the missing hours was perfectly clear and perfectly mundane.

He had tried, and failed, to finish an essay on whether Dickens could be accused of misogyny in Great Expectations. In the afternoon, which had dragged, he had gone to the cinema for an early showing of Witness, which he was sure he would have enjoyed if he had been able to focus. One scene affected him although he didn't realise why until later. He had eaten the last portion of frozen chilli, since Ash never ate anything, or offered him any food.

Now he was following Ash upstairs, unbuttoning his shirt as he went, his breath coming fast and shallow. He could understand why lust was classified as one of the seven deadly sins. Every nerve end was alive and singing with anticipation. He felt bloody fantastic.

Later, waking beside her in the dark, he knew it wouldn't last. He and Ash would never be together, not properly. John had avoided thinking about it because the whole affair was so exciting, mysterious, even dangerous. He thought back to the only scene in Witness that had stuck in his lust-addled brain. Harrison Ford's character walks in on Kelly McGillis taking a bath, and she allows him to see her naked. For a long moment, they look at each other, then Ford walks away. The emotional heft of this scene had stayed with John. Now he knew why. He related to the lust of the characters in the film—they were from very different worlds and could never be together—but there were deep emotions underpinning that lust. It wasn't like that with Ash. Theirs was a relationship built on horniness. The craving he felt for Ash was that of the junky for his fix.

It hadn't stopped him becoming obsessed with her. A few days earlier, Chris and Alison had staged what they rather grandly named an *intervention*. They had taken him down to the Trowel and Hammer, put a pint of bitter and packet of crisps in front of him, and asked him what was going on. At first, he said he was a grown-up and that his love life was none of their business. They were not satisfied with this, and they told him why: slipping grades—John had received his first C ever that month—a patchy attendance record at lectures, and a complete disengagement from his friends.

Chris was blunt. "You look like shit."

John had noticed the darkness under his eyes, and there was no getting away from the fact that he was finding it hard to concentrate for any length of time.

"I'm fine."

"You're not, mate, so stop talking bollocks."

After Chris's attempt at diplomacy had failed, Alison took over.

"Tell us about this girl. Why all the secrecy? When do we get to meet her?"

The answer to that was *never*. John suspected that such a meeting was impossible, like asking someone to see something in ultraviolet or hear a frequency outside the range of the human ear.

Looking at Alison and Chris, seeing their concern, he was ashamed at the way he had allowed himself to drift away from them. He told them about his nights with Ash. Not in detail, which left little to say. He knew nothing about her other than her name. He could describe every inch of her body, however, and had an impressive knowledge of her favourite sexual positions and variations. He admitted as much, with a little of the pride he had felt after their first night together.

Alison, whose father was a vicar, deadpanned her reply. "As it says in the bible, man cannot live on head alone."

A few drinks later, and they were back to their usual unforced intimacy. John promised them, and himself, that he would, as Chris put it, "stop being a nob."

Now, awake again as Ash breathed beside him, he admitted that his obsession with her was derailing his life. Whatever this relationship was, it wasn't healthy. It was time to break away.

Around the window frame, he could see the first hints of the approaching dawn. He would tell her when she woke up.

He must have dozed himself, because the next thing he knew, he woke from an erotic dream to find Ash's head between his legs. His body didn't consider itself bound by the decision he had made only hours before. As she moved her mouth, she started humming. In a summer full of new experiences, this one would make the top three.

"Oh," he said. Perhaps it would be better if he told her next time they met.

TWENTY-FIVE

John woke up with an erection so insistent it was almost painful. He considered taking care of it in time-honoured fashion, but his stubborn streak won out over his penis, which was, possibly, a first. He had been dreaming—however inadequate a word that might be for it—about Ash, and he wouldn't let her presence taint the real world - if this was real, and he was actually awake.

He sat on the sagging sofa and waited for the tumescence to subside. He thought about the memory-dreams. There had been details in his recollection of his student house that he hadn't thought about for years. Nigel, the out-of-date milk bottle. The particular pizza takeaway whose flyer had obscured the letter from Ash. A lingering smell of drying clothes, stale beer, and dope. The corner of his Hitchhiker's Guide To The Galaxy poster that always detached itself from the wall.

During the dreams, the replays, he could change nothing, not even the banal thoughts that popped into his mind. But he was there, too—the older John—an observer in his younger self's mind. The replays were immersive, as real as the ripped floral fabric of the sofa.

It was an exquisite form of torture, John concluded. He knew the event towards which his younger self was heading, but there was no way of sparing him the pain that was coming.

In those days, a psychotic break was still referred to as a nervous breakdown, a hangover from the days of Victorian medicine. Nerves were not involved, and breakdown suggested something mechanical. Cars break down, washing machines break down. If you know which bits to oil, which holes to weld, they could be fixed. John had once overheard a friend refer to him as 'having a screw loose'. It was comforting, he supposed, to imagine that fixing a person's mind might be as easy as finding the right screws to tighten. But John's mind didn't break down, it shattered, violently. When it exploded, he sank into the white nothingness from which he thought he might never return. If there was no John, who would return anyway? And when he came back, when he had opened his eyes to find his mother holding his hand, John wasn't the same boy who had run from Ash that night. He couldn't be. That boy, who loved the mysticism of William Blake and wrote poems he hoped one day to publish, was missing too many pieces.

He knew, months before he told anyone, that he could never go back to university. The classics of literature were dead to him, the words on the page resolutely remaining there, sparking no answering cry of recognition from his battered mind. It would be years before he would read for pleasure, and he never found himself entirely transported to a fictional world again. He needed solid, boring mundanity, not fantasy.

To look out at the world from the mind of his twenty-year-old self broke his heart, knowing the fate that awaited him, and not being able to change it.

It was still dark in the cottage. John didn't need to look at his watch to know it was long before dawn. His erection had gone, and he felt sad. Not depressed. He knew how depression felt, and this wasn't it. This was an ache of sadness for crushed optimism, for unwritten poetry, for the secret language of close friends.

He thought about making a cup of tea. As he stood up, he realised he wasn't scared anymore. He was trapped in the cottage with some sort of malevolent presence, and he wasn't afraid of it.

In an exquisite demonstration of timing that surely wasn't coincidental, a sound came from upstairs; the kind of sound an old iron bed makes when someone sits up in it. His mouth went dry. He swallowed with difficulty. Right. The fear was back. Despite the hairs on his neck and across his shoulders prickling, he walked towards the kitchen and the kettle. He was awake now. There was no one upstairs. He knew that.

Then she laughed.

He gasped, unable to stop himself. He forced himself to walk out of the kitchen and stand at the bottom of the stairs.

"Hello? Hello?"

Pipes. Old water pipes could make strange noises. It was a very old cottage. Very old indeed.

Pipes. Definitely pipes.

He sat on the sofa, an empty mug clutched in his right hand, until dawn flooded the room with summer light. Then he opened the back door and set out into the morning.

TWENTY-SIX

Evie,

The Between cannot be defined by what it is, only by what it is not. There's a branch of theology—via negativa—which takes the same approach to describe God. Or rather, to not describe her, or him, or it, or none and all of these things. See how quickly it becomes a mess? Still, it's the best we can do.

The Between is not a place, but you must go there. It is not a mental state, but you can only reach it with your mind. It does not exist, but it is there. To find it, you must look for it, but if you look for it, you will never find it.

Does all this make you want to slap someone? Me in particular? Good. You're starting to get it.

To reach the Between, you begin with intent, with a desire to be there, but as soon as you have summoned up that desire, as soon as you have focused utterly on getting there, you must let go of it completely. If this sounds difficult—impossible, even—then you are ready to start.

In Zen—a wonderful spiritual practice, I'd highly recommend you try it—there's a concept called beginner's mind. Have you ever learned a musical instrument, Evie? In Britain, children are often taught to play the recorder, much to the distress of their parents. You may have the same tradition in America. If so, I want you to remember the first time you were handed the recorder. You may not have known which way round to hold it, which end to blow into. If you had never seen someone play a recorder, you might not even have known you were supposed to blow into it at all.

Do you remember when your teacher showed you how to place your fingers over the holes? Do you remember your first attempts- probably blowing too hard before you learned to regulate your breath? And do you remember the wonder you felt when you produced your first musical note?

Good. Now rewind all that. Go back to that moment when the teacher handed you the recorder. At that precise moment, you have beginner's mind. Children are good at this. Adults have some unlearning to do before they can achieve the same state. The mind is receptive, open, non-judging. Very young children bring no mental baggage to the situation. They are detached, disinterested. It's a powerful state of mind. When you hand a three-year-old an object, she doesn't file it in a particular category. That comes later. For a baby, a wooden brick can be many things: something for emerging teeth to chew on, something for chubby fingers to grasp, a way to get attention by throwing it. For a three-year-old, that same block might be a car, a spaceship, a drum. But for all of us, at the moment before we make judgements, that wooden block, or that recorder, is a pure expression of reality. You need to find that sliver of time between encountering something and labelling it. Beginner's mind. That's where the Between is. Except, of course, it isn't.

If it were easy to find, everybody would go there.

Luckily, many centuries of Adepts have found their way to the Between, and their wisdom is available to guide us. The starting point of that wisdom can be distilled very simply: if you want to learn how to find the Between, take a nap.

I've already mentioned how important naps are. I wasn't joking. They are crucial for anyone studying the craft of magic. It's imperative you get in the habit of taking naps as soon as possible. Or, almost taking naps. I don't want you to fall asleep. You will, the first few times. It's not easy. I'm just going to give you the method that has helped your forebears.

You need to do this during the day. At night, you're more likely to nod off. Find a comfortable chair. A bean bag is perfect. I wish they had been invented when I was learning to access the Between. I used to take the pillows off of my bed, pile them up in the corner and sit there. Eyes half-closed is best. If they're closed, you'll fall asleep. If they're open, there are too many distractions. With eyes half-shut, familiar objects become strange as your field of vision is reduced. Tiny scratches on your eyeballs float in front of you.

If you're going to find your way to the Between, it needs to happen fast. If you're not there in five seconds, open your eyes and start again.

Begin with intent. You have experienced magic, so you know how it feels when the power flows through you. You remember my metaphor of the stream? Your experience of magic, when you summon it, is like moving a stone in the stream to redirect the flow of water. There's a kind of passivity to the process. That passivity needs to be the focus of your intent. I did say it was difficult. You have to passionately desire a passionless state. Once you have established that desire, let it go. Don't push it away, let it fall.

Over and over, half-close your eyes, establish intent, then let it go. Do it again and again until it makes you frustrated and angry. Then do it some more. Do it until you become so bored you forget what you're trying to do. Keep going, because you're getting close.

Suddenly, you're there. You've slipped through. You're in the Between. You'll know you're there when you reach it. How? Put it this way. The Between, the place which isn't a place, the not-there, the place which is sometimes called the Unplace, is outside of time. It's utterly still, a vast, snowy plateau in the half-light of dusk, but it's a maelstrom of constant energy. You will feel as if you've arrived at the centre of the universe, the nucleus of the divine atom, the source of that which breathes all life into being.

You can't miss it.

A place is waiting for you. This is your sanctum. The word comes from the same roots as sanctuary, and you will feel protected there. But you don't belong in the Between, and you must not forget that. Never linger. Especially the first few times. To come back, picture your body as it was when you left it. The more details, the better. Imagine yourself back in that body. That's how you return.

There's an awful wrench when you find yourself back. I've never got used to it, but it gets easier with practise.

On a practical level, you will notice, I hope, after the bliss and the shock, that you have only been in the Between for seconds. Actually, no time passes there. It's only when you return that the clock starts ticking again. Practise getting back as fast as possible. Your Warden will tell you more about this when you meet him.

The Between is always used to prepare strong magic. Skilful use of the Between is the most crucial aspect of our art. The greatest Adepts have been those who honed their skills there without getting lost. But some great magicians have never come back. Don't tarry, Evie. Once you've become an Adept, you can explore the Between. For now, just learn how to get there, and return immediately.

The next bit is the hardest part. Sorry.

I hope you didn't just screw up this letter and throw it away with a howl of frustration.

Trust me, Evie, it's worth it. It's all worth it. I know I've emphasised the dangers and the responsibility, and I have admitted that magic—albeit very rare, powerful, dark magic—is killing me, but I hope you're not getting the impression that you won't have any fun. When you sang the word of power I gave you, the magic flowed through your blood, pulsed across your skin, lit up your brain with sheer delight, and... well, there are other side-effects it isn't appropriate for me to discuss with my great-granddaughter. You'll understand when you're older.

Now for the hard part I mentioned. But only read on when you can reach the Between at will when your body and mind are relaxed. Now you must learn to get there when you are wide awake. To do this, incrementally increase the difficulty. Try accessing the Between a few minutes after you've woken up in the morning. Sit on the edge of your bed and go there. Once you've mastered that, try it standing up. Cover the floor with soft cushions. You'll fall over at first, but your body will adapt and you'll find you can stay upright until your return.

Once you've mastered standing up, you need to try it while moving. Make a path in your room with cushions on either side. Make sure the path you lay out leads to your bed. After your first step, go to the Between. Try to return before your next step.

Once you have mastered this indoors, do it while you're

out. Not while you're crossing the street—safety first—but maybe while you're walking into class at school, surrounded by noise and distractions.

Push yourself. It'll take time, but persevere. Because, one day, your life may depend on it.

When you are in the Between, your body is unprotected. The charms which you will learn to sing into your skin are useless if you—that is, your essence—is not present. During that time, you're as vulnerable as any other human being. More so, as you cannot defend yourself.

I don't want to scare you, Evie, but it would be irresponsible of me not to warn you that there will always be those who wish the Three harm. Always. This letter is a poor substitute for one-to-one training, but it will at least give you some preparation for what lies ahead.

When you can visit and return within one exhalation, even under circumstances where you are surrounded by distractions, then you will be a formidable magician. Once you are an Adept, you will spend what seems like hours gathering power, crafting spells, preparing enchantments, but you will return within that single breath.

My enemies grow stronger, and more confident. I held them off for so many years, but now they've breached my outer defences, it's only a matter of time. Already, some of my memories of the past few years have faded. I know that Sarah—your grandmother—died, but I don't recall when, or how. My time is short, but I'm exhausted. I will finish these letters tomorrow.

TWENTY-SEVEN

When John arrived at the clearing, Gai wasn't there. John wasn't even sure he was in the right place. The fallen tree trunk was in the same place, but he remembered more ivy and moss covering it. There was no evidence of yesterday's fire.

"The dime page or way skeep atone time."

The voice came from above. John looked up. In the highest branch of the tallest tree, he spotted Gai's silhouetted form.

"What?" John shouted.

"I said..." The figure dropped from the branch and plummeted towards the ground. Instead of screaming as he headed for an impact that would cause serious injury or death, Gai sang. John could hear him, apparently unconcerned, the sound getting louder as he fell. Fifteen feet before impact, Gai threw his hands in front of him. A gust of wind came from nowhere, lifting twigs, grass, fallen leaves, bark and small stones from the ground as it blew directly upward. When all of his speed had been scrubbed away by the wind, it vanished as quickly as it had appeared and Gai dropped to the ground.

He stood up, slapped the wide-eyed John on the arm and took a swig of mead from the bottle in his knapsack before offering it.

"I said the time cage always keeps its own time."

"What just happened? How did you—"

"I was showing off," said Gai. "I shouldn't, really. Being young is no excuse. But it's fun. I imagine you were the same when you were... hang on, twelve moons is one of your years, right?"

John, still bug-eyed, nodded.

"Ten, twenty... yes. I bet you were rebellious in your seventies, correct?"

John added an open mouth to his staring eyes. "You're... how old are you?"

"Seventy-four by your reckoning. Oh, right. You don't live long, do you?"

"It depends what you mean by long."

"Well, my father is..." Gai closed his eyes, "... about fifteen hundred years old. But we experience time differently, so don't get jealous."

"Fifteen hundred... and you're seventy-four?"

"I am. Now, John Aviemore, here are the facts. You're trapped in here. Me too, it would seem. No noone is ever supposed to get this close to the cage. I thought the warnings were exaggerated. Tani and Obe trying to stop us having any fun."

"Who?"

"Tani and Obe? Noone royalty, or so they'd still have us believe. Our system of government is very old-fashioned. No time for politics though. I don't know how much time we have before Astarte makes her move, so I suggest we start on the lessons."

"Who? What lessons? No. Stop. I want some answers."

"Answers to what? I told you time is flexible here. We might have all day or only an hour. Look, tonight a god might try to suck your soul out of the top of your head, steal your power and break back into the temporal world. Your questions can wait."

John folded his arms and shook his head, hoping he was looking formidable and determined, but suspecting he looked like a sulky toddler who wouldn't use the potty until he got a biscuit.

"What are the Blurred Lands? Who are the noones? What happened yesterday? I was here, then I wasn't. Am I dreaming now or is this real? What power am I supposed to have, what does Ash want with it, where's this bloody cage she's in, and are you seriously expecting me to believe she's a god?"

Gai scowled up at John, paced up and down, then faced him again.

"Sit down," he said, pointing at the log. "I will answer some of your questions, but you must shut up and listen. Then I will teach you magic. After the first lesson, I may answer another question or two."

John sat down and waited. Gai sat cross-legged on the ground in front of him.

"There are seven realms in the known universe."

"Seven what?"

"Realms. Don't interrupt."

"But I can't let you talk about stuff that makes no sense. The known universe is made up of stars, planets, galaxies, black holes, er, dark matter. I'm no scientist, but we are exploring the universe with telescopes, probes, rockets. We have data."

"Correction." Gai was holding up a finger. "Humans are not exploring the universe. They are exploring *a* universe. The universe you know is the realm we call Earth."

John put his hands on the fallen tree, the gnarled, flaking bark comfortably real as he crumbled it between his fingers. "The universe is one of seven?"

Gai's lips twitched. "We know of seven realms."

"And you come from another realm? Is that where I am now?"

"Yes, I come from another realm, but that's not where we are now. We're in the Blurred Lands. And, for thousands of years, the time cage has been here. Astarte—Ashtoreth—is its prisoner."

"But..."

Gai shook his head. "No. This won't work if you keep interrupting. Quiet."

John heard the irritation in the tone of his companion. He thought about the disappearing city and the impossible dreams. He shut up.

"Good," said Gai. "There are seven realms. Thinking in terms of physical location doesn't reflect the reality, but it is useful to imagine some being 'closer together' than others. My realm is Da Luan. The dominant species of my realm, which also contains remnants and elementals, is the noones. There have been countless encounters between humans and noones in the Blurred Lands over the centuries."

Gai stood up and stretched like a cat. "Even our name—noone—comes from your language."

John couldn't stop himself. "How do you know English?"

"Those of us who wish to explore our neighbouring

realm must know the language. It only take one trip to the Between to learn it after all."

John hoped Gai wasn't going to speak in riddles all day, but he stopped himself interrupting.

"Northern Europe has always been a well-used border. But your people have forgotten us over the last five thousand years. Hence the name. Noone. No one. It comes from the time when the realms were still withdrawing from each other. If a human met one of us, un-Glamoured, deep in the forest, we would use a charm of confusion before sending them home. *What happened in the forest? Who did you meet?* No one. Noone."

One patch of the fog clouding John's mind thinned for a second. Gai's diminutive stature, the magic, the carved wooden whistle. "Wait?" he said, "are you a fairy?"

Gai glared at him. "Did you just call me a fucking fairy?"

"Sorry, Gai, it's just that, well, er, with you being, um..." John's voice trailed away.

"Being what? Small? Found in wooded areas? Does that make me a fairy? Or a pixie, or a leprechaun? Do you think we have nothing better to do than to steal children and to dance around toadstools all night?"

"Okay, okay, I'm sorry, I didn't mean... I thought..."

"You *thought*. Spare me your prejudices. A noone hardly ever takes a human child these days. We're very strict about that kind of thing. And why shouldn't we dance around toadstools? Some of them have remarkable magical properties. Don't judge."

John took in what he had just heard. "I was right? You are a f—"

Gai made a sound like a musical grunt, and John was pushed backwards. It felt like he'd been kicked. The force of the blow was so hard that he travelled six feet in the air before landing on his back. The impact winded him, and he rolled onto his side, wheezing.

Gai jumped up onto the recently vacated log. His fists were bunched, and the expression on his face was half-fury, half-something else. Surprise, maybe. John didn't have much time to speculate, because the noone grunted again, and he was flung a few more feet across the clearing. He pushed himself up onto his hands and knees, trying to catch his breath.

Gai jumped from the log. "Interesting," he said. "My father's hypothesis was right. It makes sense now, Astarte coming after you. Ah, the famous pride of the Wardens and the Adepts. So wise, the self-appointed guardians of esoteric knowledge. They didn't listen to my father, told him he was wasting his time studying human science. Ha!"

John caught his breath. "Gai. I'm sorry if I upset you."

Gai flashed a tiny, mischievous smile. "Defend yourself," he whispered, then grunted again.

"No!" John was lifted into the air and thrown backwards. He was glad it was early summer, and the ground was soft. Frozen ground would have broken his knees when they took the brunt of the impact. He yelped in pain.

Gai walked unhurriedly towards him. "Humans have met noones in so many forms. The bad ones get respect. Ghosts, poltergeists, shapeshifters, vampires, djinn, incubi. But the ones who are friendly? Well, mostly friendly? All right, occasionally friendly. You call them fairies. Pretty little winged arseholes in gauze dresses fluttering around the flowers and talking shite since the dark ages. Defend yourself."

"What? How? Agh!" John had got to his feet when his legs were swept from under him, and he fell back to the ground. His shoulder hit first, and he screamed. He knew an impact that heavy must have broken something. He sat up, cradling his left arm, wondering how the hell he would get to a doctor when he was trapped in Leigh Woods with a violent fairy and a vengeful god.

Gai was implacable. "Defend yourself," he whispered, and drew breath for another of his malicious grunts.

As Gai made a sound in his throat, John did the same. He coughed out a sound somewhere between a paper tear and the howl of a chimpanzee. Gai was thrown up and into the trees at such speed, it looked like he had vanished. Only the sound of breaking branches as he tore his way through the old oak gave any clue to where he was.

John stood up, still holding his arm. He walked over to the oak at the edge of the clearing. Gai was now falling back through the branches, crying out as he hit each one, turning uncontrollably in the air as he tumbled.

"Ow! Argh! No! Ugh! Ooh! Agh! Plea—ow!"

There was no magical gust of wind to break his fall this time, and he hit the ground, crumpling into a heap of limbs.

John approached cautiously. "Gai?" He moved closer, bending to get a better idea of which bits of the mess were arms, legs, torso, or head. "Are you all right?"

"Bloody stupid question, human." Perhaps Gai's injuries weren't as bad as they looked. "What do you think?"

Gai rolled onto one side, then sat up. John stared at the noone as he brushed leaves, twigs, and dirt from his face and neck. No blood. No broken bones. He looked like he'd tripped while walking, not fallen twenty feet through the branches of a tree.

Gai stood up and slapped John on his broken arm. John flinched and gasped, waiting for the pain. It didn't come. He looked at his arm and gingerly moved it across his body, then down to his side. There was no break. No sign of any injury.

He looked at Gai, who was rummaging around in his bag. He pulled out a full bottle.

"Drink?" said Gai.

"Yep," said John.

TWENTY-EIGHT

When darkness came, it did so with the speed of an eclipse. John had stepped between the trees to urinate when it happened. He zipped up his trousers and hurried back, but Gai had gone, along with the clearing. In their place was the cottage. He turned his back on it and walked away. A dozen steps later, the iron gate loomed up in front of him.

"This is ridiculous." John squared his shoulders, lifted the latch, walked up the path and entered the cottage. Whatever was happening, he would not let it beat him. He would stay in control.

As soon as the door closed behind him, he heard it; the sound of movement upstairs, the creak of springs as the bed took someone's weight.

No. Just the natural expanding and contracting of old wooden floorboards. Nothing else.

"John."

He recognised her voice, but pretended he hadn't heard it. He couldn't have heard it. Ash was dead.

"John."

Knowing there was only one way to find out, John then did what Sarah had told every character in every horror film he'd made her sit through not to do. He walked upstairs. He did it quickly, making no attempt to be quiet, turning left at the top, and striding up to the bedroom door. He flung it open it forcefully, saying, "hah!" as he did so, in an attempt to dispel his fear.

It didn't work, partly because saying, "hah!" has no proven effect on fear, but mostly because Ash was sitting on the bed.

For a dead woman in her sixties, Ash looked good. More than good, John admitted. She looked amazing. Age, or death, had not altered her in the slightest from the alluring, inviting, irresistible woman she'd been when he'd first met her.

Well, that wasn't quite true, John conceded as Ash brushed back the copper hair that was obscuring one of her deep, mocking green eyes. She wasn't irresistible anymore. Not to him, at any rate. Although, he conceded, she was still an adolescent male's wet dream.

John stood in the doorway. The bedroom was carpeted as it had been during the nights he had visited her in the eighties. His new paint had gone, replaced by the cloying pink-purple beneath. The room was lit by candles and oil lamps hanging from hooks under the old beams. Heavy brocade curtains hung at the window. The bed was unmade, the dark satin sheets pushed aside as if Ash had just woken up.

"What were you expecting? A rotting corpse with staring eye sockets? My chin held on with a handkerchief like the ghost of Jacob Marley?"

John thought of his ever-mounting sense of dread since arriving at Sally Cottage.

"Something like that, yes," he said, his voice only cracking a little.

Ash stood up. She was naked, of course. Her breasts were still heavy, her hips rounded, her skin flawlessly creamy. It was a body that belonged to someone in their twenties. John looked at her and said nothing.

"You're middle-aged, John Aviemore," she said. "Not that it makes any difference. Old, young, beautiful, ugly, sick, well, I've had them all. But you were special. You still are."

"I don't think so," said John.

Ash studied him.

"You don't think this is happening, do you? You're too calm, considering the situation. Do you think you're going mad?"

"That's not quite the way I would have put it."

"Not politically correct enough for you?"

He was surprised at the expression. In his mind, Ash was stuck in the mid-nineteen-eighties.

She picked up on his confusion.

"Oh, I may be trapped here, but it doesn't mean I don't know what's happening outside. The cage is flexible, and I've learned when and how to stretch its walls. And there's always television when we're in the right time period."

John was lost by the direction of the conversation, but Ash was still talking.

"It was maddening at first, all that power, so close, I could almost taste it. You were right there, just out of reach. I didn't guess the truth. I thought I had found an Adept, considering the dormant magic I sensed in you. I was prepared for a fight. But when I saw you, that night when you were on my doorstep, I couldn't believe my luck."

If John had expected a coherent chat with a ghost, it

was clear he would be disappointed. He could only conclude that he was in shock, as he was responding to her as if this was a normal conversation, instead of evacuating his bowels and jumping through a window.

"You don't know what I'm talking about, do you?" she said. "No matter. Let me ask you this. Did anyone else at that party remember seeing me?"

John had thought his friends were winding him up when they'd claimed he'd left alone that night. He'd put it down to jealousy, considering how far out of his league Ash was. Any healthy heterosexual male would have crawled over a field of broken glass if she'd given so much as an encouraging glance.

He said nothing. Ash smiled.

"Such a display of my power did not go unnoticed. The cage adapted, strengthened itself. But I had you by then. You came to me. And here you are again."

"The letter?" said John. "Stinder Hackleworth? I thought you'd..."

"Died? No. That's not something I'm ever expecting to do."

"What are you?" said John.

Ash laughed.

"You don't even know what *you* are, John Aviemore. How can you hope to understand what I am?"

He looked at her. Ashleigh Zanash, the first woman he'd had sex with. She was hardly his idea of a god.

"You're wondering if I look like this to everyone, or just you?" Ash phrased it like a question, but it wasn't. Not really. He knew the answer, and she knew he knew it. She was his twenty-year-old self's fantasy made flesh.

Her gaze was direct and as openly sexual as it had

always been. There was nothing feigned about Ash's libido. She would take him now if he let her.

John cleared his throat and looked into her eyes. He acknowledged the invitation but ignored it.

"I was a virgin," he said.

"I know," she replied. "Delicious."

"Until I slept with a woman, my mental ideal was all I had."

"Then you met me," said Ash, one hand coming up to cup a breast in a gesture which looked entirely unconscious. Except nothing Ash did was ever unconscious.

"No," said John. "I said a real woman."

He was prepared for some anger at that, but Ash smiled, her thumb still tracing the underside of her breast.

"Hmm. That's fair. And how did a real woman compare?"

John wasn't sure what game they were playing here, but he was convinced his sanity was at stake. How he dealt with this conversation would have repercussions. He thought of Sarah, and of Harry. He thought of his granddaughter, Evie. John chose honesty.

"A real woman?" he said, shaking his head. "After you? It was a disappointment, but you know that already, don't you?"

"Yes. How could it be otherwise? You must have spent your life dreaming of the nights we spent together."

"You didn't let me finish," said John. Ash sat on the bed, then lay back, propping herself up on the pillows. She looked up at him. If any Renaissance painter had captured even a hint of the invitation in her face and body, they would have been denounced as a devil and burned at the stake.

"I'm listening," she said.

"I had a couple of relationships after you." It had been almost two years after, but he wasn't about to mention his breakdown and the hospital. "The first was a disaster. I wanted something she couldn't give me, but I couldn't even tell her what that was."

Ash nodded.

"I tried harder the next time. But whenever we went to bed, I could only think about you."

There was a kind of relief in admitting it, saying it out loud for the first time. "We broke up. I was better off on my own."

"I understand." There was no pride in her voice. John thought about the wicked queen in Snow White. The magic mirror reassured her she was the most beautiful woman in the land. Ash had no such insecurities. She knew she was the most beautiful. She definitely wouldn't like what was coming next.

"Then I met Sarah. We were married six months later. She died three years ago. Once I'd met her, I forgot about you. And, on the rare occasions I did think about you, I found you'd lost your power over me."

Now he had riled her. The amused, aroused, expression on Ash's face barely altered, but John knew he hadn't imagined the flash of anger on her perfect features.

"Tell me about her," was all she said.

John thought of Sarah, of her grin when she'd got down on one knee in a pool of spilt beer to propose to him, and of that same grin the night before those eyes closed for the last time. He took a step into the bedroom, fighting his fear. Ash, and Gai had both spoken of his power. Time to act as if he had some.

"No," he said.

"No?" Ash was comically shocked. John speculated it

might be the first time someone had ever refused her.

"You're lying," she said. "Your marriage was a sham. I was there in your mind, and in your bed, every time. You never 'made love' to your wife. It was me. It was always me."

Perhaps the cliché that some people look beautiful when angry has a basis in fact, but it wasn't true of Ashleigh Zanash. John remembered seeing this expression on her face moments before he ran from the woods, his mind already slipping its moorings as he sprinted away. The bland mask of seductive, available sexuality was gone, and behind it was frustration, rage, and hatred. It was a more honest glimpse of who he was dealing with.

She stood up and took a pace towards him. John held his ground.

"I'm not lying," he said. "You know I'm not. You might not understand it, but Sarah was all I ever wanted. And the longer we were together, the better it was. You mean nothing to me."

Ash made a noise unlike anything John had ever heard. Somewhere in the vicinity of a grunt, or a growl, but louder and stranger than either. More disturbing, and threatening, too.

As he looked at her, Ash changed. John flinched and stepped backwards, tripping, falling, and knocking the back of his head against the door frame. By the time the pain of the blow registered, it was over.

Ash was taller, shorter, fatter, thinner. Her skin was milk-white, clay-red, night-black, sea-green, rusted brown, translucent grey, tanned leather, shining pearl. Her eyes rolled through every colour John could name, and some he could not. Like riffling a deck of cards, her features flicked through a hundred changes.

Treacle-thick time slowed, the air becoming cloying and

dense. John's mind unpicked the awful noise she was making and heard it not as one sound but as hundreds of different words. Ash spoke all the words simultaneously, but not in the same language, and not even in the same voice.

She was naming herself. Hundreds of words were crammed into one dense sound.

"PRENDE ASTGHIK RATI FREYA SUADELA KUNI TIACAPAN XOCOTZIN QUETESH ÁINE TURAN ŽIVA BASTET ASTARTE ISHTAR RĀGARĀJA ASHTORETH."

The impact of the doorframe on the back of John's head was harder than he had expected. There was a crack, and—for a few seconds—he saw, or heard, nothing. Then his vision cleared. He was looking at the bare floorboards of the cottage bedroom. He could smell fresh paint.

Ash had disappeared. The bed was bare, the mattress and sheets gone. The walls, lit by the single bare bulb hanging above, were back to their inoffensive magnolia.

John scrambled backwards out of the bedroom and crawled into the bathroom, his head throbbing. He threw up, flushed it away, then carefully pulled himself upright. He touched the back of his head and examined his fingers. No blood, and the lump he'd traced on his skull was smaller than he'd expected.

He bent forward and examined his face in the shaving mirror. Unshaven, red-eyed, he looked like he hadn't slept for a week. His hair stood up in clumps, and his lips were dry and cracked.

"Hi, handsome," John whispered, but he couldn't stop the final name he had heard sounding again and again in his mind.

"ASHTORETH."

TWENTY-NINE

"Protective charms," said Gai the following day, sipping from the bottle of mead. John had noticed that, no matter how much they drank, the bottle never emptied. He had once invented a trick that appeared to produce the same effect, but it was an illusion. This was not.

"Protective charms," repeated John, as if saying the words out loud would make the concept less ridiculous. It didn't work. He felt the rear of his head, which should have had a lump the size of an egg on it after the impact with the doorframe. It was unmarked. It didn't even hurt when he rapped his knuckles against it.

"Yes. Ever break a bone? Or have any serious physical injury?"

John thought about it. "No,"

"Protective charms. I have them too. Physical damage hurts, but permanent injury is prevented."

"Protective charms," said John, again. Nope, it still sounded crazy.

"Not your own work, so someone else." Gai was mumbling to himself. "Who? A noone? Unlikely." he turned his attention to John. "Someone protected you, and they did it well. Any strong women in your family?"

"Maybe. Why?"

Gai seemed not to have heard. "Interesting. But if Ashtoreth wants something from you, you will need more than protective charms to stop her. Tell me again about last night."

John told him while the noone listened intently.

"She revealed herself to you," said Gai when he had finished.

"She definitely did that," said John, remembering the many versions of Ash that had come and gone in that terrifying second as he'd stumbled backwards in the bedroom.

John accepted the mead from Gai and took a long swallow. He trusted this creature, and he wasn't sure why. There was something reassuringly familiar about him. He had only his instinct and the evidence of his senses to go on, but they all agreed. Gai was on his side. If he existed, if any of this was real. John was now behaving as if it was. But even if Gai, Ash, Sally Cottage and all of Leigh Woods turned out to be a hallucination, it wouldn't matter if he could get away.

"I'm a human," John said. "You're a,"—Gai's face darkened—"a noone. You tell me Ash—Ashtoreth—is a god. What chance do we have against a god?"

Gai snorted. "Gods are just beings from the older realms," he said. "When Earth first became accessible through the Blurred Lands, it attracted visitors from as far as Nysa. Most did just that—visit—but some were seduced by the flow of magic in your realm, by its purity and availability. They stayed."

"Don't these other… realms have magic too?"

"Yes. Old magic, evolved magic, richer, but far less plentiful. All intelligent species can use magic in the other realms. There, they are nothing special. But when, thousands of years ago, they came to your realm, beings like Ashtoreth wielded Earth's raw magic much more effectively than humans. Their abilities were so far beyond yours, it was as if they were... well, gods."

"You said 'they' stayed. There were more of them?"

"Your planets still bear the names of some of them. Neptune. Jupiter. You tell their stories and call them myths. You even name your days after them: Odin - Wednesday, Thor - Thursday."

"But they're myths."

Gai laughed. "Want to know the difference between a fact and a myth? About three thousand years."

"So where are they now?"

Gai was pacing up and down. Now he stopped and sighed. "All right. A quick explanation, then we'll get to work."

"Do I get to ask questions?"

"No interruptions. You struggled with that yesterday. Think you can manage it now?"

John nodded, and Gai started talking.

"There was a war. The war of the gods. It raged for generations on Earth. By the time the gods took the alliance between Earth and Da Luan seriously, it was too late. When the gods were defeated, they were banned from using magic again. They are long-lived, but not immortal. They died, eventually, of old age."

"Not all of them. There's one in that cottage back there. How were they defeated if their magical abilities are so far beyond that of humans?"

Gai glared at him. "Sorry," said John.

"I said their abilities *were* more powerful," said Gai. "But it was a human who led the revolution that defeated them."

And John listened as the noone gave him a history lesson that would have been laughed out of any school curriculum.

"Astarte is from Tartarus. All the realms have names that echo through human legends and myths. Earth, Da Luan—my realm—Erebus, Tartarus, Nysa, Mu and Shambhala.

"Erebus and Tartarus gave us most of the creatures that went power-crazy in the magic-rich atmosphere of Earth. Centaurs, gorgons, sphinxes, griffins, winged horses, unicorns, shapeshifters, vampires, and the rest. The most powerful of all were treated as gods.

"Astarte started the gods' war. She called herself Queen of the gods. She was already known as the god of fertility and war, with many also calling her the god of love. Her lust for power spilled over to her followers, and she drew on their magic to supplement her own. For a while, she was unstoppable, and Earth's continents ran red with blood.

"Eve, the human who stopped her, was the first Adept. She had turned away from the gods as a child, feeling no respect for these violent and destructive entities. By the time she parleyed with the noones, she could sing words of power.

"She proposed an alliance. Her time in the Between had shown her a way to separate the realms. The noones agreed to help.

"The myth tells of Eve entering a wooded grove, digging at the roots of an ancient tree, her fingers intertwining with its roots. She sang her words, and the noones sang with her. Across the world, there were cries of fear from the gods as their realms moved away from ours. Faced with the choice, most returned to their homes as they separated from Earth.

"When it was over, only a few of the creatures and gods remained. Their exile in your realm was permanent. They agreed to live peacefully. Some resisted, but Eve and her followers subdued them. Over time—many hundreds of years—even the most long-lived of them died.

"Astarte refused to accept the agreement forged by Eve and the noones, which became known as the Accord. The god of love wanted to rule your realm. She still does. Astarte is not insane. Neither is she evil. She believes Earth would be a better place if she ruled it. The fact that you'd all be rutting like animals or killing each other would, in her eyes, be a restoration of the natural order.

The last days of the war were costly. When it was over, thousands were dead or injured. The god was defeated. Eve refused to kill her. The noones carried her to the Blurred Lands, and—using the Between—the most powerful magicians constructed the time cage.

"On the first anniversary of the end of the war, the Accord was strengthened by the formation of the Three. Three human women, of whom Eve was the first, to protect Earth and keep the peace. Da Luan agreed to supply Wardens, one for each of the Three. The Wardens live in your realm as voluntary exiles."

Gai stopped talking. "Questions?"

John didn't know where to start. "Why don't humans use magic anymore?"

"They do. But the Accord restricts its use. If not, Earth, so rich with magic, might become too much of a threat to the other realms. Magic is kept secret for good reason, John. Not that it should concern you. According to everything we know, you are incapable of using it."

"Oh?" John remembered the look of shock and delight on Gai's face when John had retaliated the previous day. "Why?"

"Because you're the wrong sex. Guess how many men have wielded magic in your realm during the last five thousand years?"

John knew a rhetorical question when he heard one. Sure enough, Gai didn't wait for an answer.

"None. But here you are. No more questions. You need to visit the Between. It usually takes two or three moons to become competent, but you have serious disadvantages. You're not only human, you're male. And we only have days. Maybe less. Let's get started, shall we?"

"Shit."

"Pardon me?"

Gai's voice was faint. The light had changed in seconds, dusk falling without warning.

John looked at Gai. The noone was fading, and something else was taking his place. Within seconds, the clearing had gone, Gai with it. John was looking at the front door of Sally Cottage.

"Looks like we'll have to start tomorrow." he said.

THIRTY

Whether he could truly call his dreams by that name any more, or whether some other word would have to take its place, John wasn't sure. He was also unsure whether he was dreading or looking forward to what memories might resurface when he went to sleep. He only knew the lines between waking and sleeping were blurring, and what he experienced during periods of unconsciousness were as real to him as his daytime experiences. Given that his days now involved talking to a magical fairy in a world where Clifton Suspension Bridge and Bristol didn't exist, it was no wonder the whole situation was confusing.

Then there was the fact that Ash was here. *In the flesh* was the expression that came to mind, but it was all wrong. The transformations she had undergone the previous evening meant she was something other than a flesh and bone being.

John had steeled himself to check upstairs in daylight that morning, only to find the bedroom back to normal. No carpet, no mattress and sheets on the bed, no subtle oil lamps, no naked sixty-year-old with the body of a twenty-year-old. No monsters.

He looked at his watch, but it had long ceased being useful. Ten past nine. It might be accurate. It was dark enough. Equally, it could be midnight or three in the morning. He just had to make it to dawn. Whether it was an ancient instinct of his species or a baseless superstition, he was sure Ash couldn't touch him once dawn had arrived.

John was determined to notice the moment his dreams began, the point at which his mind made the switch from awake to asleep. He stood in the middle of the living room, practising a yoga stance Sarah had taught him to help with his bad posture. He'd spent too many hours hunched over his desk writing, drawing diagrams, or making intricate magic props.

Planting both feet on the floor, shoulder-width apart, he lifted his toes and rocked backwards and forwards until his weight was evenly distributed from the ball of his feet to his heels. Then he relaxed his feet, pushed his hips forward, brought his shoulders back, and imagined an invisible thread coming from the top of his head, leading up to the ceiling. The mountain pose not only helped with his posture but kept him alert. He hoped maintaining it would stop him missing the moment when he drifted into a dream.

When he thought of the invisible thread, John couldn't stop himself following it through the ceiling into the bedroom above, imagining Ash holding the other end, controlling him like a puppet. He brought his attention back to the living room. It wasn't there anymore.

Shit.

John was standing in the lobby of a theatre, tucked away in a side street a mile east of Harrow. Sarah had invited him to a play. One of her friends was performing, and another was directing. John had enjoyed nothing about the play apart from the fact that he was sitting next to this incredible woman. It was the weekend after he had shared coffee and sandwiches with her in a café near the design agency where she worked. He was trying, and failing, not to have any expectations about where the evening might lead. He had always assumed someone as intelligent, thoughtful, and talented as Sarah would be out of reach to someone like him. It had been a tough few years, recovering from his breakdown and rebuilding his self-confidence. He was nervous. Too nervous considering the circumstances. He was sure Sarah must have noticed. His palms were sweating, he had spilled his drink in the interval, and when she had asked if he had enjoyed the performance, he had lied unconvincingly.

Her actor friend and the director were both men; confident, brash, charming, handsome, and intolerable. Sarah chatted with them easily, never running out of questions to ask or things to say. John was caught up in the way she moved, the sound of her voice, and the smile he feebly mirrored every time it appeared. It was only later that he realised her praise had been guarded. She never came out and said how great the play was, but she found moments within it to highlight and praise. John watched enviously as her friends enjoyed her attention, and within a few minutes, their small group had attracted more actors and crew. It was the first night, and everyone was buzzing with adrenaline.

John had drifted to the edge of the group, and when a tall man carrying a bottle of bubbly elbowed him aside to offer the cast a drink, he said nothing. They were discussing going on for a drink somewhere, and he heard Sarah agree. He was miserable. He found a table near the entrance, put his empty glass on it, and pretended to look at the upcoming events poster. Five minutes, that's how long he'd give it. Then he'd make an excuse and go home.

"Bailing out on me?" Sarah held a glass of bubbly. The good mood and excitement of her friends had rubbed off on her. She looked happy. There was a tiny smudge of lipstick on one of her front teeth. John wanted to kiss her more than anything else in the world.

"Sarah!" The voice came from the far side of the room, from a woman in a purple caftan. "Come on, we're off to the pub. Jack says he's getting the first round in."

"That's Ailsa," said Sarah. "We were at university together. I haven't seen her for about a year."

John had lost his grasp of the social niceties and didn't know what to say to that. "Oh, you should go, don't let me stop you. I have a couple of things I need to do at home, anyway."

What John wanted to say was, "Don't leave. Let your friends go to the pub even if you haven't seen them for years. I've only known you for a week, and I want to see you all the time. Come home with me."

Too late. He waited for her to answer, wondering if he imagined the disappointed dip of her head at his words.

"Okay," she said. "Okay. But let's chat soon. Call me." And with that, she was gone. Not wanting to be there when the laughing, shouting group left for the pub, John pushed through the door with a half-wave to Sarah.

On the tube, he went over and over that last exchange in his mind. He wanted to believe Sarah meant it when she said he should call her, but it was more likely she was just being polite. The thud and clank of the wheels on the track as the empty carriage rattled underneath London chanted what John thought of himself.

"Idiot, idiot, idiot, idiot, idiot, idiot, idiot..."

On the top floor of a bed-and-breakfast on the outskirts of Manchester, John paced backwards and forwards, moving from the window to the bed. The end of the bed afforded the best view of the television, which could only pick up BBC Two and ITV. This meant a choice between wrestling or watching the Lavender Hill mob for the fourth or fifth time, which was no choice at all. But even Alec Guinness and his cronies couldn't stop John getting up every two minutes. From the window, he could see the small car park where Sarah's Mini Metro would pull up.

She had been gone since lunchtime. Two hours had been her guess, three at most. It was now four-and-a-half hours since John had seen her beige hatchback nose into the traffic on the ring road and drive away.

Sarah's ex-boyfriend was in town. They had been childhood sweethearts from the age of fourteen until Steve had taken a year in Canada as part of his degree course. He'd decided to stay there.

Sarah had told John the story. She hadn't concealed the fact she was still hurt by what Steve had done. He had been her first love, and—at one time—they had both assumed they would end up married. After six weeks in Vancouver, Steve had fallen for someone else. He hadn't told Sarah until another six months had gone by.

Naturally, John hated Steve. It was a given, considering how he had treated Sarah. However, Sarah had agreed to this meeting when Steve called out of the blue to say he was in the country for a few days. John didn't know what to make of that. On the one hand, a six-year relationship meant they had been best friends as much as boyfriend and girlfriend. On the other hand, why would she want to spend any time with someone who had dumped her? John had said nothing. It was Sarah's decision, and when she suggested they make a weekend of it together, he agreed. Not that he didn't trust her. Not that he wanted to be close enough to keep an eye on her. Nothing like that.

The rain was getting heavier, and long slanting drops of water ran down the window. He followed the progress of every light-coloured car, only to watch them drive past without slowing.

Exactly five hours and eight minutes after she had left, Sarah's Metro turned left into the driveway and parked in front of the bed-and-breakfast. John watched her get out, lock the door, and run through the heavy rain towards shelter. Two floors down, he heard the front door open, then her footsteps on the stairs.

He felt jealous, helpless, angry at himself. The truth was, he could no longer imagine the future without Sarah, and that frightened him. He had never been happier. He was scared out of his mind that seeing Steve again might convince Sarah that John wasn't right for her. Maybe Steve had flown back to admit his mistake, beg for forgiveness and profess his undying love for her. John knew how easy Sarah was to love. Surely, Steve must have realised his error?

The door opened. Sarah's hair was stuck to her face, her mascara was running, and the suede jacket she had worn was ruined.

"Sorry I'm late, only the art gallery next door had a Basquiat exhibition, so I nipped in and lost track of time."

John's heart felt like a lump of lead in his chest. Did she look guilty? Happy? What had happened? He didn't want to appear a fraction as needy as he actually was, in case it scared her off.

"How's Steve?"

Sarah had unhooked the towel from the back of the bathroom door and was rubbing her hair. She stopped, her hair sticking out at all angles. She looked beautiful. "Oh, he hasn't changed at all."

John swallowed. "Oh."

"Yep," said Sarah leaning forward to kiss him, "he's still a twat."

John opened his eyes to find dust mites floating through the sunlight that streamed across the cottage living room. He groaned. He could still taste Sarah's kiss on his lips, still remember the rush of emotions that had assaulted him that afternoon in Manchester. Once again, he had been an observer in his own memory. It had been every bit as real as it had been the first time. He had forgotten how jealous he had been. He had hoped to be a better man than that, and the physical way jealousy had affected him, causing stomach cramps and a dull, thumping headache made him feel weak-willed and useless. During those hours in the bed-and-breakfast, hundreds of scenarios had played out in his mind, all of which led to him losing Sarah. The intensity of it all was almost overwhelming. And the earlier memory, the first date at the theatre, was not much better. When he looked back on how paranoid and suspicious he had been, he was amazed Sarah had come back for more.

He went to the kitchen to make himself tea, and while the kettle was boiling, the grief—which never went away, just lay in waiting for the next opportunity—ambushed him and forced him to his knees. He didn't cry, just moaned as the reality of a world without Sarah made itself newly clear to him. John had learned grief was a wound that never healed; it just left longer gaps between making its presence felt. The agony was as sweet and sharp as ever. By the time it had passed, or, rather, reduced in intensity to a level where he was numb, he stood up, re-boiled the kettle and turned his mind back to his predicament.

He missed Sarah. She would have known what to do.

THIRTY-ONE

In the clearing, Gai was already waiting. John sat down.

"More dreams?" asked the noone.

John had told the noone about his dreams. This time he was noncommittal. "Nothing that could help us work out what she wants."

"I need to get you into the Between," said Gai. "Whatever Ashtoreth is planning, it will give you a chance to fight back."

"One question."

"It had better be good."

"What the hell's the Between?"

Even the short version took Gai half an hour to explain, and, by the end, after various warnings about the potential dangers, John was as confused as when he'd started.

"You want me to go somewhere that doesn't exist where I can learn magic?"

"Correct."

"And it can take weeks to learn how to get there?"

"But once you've succeeded, it's easy to get back."

"Doesn't help if I can't get there for weeks."

"Ah." Gai took a small glass vial out of his knapsack. "But you will take a shortcut. Humans might take an age to master getting to the Between, but noones have been doing it for millennia. We drink sap."

"Sap? Sounds tasty."

Gai uncorked the vial and handed it over. It was odourless. "Can't tell you how many rules I'm breaking," he said, chuckling. "Drink up."

Whatever form John had expected the Between to take, it wasn't this. A moment earlier he had been leaning back against the soft, moss-covered trunk of a whitebeam in the clearing with Gai. The sun had passed its zenith and was warming the left side of his face more than the right. The sap, as tasteless as it was odourless, had made him drowsy. A twig was caught in his hair, and he had been thinking about opening his eyes and removing it.

That particular thought had been the tipping point. It had arisen just as he was about to fall asleep, and it had brought him back to a state of self-awareness. He opened his eyes without opening his eyes and found himself in the Between.

John was sitting in an armchair in front of a log fire, which crackled as it gave off the perfect amount of warmth. The chair was wing-backed, leather, dark green, and extremely comfortable. This, as much as any of the other impossibilities he was about to encounter, was enough to convince John that he was no longer on Earth. He had spent much of his adult life trying to find just such an armchair. In his childhood, after seeing an illustration in a Dickens, or MR James book, he had set his heart on owning what he later described as the Platonic Chair. Plato wrote that everything in existence was an imperfect example of an ideal. Every dark-green leather armchair John found fell short of the Platonic Chair. The shade of green was wrong, it was too high or too low, the arms were incorrectly positioned; the cushion slipped when he leaned back, the metal studs dug into his elbows. Mostly, they weren't comfortable to sit in. At all. John had wasted a great deal of time and money before giving up, the final green monstrosity still sitting in his Wimbledon study like a monument to bad design.

But this chair, in front of the improbably perfect fire, was the Platonic Chair, without a doubt. If only Sarah could have seen it. She would have been as happy as he was, maybe more so. John smiled for the first time in days. He looked down. He was wearing pyjamas and a paisley dressing gown. His toes, when he flexed them, were encased in warm, comfortable slippers. Perhaps this wasn't Dickens at all, but Wodehouse.

There was a book on the polished wooden table near his right elbow. It was an old hardback, the kind of book John would scour second-hand shops and boot sales in search of, its thick cream pages hand cut. On the cover, in ornate embossed gold letters, was printed John's favourite quote about the art of conjuring: The More Secret Things Are, The More Beautiful They Are. It came from Luca Pacioli's De Viribus Quantitatis (On The Powers Of Numbers), the earliest known book on conjuring and deception. The only copy had languished in the vaults of the University of Bologna for over five hundred years. Another Platonic ideal, John supposed.

He opened the book. Every thick, creamy, textured page was blank. Disappointed, he placed it back on the table. As he leaned forward, he saw what he at first assumed was a floor-to-ceiling window to his left. He stood up and grabbed the top of the chair in fear as a wave of shock and nausea swept over him. The window was not a window. The entire wall was missing as was every other wall. When he looked down, instead of a carpet or floorboards, he saw straight through to the open ground beneath, some twelve feet below where he appeared to be standing on air.

He closed his eyes, then reopened them. Nothing changed. Taking his right foot out of its slipper, he put his weight down on it. He felt soft fibres tickle his toes, then a solid floor beneath the ball of his foot. He was standing on a carpet. The only problem was, he couldn't see it. What he could see, clearly, was snow. The ground below was covered in it and, as he watched, more flakes appeared a few inches under his feet and descended slowly to the whiteness below.

Lifting his head, he looked at the fireplace. That, at least, was reassuringly solid, as was the wall behind it. The closed door, four feet to the right of the fire, was constructed of dark wood and looked like it had been there for centuries.

John looked back at the missing wall on his left, then across to his right. Finally, he turned, still gripping the top of the armchair. The wall behind him was also missing. The landscape beyond the floating room was almost featureless. He was looking at a field blanketed with snow. The quality of the light suggested it was night, but the reflected brightness on the surface of the snow was so bright, it seemed spotlit. Turning to check every wall, John could see no roads, no hedges, no movement other than the constant, slow fall of the snow.

He took a cautious step towards the fire, not letting go of the back of the chair until he was sure the invisible floor would bear his weight. Once he had released the chair, he became more confident, finding the courage to take a second step, then a third.

Directly in front of the fire, the warmth it gave off was the same as it had been when John had been seated. It was neither too hot nor too cold, just as the cushion on the chair had been neither too hard nor too soft.

It's a Goldilocks room.

John thought back to Gai's words.

"The Between is where your mind intersects with no-time and no-space. What you'll find there is your sanctum, which is yours, and yours alone. No one can follow you there, but when you travel back to our reality, you will be unprotected, and vulnerable. Time does not exist in any recognisable sense in the Between. You could spend days there and return before you drew another breath here. You would be ill-advised to do so, John Aviemore. The Between has its own dangers. Learn from it and, once you start to get comfortable, return."

John looked up, expecting to see either a plastered ceiling or a star-studded sky and a low moon. What he saw was neither, and the sight made him draw a long breath full of awe.

It was night sure enough, but the heavens contained a cosmic display that would have made an astronomer hyperventilate. There were more stars than John had ever seen, far more than he knew were visible from Earth. He saw layers upon layers of stars of varying brightness, most white, but some yellow, red, or blue. As he watched, stars disappeared and others took their place. He saw a moon, then another. A third described a long arc, turning as it went, before vanishing. There were planets, too, some so close, they reminded him of photographs from the Hubble telescope. But these planets were unfamiliar. There were galaxies which, as he focused his attention on them, faded or flared brightly and disappeared. There were areas of nothingness, too, which John thought might be black holes, the points of light around them being sucked into darkness like soap suds circling a plughole.

He saw other sights that made no sense to him and which, as soon as he looked away from them, were forgotten as if they had never existed. His mind could not relate them to anything he had ever encountered.

By the time he looked away, John was filled with such wonder that he could not move for a few minutes.

Reminding himself of why he was here, John walked to the door and pulled it open. It led to a long corridor, lit at intervals by oil lamps. Pairs of doors led off on both sides, but he could see no rooms beyond the transparent walls, just the falling snow and the undulating whiteness.

John stepped forward onto what felt like polished floorboards. He tried the first door on the left. It was locked as was its companion on the right. The third door he tried opened smoothly inwards and, as it did so, the room beyond appeared.

It was a small room, the size of the average single garage. The floor was visible, covered in a rough kind of hemp. At its outer limits, the snowy landscape could be seen. It was as if the room had sprung into existence and defined its shape the moment John opened the door.

He stepped inside. The room, despite the lack of any heat source, was the same temperature as the first, which John was already thinking of as his study. He stepped out of his slippers and left them by the door. The rough fibres under his bare feet might have belonged in a temple or a gym. As he walked, the room stretched, meaning he got no closer to the snowy view. He broke into a brief sprint, but it made no difference. When he looked around, he was now standing in an area the size of a school hall. The room had grown in all directions simultaneously.

More surprising than the expanding room, when he stopped to think about it, was the ease in which he'd broken into a sprint. Never particularly sporty, John had, nevertheless, tried to stay in reasonable shape. At home, he ran to keep his heart and muscles working, not to set any records. On the few occasions he had pushed himself for the last quarter of a mile, he had finished as a sweaty, shaking wreck, lungs burning, hands on knees as he tried to catch his breath. Not here. His sprint had been effortless, and his breathing had been unaffected.

In this place, in the Between, his body was as much an artificial construct as the floating house.

With a whoop, he sprinted towards the receding wall again, then turned and ran back to the door. Was this what top athletes experienced when they were at their peak? Every muscle, every sinew, every joint was powering him forward in the most efficient way, his arms pumping and the balls of his feet barely touching the matting.

For a few minutes, John relived what it was like to be a child, released from a stuffy classroom into the open air. He ran, jumped, rolled, did handstands, cartwheels, front and backflips simply because he could. When he stopped, he wasn't sweating, and his pulse was normal.

He walked back to the door and stepped into the corridor. He mentally named the room his dojo.

The next door was locked, but the final door on the right was open. The corridor darkened past that point, and although John suspected there were more doors he couldn't see, he thought his sanctum would reveal more of itself when he was ready.

He had already accepted this place and was thinking of it as his own. When he stepped through the door into the next room, the process was complete. John belonged here.

THIRTY-TWO

It was a library. Not just any library. Unlike the other rooms in the sanctum, John could not see the landscape beyond. There were no windows. The room was vast, built of stone, and had the scale and ambience of a cathedral. But there was no altar, no nave, no pews. This was a cathedral of reading. Vast shelves filled the hushed space, towering over his head. The smallest shelves were twenty feet long and ten feet tall. They were dwarfed by some of those lining the outer walls. John couldn't see the tops of those shelves, which vanished into impenetrable darkness above.

The library was the darkest room in the sanctum. More lamps flickered on brackets at intervals, but the room was too large for their light to make much headway in the thick darkness. In front of John was a low table on which a lit candle in a pewter holder gave out a comforting glow. John picked it up and followed the outer wall to his right, until a gap opened between the shelves, leading further into the room. He stepped through.

The books he could see were all ancient hardbacks.

Most of the spines were black, although there were a few muted browns, greens, and reds among them.

John turned left and walked between two stacks. It didn't seem right to touch the books, so he contented himself with pausing and looking at the gold lettering of their titles. They were written in no language he had ever encountered. Even so, they communicated something of their contents. One dictionary-sized tome gave off such an air of menace that he hurried away after examining it. Another slim volume made him think of young love, a delicate perfume wafting from its place on the shelf.

Soon, John was presented with a choice. He could either keep following this corridor of books or head towards the centre of the room. Stepping between the shelves, he looked left and right. Another book corridor, this time with gaps on both sides leading to still more shelves. He turned left, then right, finding a long corridor of shelves taller than his Wimbledon house.

It was a maze. A maze made of books. He smiled at the idea. Then he thought back over the turns he had taken so far and wasn't convinced he could retrace his steps. He stepped back into the corridor he had just left, followed it for a while, then took a turn leading towards the outside walls of the room. He held his candle high to see if he recognised any of the books as he passed, but none looked familiar. One more turn, and he knew he had gone wrong somewhere. He wasn't heading towards the outer wall, but further into the library.

Another few minutes of walking, and he was in trouble. He looked at the candle, which was still burning, and hadn't reduced in size. Gai had said time didn't exist here until the moment he travelled back from the Between. The everlasting candle was a reminder of this, and John, when he thought about it, found his own experience of time had been distorted. One event had followed another. He had arrived in the study, sat in the Platonic Chair, found the corridor and the dojo, and entered the library. Yet all these experiences occupied the same place in his mind as if they had happened simultaneously.

Experimentally, John waved his fingers over the candle flame. There was a sensation of heat. He moved his fingers closer. No hotter. Closer still, until his forefinger was in the flame itself. No more heat, and no pain. He snuffed out the flame. It continued to burn. He blew it, hard. The flame wavered and burned on.

Gai's advice was to come back quickly this first time. John knew he should be concerned. He was lost in a maze inside a cathedral of books, and he had no idea how to get out. But he wasn't worried. He was safe. The word sanctum was wisely chosen. Nothing could touch him.

On a sudden whim, he reached out to take a book at random. His fingers passed straight through the spine. The sensation was like putting his hand into water. The book and its immediate neighbours even rippled like the surface of a pond. John half-expected his hand to be wet, but his fingers were dry. He tried two more books with the same result.

He strolled around the shelves. Despite the fact he couldn't touch the books, he was comforted by their presence. He knew he was surrounded by a repository of knowledge larger than any that existed on Earth. It was as if the internet had been crammed into this still, stone place. Unlike the internet, though, the information contained in the billions of pages was arcane, powerful, and all of it was useful. The books whispered of knowledge to enrich minds, of secrets untold for countless centuries, and of power available to those who knew how to ask the right questions.

Acres of books, mountains of books, streets, passageways, alleys and thoroughfares of books. The air itself rich with hints, snatches of ideas, vast concepts that floated through the cathedral-like clouds. Shadows trailed promises of enlightenment, the odour of stone and fusty wood lured the wanderer onwards, inwards, the search its own reward.

It was a memory that saved John from getting lost in the Between.

A mobile library parked outside the primary school. Harry, six years old, thrilled that a library could have wheels. "The books are coming to find us, Daddy, they're coming to find us." Following Harry up the two metal steps into the tiny space, the children's section just five shelves, only one of which was suitable for his son's reading age. Harry's excitement and delight at finding a Roald Dahl book he had only read four times. The smile John had shared with Sarah as they had watched their boy, too delighted to wait, flop onto the floor and start reading.

John looked around him. He must have stopped walking. He was standing very still, blinking rapidly, the candle still burning. The lack of a sense of time confused him. How long had he been standing there? Seconds? Minutes? Hours? The thought of his wife and son had brought him back.

He bounced on his toes and shook his head like a dog drying itself. He remembered Gai's warning, back in the clearing.

"The Between is seductive. Once you're there, I can't bring you back. You have to decide to come back."

The thought of Harry brought on a twinge of guilt. John, hurt by his own mother's distance, even after the death of his father, had made the same mistake with his own son. He had tried to be closer to Harry, spend time with him, play with him, but he had always sensed a gap, a deficiency, a lack of something he couldn't fake. It was to Sarah that Harry went first with his stories from school, his success and failures, his scraped knees and wounded pride, his hopes and dreams. John loved to watch them together. He wasn't bitter about the distance between him and his son, just sad.

John resolved to spend time with Harry and Evie when he got back.

If he got back.

At that thought, he did what Gai had taught him. He sat down and leaned against the nearest wall. Closing his eyes, he imagined the bark of the tree pressing against his back, tried to feel the warmth of the sun on his left cheek. He remembered the twig in his hair, scratching at his scalp.

In the uppermost right hand corner behind his eyelids, he saw faint lines, sharpening and growing. The lines became branches, and as he looked up, leaves appeared. Shades of green, yellow and blue warmed the image. Other patches revealed themselves as the picture took on more definition. The clearing was taking shape around him. It was working, he was returning, travelling back from the Between.

With that, he opened his eyes.

Something was wrong. Very wrong.

He was moving along a tunnel, at the end of which was a pair of grey eyes. There was a roar, increasing in volume, as if he had stuck his head into a waterfall. He tried to draw breath, but something was wrapped around his neck, constricting his windpipe. He couldn't breathe. He couldn't breathe. Panicking now, he thrashed upwards with his arms, but they were lead-heavy and weak. Much too weak. The roaring got louder. The world darkened around him.

I'm going to die.

THIRTY-THREE

"I could have killed you. You gave me plenty of time."

John heard the words but didn't acknowledge them. He was on all fours, coughing.

Gai was standing over him, his voice as unconcerned as if he were discussing the weather. "You would have died if I had been your enemy. So many ways I could have killed you."

"Wh—wh—why...?"

Gai ignored the interruption. "Could have stabbed you, gutted you, dropped a big rock on your head to crush your skull. Could have smothered you, poured poison into your stupid open mouth, gouged your eyes out. Even cut off your legs and beaten you to death with them. Options, options."

John rolled onto his side. He tried to speak again, but his throat was raw. Gai tutted, held his hand out and hummed. He passed the bottle of mead. John swallowed with relief. He glared at the unconcerned noone.

"You arsehole. Why did you do that?"

"'That, my boy,"—which sounded odd coming from someone who looked like a child—"was me saving your life."

"Funny," said John, his fingers tracing the skin on his neck where Gai's hands had squeezed, "because, from where I was sitting, it felt like the opposite."

"What did I tell you about the Between? The dangers, I mean."

"Not to get too comfortable," said John, like a sulky teenager being told off in front of the class.

"And?"

John mumbled, "to make the return journey as quick as possible."

"What was that? Didn't quite catch it."

"The return journey. I was supposed to make the travel time as short as possible. I get it, okay." John was on his feet now, towering over the noone and pointing at him. "I listened to what you said, and I knew it was important. But that was the first time I've ever been to the Between. Do you remember your first time there, Gai? It must have been easier because you believe in magic. You didn't grow up on a world where it doesn't exist. Or, rather, where it does exist, but your own mother kept it secret from you."

John paused for breath. Gai took it as a cue for him to speak, but John's finger jabbed forward until it was an inch from his nose.

"I haven't finished. Let me tell you how I earn my living. You'll love this. I'm a magician. A conjurer. Someone who pretends magic is real. I can read minds, make items disappear, pass one solid object through another. Watch."

He picked up a stone and held it up between his left thumb and forefinger. Although he appeared to take it in his right hand, he let it fall behind his left fingers, then allowed the hand to fall to his side, giving all his attention to his empty right hand. Apparently, a noone was as easily misdirected as a human, and Gai watched John's fingers curl open to prove that the stone had gone.

The noone leapt forward to look more closely at his palm. "Remarkable! How is it possible? I have seen nothing like it. You have abilities I have never encountered before. You didn't whisper a single word of power, didn't sing a charm. I was watching you. How? How did you do it?"

"It's not real. The audience knows it, too. They play along because they'd love to think magic is real."

Gai was still looking at John's hand, eyes wide.

John looked at the excited noone, then sighed in exasperation. "It's in my other hand." He opened it to show Gai the stone. "It was always there."

Gai examined the stone. When he was satisfied that it was the same one, he looked aghast. "You cheated," he said.

"I cheated."

"But... why?"

"Because I'm a magician. And that's what a magician does in a world without magic."

Gai looked crestfallen, a kid who'd just found out the truth about Father Christmas. "I don't understand."

"I don't expect you to. You haven't grown up in my world. Maybe that's why people like me become pretend magicians, and why other people pay to see me cheat. Because, deep down, they know the impossible is real. You told me we were all magicians, thousands of years ago. Now none of us are. Well, virtually none of us."

John sat down on the fallen log and looked out into Leigh Woods. "Yes, I got too comfortable in the Between. In fact, I almost lost myself there. What did you expect to happen? I've just been to a place that should only exist in dreams, but it was just as real as this stone. I don't expect you to understand."

He let the stone drop. Gai watched intently as if expecting it to disappear again. "I'm sorry, John. You're right. I don't understand. But I hear the pain in your words. I hadn't anticipated how overwhelming the Between might be for you."

"It was incredible," said John. "All of it. Especially the library. It was the size of a—"

Gai hissed, waving his hands. "No. Don't tell me about it. The place you build in the Between is *your* sanctum, John. It is the most private of places. You must not share its secrets, even with me. Whatever form your sanctum took, it should have contained a place of knowledge and a place where you can practice putting the knowledge to practical use. Yes?"

The library and the dojo. John nodded.

"Good. It is up to you to discover how they work in your sanctum. You will need to go back. But remember, you are susceptible to the dangers there. There is a part of us that does not want to leave the Between. But we don't know how long we have. So you must go back. Stay in your sanctum at all times, John. It's not safe for you outside. Not yet."

John rubbed his throat. "Promise not to kill me while I'm there?"

"I promise to only hurt you. Hopefully, you won't die."

"Oh, well, thank you. That's very big of you."

The noone glowered at him from under his untidy eyebrows.

"It's just an expression," said John.

"Next time, come back faster, or I'll jump up and down on your reproductive organs."

John paled. "How can I get back faster?"

"Work on your visualisation. Make it vivid, detailed, and real. When you travel from the Between, you have no charms, no magic, no physical defence. You can be killed as easily as a helpless child. When you came back this time, I called your name, slapped your face. It took you at least ten beats to return. I could have chopped your head off."

"So you said. Beats?"

"Heartbeats. Ah. You say seconds. Ten seconds. I've been meaning to ask, why do you say seconds when there are no firsts? Maybe now's not the time. You need to come back faster. Slowly is no good. It needs to happen like waking up when someone shouts in your ear. From one state to the other in an instant. Asleep, awake! Got it?"

He clapped his hands twice to emphasise his point. "Between, back here! Otherwise, you wake up dead with a dagger in your throat."

John wanted to ask more, but Gai held up his hand for silence, his head tilted to one side, and his eyes shut. When he opened his eyes, John saw fear there.

"Move," said the noone, picking up his knapsack. He ran to a large oak and stood with his back against it, motioning John to do the same.

"Sing with me if you can," he said, "then stay absolutely still. And not a word, understand?"

Without any further explanation, he sang. The melody, although simple, was made discordant by the guttural accompaniment that came from another, deeper sound. The low pitch of this counter melody was surprising not just because of the way Gai sang it simultaneously with the first tune, but also because the timbre of the sound seemed impossible from such a small body. John's solar plexus vibrated as if he were standing next to a powerful bass speaker.

The air around them vibrated, and John's vision blurred. He tried singing with Gai. At first, he felt like someone trying to sing in a different language. Then, of its own accord, his body produced a second melody just as Gai's had. Within three seconds of their voices joining, the vibrating air snapped into solidity. John could see the open space, the leaves and stones on the ground, the fallen log and the surrounding trees, but no sound reached him. He moved his right hand forward and encountered resistance. It was like pushing on a trampoline.

Gai grabbed his wrist and squeezed. John looked back up at the clearing and froze.

From the north, something was coming. No, not something, some*things*. John watched the first creature unfold, then refold itself as it moved closer, followed by a monster that slithered like a giant worm across the sun-warmed earth.

John stared in horror as more nightmare creatures entered the clearing. He recognised most of them. They weren't creatures from any old nightmare, they had crawled straight out of his mind. They were the monsters from the Charleston Hotel.

THIRTY-FOUR

In horror films, monsters lurk in the darkness, so the viewer's imagination can conjure something scarier than the special effects department can come up with. Which should have made what John was looking at easier to deal with as the creatures entered the clearing. But it didn't. Daylight revealed his worst imaginings as real.

Even so, there was something inherent in the creatures that shunned the light, and the party making their way through the woods carried something of the night with them.

The hideous metallic mantis came first. When John had first seen it in the Bloomsbury Suite, it had given the impression that it grew taller with every step. Now he saw he had only witnessed part of its system of movement. For three long, jerky steps, it unfolded and grew in height, its many-jointed legs sliding together like pistons. Its blunt, shovel-shaped head was covered in dark dots, which John at first took to be markings. As the head swung from side to side, tilting, John saw that the dots were, in fact, hundreds of eyes. Over the course of a few more jerky steps, the mantis folded back into itself, halving its height until it stood about five feet tall, its thin limbs creased together. Then the process began again.

Not all the creatures John had seen that night were here. He recognised the cloven-heeled women, three of them this time, their features pinched and cruel, eyes positioned so far apart their faces looked more animal than human. After them came the horrible child-shaped thing in pyjamas, its blood-filled eyes swivelling left and right, its mouth closed, hiding its two sets of vicious teeth.

The man that wasn't a man was next, not in a business suit this time, but wrapped in a grey cloak, a hood keeping most of its face in shadow. John could still see the side of one cheek, the jawline and part of its neck. The skin looked wet. He was too far away to see clearly, but John knew it wasn't liquid he saw on the hooded figure's skin, because it had no skin. Such light that reached under the hood was reflected by the millions of ants crawling constantly around the 'body', maintaining the illusion of a walking man.

Gai had remained calm as the grotesquerie made their way through the clearing, but when the final figure appeared, his grip tightened on John's wrist.

The noone who had followed the beasts into the clearing was old, bald, and ugly, with yellow eyes.

Gai whispered something so faint it was barely audible. The air in front of their hiding place shimmered, and the old noone was gone. In his place was the dark-haired woman who had sat closest to John that night in the Charleston Hotel. It seemed like years since he'd seen her, but he'd never forget the moment she blew black dust into his face. She was even smaller than Gai.

After sniffing the fallen tree, she licked it, her tongue darting out like a lizard's. Her chin tilted back, and she shouted something. Whatever magical device Gai had constructed, no sound penetrated it. But the creatures heard and responded, turning and coming back to the centre of the clearing. John's breathing was becoming shallow. What if there was only limited air in their magic bubble? And what if it were running out already? His shirt was clammy where he'd begun to sweat. He gasped quietly and shifted his feet a fraction of an inch.

The reaction from the woman was instant. Her head snapped up, and she looked towards their side of the clearing. She spoke, and the three cloven-hoofed women trotted closer, nostrils flaring.

Their hands, John noticed, were human enough, hairy and large, the skin tough and weathered. The hair on their lower body became less coarse at their hips, thinned across their stomachs, and became a fine down on their breasts and shoulders. He had assumed their hair was cut short, but now he saw it was more like the fur of an animal, following the contours of their skulls.

Centaurs. Satyrs. Or fauns. Centaurs had four legs, didn't they? Fauns and satyrs were more human in appearance according to the myths and stories. John could see little he could relate to in those wide-set brown and yellow eyes. He settled on thinking of them as satyrs. The latent menace coming off these beings like a bad smell did not sit well with the cuddly image John associated with fauns.

Two of the creatures missed John and Gai's hiding place, but one came towards them. As she did so, Gai's grip on his wrist loosened marginally. As signals go, it was subtle, but John understood. He needed to calm down, breathe more deeply, not panic. He made himself take a slower, longer breath and hold it for a second before exhaling. Another breath, and his body relaxed, his teeth unclenched and his shoulders sagged. He told himself none of it was real, but he didn't believe it.

The satyr sniffed around them, looking at John's chest. This close, he could see—nestled in the fur on her head and close to the skull—two small horns, yellowed like ivory. The satyr moved closer but, seeing and smelling nothing, moved on to the next tree. As she did so, the worm-like creature passed by, missing their position by inches.

A minute later, the satyrs reconvened by the fallen tree. After a brief conference, and a last, long look from the dark-haired woman, they continued their journey.

Gai remained as still as a statue for another five minutes, then relaxed his grip on John's wrist and sang a two-note phrase. The sound of the woods returned, and John stepped forward without meeting any resistance.

Gai spat on the forest floor. "Pan," he said with rancour. "I might have known she'd want to be in on this."

"Who? I thought Pan was male. Like the faun in the Narnia books. Or is she a satyr?"

"Your ignorance about things any child knows amazes me," said Gai. "Pan is no satyr, although you named them correctly. And Pan is sometimes female, sometimes male." He caught the look on John's face. "The name *Pan* is more of a title carried by her family. When she dies, her daughter or son will take on the role. Pan is unpredictable. She might save you from drowning in the morning and stab you in the afternoon. It's all a game to her. She would love to see Ashtoreth come back and turn everything upside down again. No doubt, she thinks once the god is finished with her initial killing spree, and half of your realm lies in ashes, she might give Pan a piece of what's left. She's brought Astarte some of her old pets to greet her when she's free."

He spat again. "Pan."

John looked across the clearing to the spot where they'd disappeared. "Then who was the old man? The old noone, I mean."

Gai grunted. "That was her. You couldn't see through it?"

"See through what?"

"The Glamour."

John pictured the lined, warty, bestial features of the old yellow-eyed noone. "Glamour?"

"With a capital G. A charm used to disguise someone's true form. Particularly effective against the weak-minded."

"Oh. Thank you."

"Nothing personal. Humans don't even know to look for it. Visitors to your realm use it all the time. It's very useful, especially if it shows you what you..." His voice trailed off, he scowled and shook his head.

"I've seen her before," said John. "In a dream. Sort of a dream. It might have been real. I've lost track."

Gai pulled at his sleeve until he faced him. "Time to stop thinking of dreams as unreal. They are as real as this tree, this leaf, and this stick I'm poking in your side."

"Ow."

"We should be long past the point where you think reality happens when you're awake."

"I'm trying, Gai."

"Tell me about the dream."

"I was performing. Magic - conjuring, not real. She was there. So were those things. She was sitting with a massive man with a huge, messy beard, a guy with a shaved head who looked like a model, and a red-haired woman who dressed like a pole-dancer."

"The Green Man," said Gai. "She has always had a hold over him, but I am disappointed he is involved. I'm not surprised by Oberon and Titania. Power-hungry parasites."

"Oberon and Titania?" John continued without thinking. "But aren't they the king and queen of the fair—"

Gai waited for him to finish the word.

"Sorry," said John. "Force of habit."

"They were royalty once," said Gai, "and they'd like to be so again. But our realm overturned the feudal system about a thousand of your years ago. Not that you'd know it if you asked Tani and Obe. They act like they run the place and still expect us to behave like we're their inferiors. The present queen, which is how she chooses to style herself, is the niece of the Titania who was toppled from the throne. Oberon is a cousin of the last one, I believe."

John's mind was whirling. "What the hell were those other things? The foldy praying mantis, the pyjama monster?"

"Other than the satyrs, they are Remnants. In your realm, creatures are born out of other creatures, correct?"

John thought about plants, bacteria, and the articles he'd read about certain lizards, insects and fish that had reproduced without a mate, but said, "Yes, pretty much."

"We are the same, mostly, but there are also creatures born of magic. Travel between realms is dangerous, John. If a native of one stays too long in another, they become trapped there. We call them Remnants. What you saw are Remnants from more distant realms. A few magic-born still try to reach Earth, even now. Some live disguised among you. The Adepts, when they find them, destroy or banish them, but they cannot return to their own realms. They live in the Blurred Lands. For the most part, they keep themselves to themselves, but you wouldn't want to bump into one after dark. Or during the day."

Gai built another fire and lit it with a gesture. "Let's eat."

"Hang on," said John, as Gai produced his wooden whistle and lifted it to his lips. "Earlier - when you told me about Glamour, there was something you weren't telling me."

Gai acted as if he hadn't heard him, blowing a few notes on the whistle, but they didn't have the same haunting quality of the first time John had heard him play. After a few seconds, he stopped. When he spoke, he didn't look at John, keeping his face turned towards the edge of the clearing.

"Glamour is a simple charm, but it can be very effective depending on who's looking, and on *how* they are looking."

John didn't prompt Gai when he fell silent, knowing there was more.

"For instance, if you were walking alongside a river in your realm at dusk, and, as you passed a bridge, you saw someone squatting there, would you think it was a troll? No. What would you expect to see there?" Gai tilted his head to indicate the question wasn't hypothetical.

"Um, someone fishing, maybe?"

"A reasonable supposition. But wrong. It's a troll. A troll in your realm needs a disguise, and it would use your assumptions to choose one. Glamour is most effective when it shows you what you want to see. Your expectations feed the charm. You see someone fishing rather than a semi-intelligent carnivorous killer on the hunt for trinkets."

Gai sighed. "But a noone should know better. We are the masters of Glamour. Stupid, stupid, stupid."

"Who is?'

"I am. Thinking my father would encourage me to come here after he'd always warned me off. I wanted him to trust me, I wanted him to believe I was capable of looking after myself. So when he said I was strong enough to resist the effects of the time cage, I was completely taken in by her."

"Her?"

"Pan." Gai spat again. "S*he* sent me here, Glamoured to look like my father, And, like a fool, here I am. Which means Ashtoreth wants me here, a noone who is fascinated by humans. A noone who might teach a natural magician how to use his powers. She *wants* you to unlock your potential and become more powerful. We're both being used, John."

"So what do we do?"

Gai held the whistle to his lips again, then paused. "We do what she wants, and we hope she's underestimated you. What else can we do?"

THIRTY-FIVE

"I have a theory," said Gai, walking up and down in front of the fallen trunk, one hand stroking his chin, like a lecturer in full flow. "But I need to hear it from you. Tell me what happened when you escaped the first time. I was there, you know."

"What? That was thirty-two years ago."

"Less than a moon ago for me. The cage distorts time for those in its field of influence."

John thought of the missing city and suspension bridge. He told Gai about it.

"Exactly my point," said the noone. "We could be anywhere."

"Before the bridge was built, you mean?" asked John.

"Yes - in the distant past. You said there was no trace of a settlement on the far bank of the river?"

"Nothing."

"But the trees were the same?"

John tried to remember. "More dense."

"Perhaps, then. But you may equally have been looking at the distant future."

"But there were no humans, no noones. No animals."

Gai shrugged. "One possible future. I do not know."

John stopped thinking about the implications. There were more pressing problems.

"You said you were there when I escaped from Ash the first time. What did you see?"

Gai had an odd look on his face, one John hadn't seen before. Was he embarrassed?

"Ah, you won't like it. I've heard how touchy humans can be about certain subjects."

"Touchy? About what?"

"Well, look, I heard you half a league away. It's not as if you were trying to be quiet. I followed you, then climbed the highest tree I could find. There were other creatures concealed around the clearing, which was a little like this one. There was wood piled up in the middle ready for a fire."

John realised what he was saying. "You mean, when I got there with Ash, we weren't alone? You were watching when she, when we...? When...?"

"Yes. Me, maybe Pan, and some Remnants. Nasty creatures."

"You watched us? Enjoy the show, did you?"

"Oh, don't be like that. I have no particular interest in your sticky-out bits and where you put them. You should be more annoyed that I didn't help you when she cursed you."

"I am. Excuse me? When she what?"

"Cursed you. While you slept, she prepared a powerful enchantment. At that stage, I could not know what it was. It was only when she delivered it that I realised. By then, it was too late. If they had seen me, the Remnants would have ripped me apart. Still, you survived, against all my expectations. And here you are. Astarte calmed down quickly after you ran. She was confident you would be back, with your mind wiped clean."

John experienced an awful moment of cold clarity. "What was the curse supposed to do?"

Gai's eyes, usually impish and amused, were clouded and downcast as he remembered.

"It was a curse of unravelling. I heard her sing it. I never knew I could be so afraid and so helpless. When she sang, it was as if she sucked all the happiness out of the world. My body was heavy, I began to question the point of my existence. Then she drew it all together into a ball of pain, and she moulded it in the fire, using the agony of the flames on her skin to feed the curse she had brought back from the Between. When you woke, she sang it into you."

John remembered Ash turning from the fire that night. He thought he must have imagined her putting her arms into the flames because her skin was unmarked. As she had reached for him, mumbling something he did not understand, he had heard a roar in his head as if a hurricane had come from nowhere. He had slapped her away—his fingers burning where they touched her—and run.

Gai looked up at him. "It should have unravelled your mind, thought by thought, memory by memory, growing stronger as it fed on your consciousness. Even the strongest protective charms could only delay the inevitable. It should have been unstoppable, John Aviemore. A curse like that cannot be lifted. I do not know how you survived it."

John thought of the hospital, of the conversation he'd overheard between his mother, Augustus, and a stranger.

"Can someone else take on a curse?" he whispered.

Gai shook his head. "Unlikely. The god may be weaker, but she's still a god. In your realm, only an experienced Adept could absorb a curse that strong. Even then, the curse would still be alive. To destroy it once it had started its work, well... I don't think it's even possible. John? What is it?"

John was slumped against the fallen trunk, thinking of the yellow walls of Fir Trees Care Home, of the tired, hopeless look in the eyes of the other families he sometimes saw there, as they lost a loved one to dementia.

"My mother," he said. "She took the curse from me."

He knew now what he had avoided hearing when he'd phoned Fir Trees, the truth that should have been clear from his dreams that night. His mother was dead. He wept, and when the old man who looked like a boy knelt beside him and put a hand on his shoulder, he did not push him away. He sobbed like a child for the lost chance to tell his mother he loved her, and for the way he had interpreted her distance as lack of love when it had been the opposite all along.

When John had stopped crying, Gai created a fire and hung a wooden kettle filled with stream water and dried leaves above it. Despite the obvious flaw with a wooden kettle, John was unsurprised when the flames left no mark on it as the water boiled. Gai poured two cups. The tea was rich and complex; bitter to the taste with a sweet finish.

"Magic use is restricted to three families on Earth. Your family is one of the Three. Your mother was an Adept."

John knew it was the truth. He had surrendered to the illness, or, as he knew now, the curse, sinking away from his life, and his mother had pulled him back. She had searched for him in the white landscape, cradling her son like an infant when she had found him. John had opened his eyes in a hospital room.

He finished his tea, and Gai refilled his cup. "My

mother lived with that curse for three decades before it destroyed her."

"Then she was truly powerful. I wish I could have known her."

"What does it mean, to be an Adept? What do they do?"

"Your mother maintained the Accord, along with the other two Adepts. The Three use their ability, when necessary, without exposing the existence of magic in your realm."

"And that's what I am? One of these Adepts?"

Gai's mischievous smile was back. "Well, you're a riddle, John. The Three, the noones, all of them would answer no to that question. In fact, they'd go further. They'd insist, because you're male, that you are genetically incapable of using magic. My father will be delighted that you can. His theory was right. He's always been derided for his interest in human science. Now he's been vindicated." Gai took another sip and frowned. "That's bad, actually. He'll be insufferable."

"What theory?"

"Oh. Right. Well, I am yet to study humans in the same depth as Father, so my knowledge is a little patchy, I'm afraid. As far as I understand, every human is born with two crime zones, correct?"

"Two what?"

"Er... crime zones? Creamy sons? Damnation. Tiny things that tell you, when you are unborn, whether you should be male or female. They are why, and they are hex."

John's blank stare changed to dawning realisation. "Chromosomes?"

"That's what I said, yes, good. Crummy zomes. Saying hex and why."

"X and Y. Women have XX, men have XY."

"Yes, yes, of course." Gai was becoming animated, pacing around the fire and illustrating his points by jabbing a stick in the air. If he hadn't been sure before, John was now convinced Gai had only the vaguest idea what he was talking about.

"Now, females are the only magicians in the Earth realm because of the way they mirror the natural order within their bodies. Or so we've always believed. Like the moon, females follow a monthly pattern. The story of life and death is re-enacted inside them every moon. What they take from the earth in food and drink, they give back in blood. The female can grow new life, containing it inside her."

John looked unconvinced, and Gai, noticing, poked his arm with the stick.

"Father said it was rubbish. He thinks it's all down to this why crummy zone. It prevents a man from using magic.

"Okay," said John. "But if your father is right, that doesn't explain me. I have a Y chromosome as far as I know."

"Ha!" said Gai, with a flourish of his stick. "You have one, yes. But your scientists have discovered that the why chrome thing has gradually been weakening. Not disappearing, but losing its purpose. He says it's like an organ in the human body. The foreword? No, the epilogue? No. What is it, come on, the useless organ, what's it called?" He prodded John in the stomach.

"Appendix?"

"That's the fellow! Yes, it's like the appendix. Or, rather, it will be like the appendix, eventually. It's heading that way. It's still present, but it is losing its usefulness. Father said there would be individuals who would leap forward, whose why chromosome—that's it, told you I knew what it was—would become redundant early. That's you! You're a mutant!"

"Thank you so much," said John. "So, there will be others?"

"Other mutants? I don't know. Very unlikely any other mutants are the sons of Adepts though."

"But when the Y chromosome has gone, all men will be able to use magic?"

"Yes. Father said it'll happen in about...," Gai screwed up his face, "a hundred million years."

"Right. So for now, it's... just me?"

"Almost certainly," said Gai. "The first male Adept. You're making history. If you survive."

"Thanks for that."

Later, after Gai had shared a loaf of flatbread flavoured with herbs, John found his instinct for self-preservation had been joined by a wish to avenge his mother.

"Tell me about the time cage," he said.

"It's designed to imprison a being with significant magical power. The cage is kept within the Blurred Lands so that Earth's magical resources can maintain its integrity. If Astarte can't break out, the only feasible way she might escape would be if another powerful magician took her place. When you were younger, she must have thought she could make you so obsessed with her you would be willing to sacrifice yourself. She is the god of love after all. What chance would an unprepared human male have against her allure?"

"She wasn't easy to resist. But she hadn't reckoned on Chris and Alison."

"Who?"

"Friends. They reminded me that there was a world outside of Ash's bedroom. A world I realised she was no part of. I split up with her. That was the night she cursed me. I should have written a letter, but some stupid sense of honour made me want to tell her face to face. This is all my fault." John experienced a moment of shame and horror. He wasn't being entirely honest. That sense of honour hadn't been the reason he'd come back that final night. It had been lust. It had almost cost him his sanity and, in the end, it had cost his mother her life.

Gai shook his head. "When the god of love has sex with you, you are connected to her forever. That you resisted her at all is remarkable. For you to have transcended those bonds and rejected her is, I think, unique. Do not blame yourself."

"But here I am again. I'm not sleeping with her this time, but I'm trapped. You said the only way she can escape is if another powerful magician takes her place. And you think that's me?"

"I do."

"Well, if she can't wipe my mind to do it, I'm hardly going to volunteer. So what's her plan?"

"I don't know," said Gai, "and that's what worries me. Now, get back to the Between. If you are to master magic in any meaningful way, you need to get there at will. While you're there, you must learn how to use its knowledge. When you fought me, your defence was a mixture of protective charms and instinct. That won't be enough to defeat a god."

"What will be enough?"

Gai grinned. "It's time for you to learn a spell. And we're going to skip all the elementary lessons and go straight to the dangerous stuff."

John tried to look less scared than he felt. "I'm ready. Teach me."

"Not me," said Gai, walking over to the whitebeam and waiting for John to sit down. "I can tell you what to look for, but I can't teach you anything. Your sanctum will do that. Find a holding spell, John. A spell to prevent Ashtoreth attacking us. Let your sanctum train you until you're ready. No sap this time. You can find it yourself."

He told John what to look for. John sat down, leaned back, half-closed his eyes and took a slow breath, wondering how long it would take him to find his way back to the no-place. Then he heard the crackle of a fire and opened his eyes.

He was in the Between. And, this time, something was calling him.

THIRTY-SIX

John sat upright in the Platonic Chair, listening. Whatever was calling, it wasn't doing it using sound. It was more of an insistent thought, a nagging sensation, like going on holiday and spending the journey wondering if he'd left the freezer door open.

He stood up. The study was the same, and the same slow-falling snow danced hypnotically beyond the non-existent windows of the house.

In the corridor, John ignored all the other doors and made straight for the library. Whatever it was that wanted him was there.

Once inside the cavernous stone space and its vast stacks of books, John picked up the lit candle and set off. There was no confusion, no sense of aimless wonder this time. He walked on with a sense of purpose, his slippered feet slapping on the dusty stone.

Gai had told him what he needed and, although he hadn't fully grasped what the noone was talking about, it appeared that his sanctum understood perfectly. Without any conscious thought about where he was heading, he allowed himself to be led between the shelves, further and further into the maze.

His relationship with the books was different this time. John had sensed an atmosphere from some of them on his first visit, but this time, the atmosphere seeping out of them was redolent with power, or—rather—with the potential for power. Each book was a tightly compressed source of energy waiting to be unleashed, and as he passed them, John sensed what some of those powers might be. As he walked, he sometimes rose from the floor and flew a few paces, or heard the distant scorched roar of an angry dragon. Passing one shelf was like walking by a half-open bedroom door and glimpsing an orgy in progress.

The temperature dropped in one corridor of books where some of the tallest shelves disappeared into the darkness above. Even as he followed the call, John was tempted to stop there. He fought the urge, but his steps slowed, and damp tendrils caressed him, sliding around his body, whispering their nihilistic message. To linger would be to risk giving in to despair. John pressed on, his mood lifting the instant he turned the next corner. He would have to learn to close himself, to block some of the more powerful books, he knew, or each trip to the library would be dangerous.

A third of the way into the spiralling maze, as he approached the centre, John stopped. The call was close now. He turned slowly, looking all around him. The light of the candle reflected on the gold letters on the spines, making their incomprehensible titles look like Christmas decorations.

The second shelf from the floor, to his right. He was certain. John put his hand out towards the books. Exactly as before, as his fingertips reached the first hardback, a dark-blue volume which smelled like the sea, there was a liquid sensation, and his hand went straight through, up to his knuckles. This time, John did not withdraw his hand, instead moving it along the shelf from right to left, his flesh passing through the books, each one giving a brief impression of what might lie within. Much of it made no sense to him. Rain, badeye, goldeater, sunburst, the curious madness, poison bringer, safety stones.

Then his hand hit something solid. Near the end of the shelf, a thick black book prevented John from moving his hand further. The call he had heard had fallen silent. He had found the book that wanted him.

He wrapped his finger around the spine and pulled. It didn't shift. It was stuck. Placing the candle holder on the floor, John reached out and got a good grip. But he still couldn't make it move, even when he rocked back on his heels and used his full weight. It wasn't coming out. Dismayed, John knelt in front of the book and tried to interpret the gold letters, hoping he might find a clue there. It didn't help. The lettering was rendered in stunning gold leaf. Some of the magic books Augustus sold in Bonneville's were beautifully bound, and John could never resist touching them.

He let the forefinger of his right hand make contact with the lettering. With a yell of surprise that echoed around the old stone walls, he jerked his hand back again. Something had moved, crawling across his fingertip. He looked at his finger and yelped again. It was covered in an intricate tattoo, so fine and complicated that it should have taken many hours to complete. But it hadn't been there before he touched the book.

Holding his finger close to his face, he studied one of the tiny letters there: a shape like a capital Q, but whose tail looped back over the top of the letter before penetrating the circle within. He looked at the gold writing on the spine again. The same symbol was in the title. There was no sense of danger, and whatever had happened to his finger had not hurt him.

This was a library of magic. He was here to find a spell. Did he expect just to pick up a book and follow instructions?

Trusting his instincts, John lifted his right hand again and, this time, placed all four fingers and thumb on the letters. The process began immediately, and he watched with fascination as his other fingers, then his hand, filled with the secret language of the book. Pulling at the sleeve of his dressing gown and pyjamas, he saw the black ink spread its thousands of tiny letters over his wrist and onto his forearm. Just before reaching his elbow, the tide of words stopped. At the same moment, the book lost its solidity, and John's fingers passed through it again.

Picking up the candle, he retraced his steps with no wrong turns and returned to the study, still allowing his instincts to guide him.

Sitting in the Platonic Chair, he picked up the book that had been there on his first visit. He flicked through the pages. As before, they were all blank. Once again leaving the decision-making to his gut, he opened the book at the first page and placed his right fingertips on the thick, textured paper. As he watched, the process he had witnessed in the library reversed, the letters crawling rapidly down his arm and onto the paper. When it was done, eight pages were filled with writing.

John leaned back in the chair, the book on his lap. Although the only source of light in the room was the fire, a soft yellow glow illuminated the pages. John looked up, then wished he hadn't, as the same mesmerising display of stars, planets, and galaxies filled the sky above him. With an effort, he wrenched his gaze away and back to the book. In a floating room in a place where time had no meaning, John Aviemore tried to learn a spell.

The words still didn't make sense. John had hoped that the next miracle would be a translation into English. Instead, the tiny, ornate letters were as impenetrable as ever, their secrets locked within a language he couldn't understand. For a few minutes, he examined the script, looking for repetition. The most common letter in the English language was 'e'. Perhaps there would be a common letter here. He gave up quickly, unable to find a single symbol that repeated, which seemed impossible. What kind of language used unique letters for every word? How could anyone ever learn to read it?

What made the task even more difficult was the way the letters and words were arranged on the page. Not a single line was straight. Instead, the author favoured an undulating movement, the sentences covering the distance from spine to edge-of-page like worms twisting in the beak of a bird. Even in the middle of a word, a letter might dart up half an inch from the one preceding it, then be followed by three letters forming a ramp down to the next word.

John put the book on the table, rubbed his eyes and stood in front of the fire. Subconsciously assuming the customary position of a British man in front of burning logs at night, he put out his hands and rubbed them together, despite the temperature already being perfect for his comfort. In the same unnecessary way, he turned his back on the flames to warm the other side of his body.

How was he supposed to learn magic written in an alien language? Gai had said everyone who visited the Between constructed their own sanctum to make sense of the no-place. The noone had said nothing practical about the method of learning a spell because the unique character of every sanctum meant there was no advice he could give.

John was on his own. If this place was constructed by his own mind, then his mind was being unhelpful and obstructive. Conjuring, the profession John had pursued for most of his life, was straightforward. You bought a book, or a trick with instructions, practised until you could do it blindfolded, then showed your long-suffering family members before unleashing your miracle upon the world. John's preferred technique, when he invented his own illusions, was to read the description of an effect, then close the book and try to devise a method of achieving the same result. By the time he had finished, he had often invented a new effect that bore no relation to the one he had read.

Perhaps that was the problem. Maybe he was supposed to come up with his own method first after which the book would make sense. But how could he? Gai had told him he needed to learn a holding spell. According to the noone, each spell's potency depended on the power of the magician wielding it. The holding spell would slow down, or halt, the mental processes of the victim, damaging any magical defences and preventing attack.

It had all sounded straightforward back in the clearing. It wasn't straightforward now. This was real, organic, magic drawn from the earth, not *pick a card, any card.*

He looked at the offending book. Upside-down, and from his standing position by the fire, the writing didn't look like writing at all. John remembered the flute Sarah had kept from her school days. She would occasionally set up a music stand and play. John, who had never learned an instrument, had sometimes looked over her shoulder, trying to follow the rise and fall of the notes, marvelling at the complexity of melody that could be communicated by black splodges on five lines.

The words of the spell rose and fell like written music. And the magic Gai used, and that John had begun to discover, involved something close to singing.

With mounting excitement, John picked up the book again, looking at the first line on the page. If this was music, then it was far more complicated than the flute part of Fauré's Pavane. He wondered how each squiggle might relate to sound, meaning a shorter note, or louder, or held for longer. He couldn't work it out. The only immediate musical possibility that presented itself was pitch. What if the symbols that were higher meant just that - that they were higher in pitch? The same logic for those that were lower.

Glad no one was there to see or hear him, John held the book as he had seen choristers do, and sang a note in his uncertain baritone. He traced a finger along the symbols, guessing at note lengths, following the rise and fall in pitch suggested by the position of the symbols. At the first break in a line, he paused and took a breath. Nothing had changed. He continued, then stopped. His gut told him to go back, try the first line again. He was learning to trust his gut.

This time, after singing four notes, there was a change. Almost imperceptible, but he knew it was happening. He had got closer, sung something that made a little sense. He started again. Now he was sure. The third attempt was accompanied by a sensation unlike any other John had ever experienced. As the melody played in his head and through his voice, an area of his brain blossomed, bursting joyously into life.

John and Sarah had once visited Hayward's Heath to

see a hundred-year-old Chinese tree. Its flowers were blooming for only the third time ever.

"It's sad, don't you think?" John had said, staring up at the shock of tiny white flowers. "That it blooms so rarely."

"Don't be a curmudgeonly old fart. I think the opposite. It's wonderful. This tree is a long way from home, it's alone, and just look what it's capable of. It's inspiring."

Remembering that moment, John, a fifty-one-year-old widow who had just become a real magician, dropped his customary cynicism and embraced Sarah's joy at the unexpected.

"I can do magic, Sarah," he whispered, book in hand, standing in front of an open fire in a place that doesn't exist.

Once he had found the secret, the text came alive, working with him as he not so much learned the spell as co-created it. The more he sang, the more he understood what the symbols required of him. He didn't need to turn the page, as the process deepened and evolved into a conversation, a dance, or, more accurately perhaps, an improvised piece of music based on a common theme.

When his last note faded and John looked back at the book, the letters had gone, the pages blank.

He knew where he needed to be. He walked back to the corridor and headed for the dojo. The new sense that was still opening its petals in his mind told him to go there.

Someone was waiting for him.

THIRTY-SEVEN

He knew she was in the dojo before he opened the door and stepped onto the matting. Even so, he swallowed nervously when he saw her. John had to remind himself that the real Ash was still in the cottage. This version of her was straight out of his subconscious, but that knowledge made her no less disconcerting.

Ash wasn't naked this time, she was wearing a long, green dress with hanging sleeves. Her copper hair framed her perfect face, and the way the dress clung to her form did nothing to diminish her innate sexuality. Ash exuded sex, passion, wantonness, and availability. That was powerful enough, but when she added the suggestion that the person she was looking at was the sole focus of her desire, she was impossible to resist. Almost. Almost impossible.

John knew the truth behind that seductive sheen. He had seen the real Ash the night she cursed him. And yet, he had come back to the cottage three decades later. Partly because Helen's professional opinion had suggested confronting his fears, but that wasn't all of it. He had lied when he told Ash he had never thought about her. It had happened rarely, but it had happened. Perhaps a dozen times during his marriage, he had woken in the middle of the night, aroused and confused, only to find his sleeping mind had betrayed him, led him back to that iron bed.

Guilt had inevitably followed the dreams, despite the fact that his betrayal had been unconscious. Sarah would have understood if he had told her, but he found that he couldn't. On the few occasions it happened, he had buried the memory and re-focused his attention on the woman he loved.

Now, though, that blossoming part of his mind, which was unfurling its petals and sending its perfume to every corner of his consciousness, gave him the capacity to understand his past afresh. Sex with Ash had never just been sex. For her, each act of copulation had been the gradual weaving of a series of charms. Sex charms were powerful indeed, and Ash had used all her experience to loop bonds around John Aviemore, tying him to her, making it impossible for him ever to be fully free. Only her death or—far more likely—his, would cut the invisible cords that bound him.

If John had been from any other family, he would never have been able to leave Bristol the first time. As it was, when Ash had been thwarted by his natural defences, she had resorted to the unravelling curse. But the bonds with which she had ensnared him during sex had only been weakened by John's escape, not severed.

John saw it clearly now. The news of Ash's death had convinced him the cottage was safe. Helen's intervention had allayed his mental health fears. But the strongest reason for his decision to return had been the work of the charms woven decades ago by a trapped god.

Well, maybe she would get more than she bargained for.

He kicked off his slippers, removed his dressing gown and walked across the hemp floor to face the avatar. Although it wasn't Ash, it was imbued with all the power his subconscious feared.

She licked her lips. "Hello, John. You can't stay away from me, can you?"

He cleared his throat nervously and raised his right hand. She chuckled at that.

"Oh, I see. A male magician, how fascinating. Come on, then. Show me what you've got."

The spell he had absorbed was ancient, powerful, and complex. Gai had assured John he was capable of casting it, but before John had travelled to the Between, the noone had put a hand on John's shoulder, all his mischief gone.

"What you're about to learn is beyond all but the most gifted magicians. You have to believe, deep down, that you can do it. If not, you will never be free of Astarte."

John had nodded in response, but Gai had shaken him until he met his eyes. "Swear to me."

"What?"

"Swear to me on the memory of your wife that you will not return until you have mastered the spell. However long it takes."

"But I thought I wasn't supposed to stay there long. You said I shouldn't get too comfortable."

Gai's expression had been hard to read. "Don't worry. You won't get comfortable this time. Now swear it."

Looking at Ash's avatar, waiting for him to cast the spell, the look on Gai's face rose unbidden in his mind, and he recognised it. It was pity.

John focused his attention inwards, summoning the power that would cast the spell. The sensation was not cerebral, but physical. It started in his solar plexus, with an uncomfortable warmth and tightness. The warmth, which he visualised as a blue light, pulsed in his gut, and expanded, sending connections outward. Blue lines linked his solar plexus to his heart and groin, then a thread stretched up, wrapping itself around his spine. His brain glowed with the light, and the world around him came alive in a way he had never experienced. Under the soles of his feet and between his toes, every individual fibre of the matting was present to him, as was the material of the cotton pyjamas against his skin. His own body was laid bare to his heightened awareness; every organ, muscle, ligament, and nerve, every cell, even down to those on the outer layer of his skin as they died, detached and floated away, was intimately observed and understood.

The sensation was so unlike anything that John had ever experienced that he felt adrift, as if he might forget what it was like to be himself. He wasn't just John Aviemore anymore. He was all men, all women, all life. The force that animated patterns of matter and gave them the semblance of individuality was now his to command. This was what it meant to be a god.

Five yards away, Ash yawned. "Getting bored now," she said, her voice honeyed poison.

John had sung the spell of holding in the study. It was time to use it. The chain of light in John's body flared, and he raised his palm towards Ash, opening his mouth to release the spell.

He exulted in the power as it flowed through and out of him.

He was unstoppable.

The lights went out, and the dojo flipped upside-down. The blue glow vanished. There was pain. A great deal of pain.

John opened his eyes. Unfocused browns and reds. His eyes were stinging. His nose... something bad had happened to his nose. He was breathing through his mouth. He tried taking a breath through his nostrils. As far as bad ideas went, it was an award-winner. Much of the cartilage had been broken when he had hit the floor face-first. Now the shattered fragments of bone floating untethered in the blood and gristle where his nose used to be were sucked up and into his nasal passages, causing white-hot needles of pain to lance behind his eyes.

He screamed and passed out.

When he regained consciousness, the pain was no less tolerable.

I can control this. This is my sanctum. The pain isn't real. It's not real.

Mentally repeating this mantra, he rolled onto his side. This was as bad an idea as breathing through his nose. One of his cheekbones had shattered, and there was a fifty-fifty chance he'd roll onto the wrong side of his face. Luck wasn't with him.

He passed out again.

When he came to a second time, he opened his eyes and saw white and red objects scattered on the floor. He couldn't imagine what they were. Then he ran his tongue around the inside of his bleeding mouth, and found the gaps. They were his teeth.

"Are you going to be long? Only I'm having my nails done later."

The voice came closer until Ash was standing over him. "Oh dear, oh dear. This doesn't look good for you, does it? I'm just an avatar pulled from your mind, John. The real me will be much tougher. Perhaps you're not cut out for this. No one would blame you if you gave up."

John lifted his head, slowly. The pain flared immediately, but it was bearable. There was a sound like parting velcro as John's bloodied hair peeled away from the matting.

"The world won't end if I escape the time cage." Ash's tone was quiet and reasonable. "I won't lie to you, John. People will die when I reveal myself as their god. Others will accept me. More than you might think. With all their talk of freedom, many humans secretly yearn for a life where someone else is in charge and tells them what to do. Your realm is too fertile, too rich in magic to be wasted on a backward species which is barely aware of its wonders. In their own small way, every woman in your realm can use magic. I will allow some of my followers to enjoy their birthright. Is that your problem, John? Scared of women having the power?"

John was on his knees now, his ruined face sending messages of agony back to his brain. He understood that what Ash said was also part of his training in the dojo. He couldn't hope to stop her if she could persuade him that her cause had merit.

"You're no friend of women," he managed to say, his voice thick. "You don't care about anyone except yourself."

"You're wrong, John," she said as he stood up and faced her.

The blue light flickered in his solar plexus, and all his pain disappeared. John looked at the floor. His teeth were gone. He brought his fingers to his mouth and touched his cheekbone. His teeth were back in place, and there was no swelling on his face. When he spoke, his voice shook.

"You destroyed my mother's mind. You killed her."

He raised his hand again. Ash smiled. "Are you sure about that, John? I cursed you, I admit it. But I didn't curse her. If you hadn't fought me, your mother would never have had to take the curse from you. Only an Adept could do that, and I didn't know she was an Adept. How could I? It was your power that drew me, not hers. I'd say you cursed her, really. Wouldn't you?"

"No," said John. The power was back, the pain of moments earlier wiped out by the blue light coursing through his body. "No, I wouldn't."

He cast the spell. He was quicker this time, exulting in his heightened awareness.

Ash swatted his spell away like an insect. John's head snapped to the side, and he both heard and felt something stretch too far and break in his neck. As he fell, his arms dropped uselessly to his sides, and his legs crumpled.

When consciousness returned, he waited in agony until the blue light did its work and his injuries healed.

He stood up and faced her, but the memory of the pain made him hesitate. Ash saw this, and her smile broadened.

"Come on, lover." Her lips parted, her eyes glazed with the same frank desire that had drawn him to her all those years ago. "It doesn't have to be this way. Time doesn't exist here. Nobody's watching. We can do whatever we like, however many times we want to. What's your fantasy, John? Do you want me to submit to you? I can do that. Do you want me to dominate you? I can do that, too. Do you want me to look like someone else? Do you want to make love to two, three women at once? Do you want to try a man? We have eternity. What do you want?"

If she wasn't genuinely aroused by her own words, the avatar was so convincing that John didn't doubt it for a second. Her pupils were dilated, and she was breathing heavily.

"I want you to fight me," he said, raising his hand.

Her face changed instantly, hard rage etched on her

features. In this avatar, John saw clearly what Ash tried to hide from him in the real world. By any definition of the word, she was no longer sane. "I can do that," she said, and before he had time to sing, she grunted something that blasted into him like a wrecking ball, crushing every rib, causing immediate and massive internal bleeding. He dropped to the matting.

Seconds, minutes, or hours later, he opened his eyes and tried to breathe. Every inhalation, however shallow he tried to make it, caused such a wave of agony in his chest and across his back that he wanted to die.

John understood now why Gai had made him swear, on Sarah's memory, that he would stay in the sanctum until he had mastered the holding spell.

This was going to be a long day.

THIRTY-EIGHT

As each attack he mounted was deflected, Ash became creative with her counter-attacks. She made his bones weak and brittle so that his feet gave way, followed by his knees breaking when he landed on them, and his pelvis, ribs, and skull joining in as they hit the floor.

She caused the blood to warm in his veins, then boil.

She flayed him from his neck to his testicles.

She punched a hole through his chest as wide as a cantaloupe.

She paralysed him and punctured his body with a hundred long, thin needles.

She induced a seizure. He swallowed his tongue.

Every time, as his body healed and he forced himself to stand, she spoke her poison and told him it didn't have to be this way.

If hell existed, this was surely it. Or, at least, it would be if it wasn't for the memory of Sarah. And Harry. And Evie, the granddaughter he had spent so little time with. That would change if he defeated Ashtoreth. This was something Ash couldn't touch. Something she didn't understand.

Ironic, really, that the god of love should know nothing about it.

Every time John opened his eyes to find himself back on the hemp floor, his body screaming in pain, he turned his mind to his family. It wasn't as if he and Sarah were the perfect couple, however tempting it was to airbrush the bad times out of the picture. They had disagreed regularly, and there had been the occasional row. There had been one terrible period when they had almost allowed themselves to become strangers, not noticing their paths were diverging until it was nearly too late. When they did notice, they had talked through the night, ending up having sex like teenagers, half on and half off the sofa, clinging desperately to each other.

When John thought of Harry, the beautiful boy they had created together, and to whom he had never been a good enough father, he swore he would make amends. If it meant moving to Los Angeles, he would do it. And he would see more of Evie, his quiet, solemn granddaughter who loved to draw, and whose smile reminded him so much of Sarah.

If he wanted to do any of those things, he had to work out how to defeat this avatar, because the real Ash would be worse.

Which attempt was this? The hundredth? The thousandth? Something had changed this time. He wasn't afraid of the pain. No, that wasn't quite it. He *was* afraid, how could he not be after the torture he had suffered over and over again? It was more that he was able to separate his decision-making process from the fear, not allow his judgement to be clouded by the anticipation of agony. The other emotions that coloured his thoughts were more manageable too. Anger, shame, guilt, regret, sadness, along with hope, courage, excitement, and love; they were all present, but he was able to observe them, acknowledge them, remain separate from them.

He looked at his emotions, his thoughts, and his memories. His mind relaxed its grip, made space, cleared the way. And, once the route was clear, an idea so direct, so simple, and so right made itself known.

It popped into his mind as a picture, brightly coloured. Playdough extruders. Harry had loved them when he was a toddler. The concept was simple. The extruder looked a little like a wide syringe which you filled with coloured dough. Instead of a needle, the end opposite the plunger pushed the dough into a variety of shapes: spaghetti, hearts, cylinders, stars.

John smiled. A true magician didn't wield power, didn't cast spells. True magic was channelled. Earth provided the raw magic, stronger than anything he could summon from his own body. The spell would shape the flow of magic.

Ash saw the change in him.

"Time to give up? No more tricks left in the old dog?"

"One more, Ash," he said, raising his hand. "One more. Ever heard of playdough?"

This time, instead of attacking as he might with a physical weapon, directing it physically and mentally, John stood aside, allowing the raw magic to pour through the opening he had cleared and be shaped by the spell he had absorbed.

The change in his own perception was instant. No longer powerful, John was weak, empty. The more that he had imposed his small sense of self onto the process, the less power had been available to him. What he had suffered in the dojo since confronting Ash would have led to his death if it had been the real world. He had died, over and over again. And, in dying, he had finally embraced the paradox at the heart of the most powerful magic. To wield true power, he had to become powerless.

Ash deflected the attack with the same dismissive gesture that had preceded every previous encounter. This time, as she pushed aside the spell, it was as if she were swatting a hurricane. Quick to react to the change, she raised both of her hands, bracing one leg behind her as she leaned in and pushed back. She hummed, sang, and whispered. The air around her thickened and rippled as great forces met. Then she sagged, incredulous at her defeat as she struggled helplessly against her invisible constraints.

John knew it wasn't over. The holding spell hadn't removed her abilities. It was the magical equivalent of pinning her arms to her sides so she couldn't punch anyone. She had to be kept there. In the dojo, it was straightforward. John could detach his attention from her once the spell was in place, having to return occasionally to refresh the flow of magic. It was like spinning plates. He was grateful there was only one plate to spin.

An impact on the back of his head cracked his skull, and he fell to the mat again.

He saw bare feet. Two pairs of bare feet. Before blacking out, he watched two new versions of Ash join the first avatar. One of them laughed. "You didn't think it was going to be that easy, did you?"

John shut the door of the dojo behind him and stood in the corridor. The no-time of the Between distorted his memory of what had just happened. When he had been inside, it had seemed like days had passed. Now, he remembered the moment he had walked into the dojo as if it were mere seconds ago.

Time to go back to Leigh Woods.

John opened his eyes. Gai was holding a moss-covered rock above his groin. He rolled, sweeping the noone's legs out from under him.

"Aagh!" Gai hit the forest floor gracelessly, wheezed, then chuckled. "Good. Good! Much better. Still too long, though. Four beats. Plenty of time for me to attack you. I was being kind."

"By crushing my balls? Very kind. Thank you so much."

"Ach. Your protective charms would have kicked in. They wouldn't have been crushed. Dented, maybe."

"That doesn't sound much more appealing." John stood up, offering the noone a hand. Gai accepted and regarded his protégé thoughtfully.

"You're different. How long were you in there?"

"Long enough to know I'll never be ready."

Gai studied him for a short while, then walked across the clearing. When he reached the far side, he called back.

"That sounds like the beginnings of wisdom, John." He bent down and picked up an acorn. "There can be no hesitation when you wield the holding spell. Show me your progress."

He held the acorn out at waist height between finger and thumb.

"When I drop this, I want you to use the spell. The moment the acorn hits the floor, I will counter-attack, and I will not hold back. This,"—the noone made no attempt to hide his amusement—"will hurt considerably. Brace yourself."

John didn't move, other than raising his right hand six inches from his side.

Gai raised his eyebrows. "I apologise in advance for your injuries. Sure you're ready?"

John said nothing.

"Right, fine, here we go then. Three, two, one."

Gai released the acorn. Before gravity had asserted its claim sufficiently to cause it to break contact with the skin of the noone's hand, John allowed the flow of Earth's magic to rise and fill him, channelling it across the clearing. By the time, a quarter of a second later, the acorn had bounced once and settled on the soil below, Gai's face was set in a mask of shock and pride. Only a slight tremor in his arms betrayed how hard he was trying to fight back with magic of his own, to no avail.

John released him, allowing the spell to dissipate, become mist.

Gai took the bottle and a loaf of flatbread from his knapsack. He tore the loaf in two, giving half to John along with some mead, raising his own cup in a toast.

"To the first male Adept."

John shook his head. "I don't want to be an Adept, Gai. I just want to go home."

Gai sipped at the mead. "We don't get to decide what we are, John Aviemore. That's a misconception that's caused untold misery. You are an Adept. What kind of Adept you will be... that's the choice before you now."

John ate some of the bread. It was flavoured with herbs and quite delicious. He washed it down with a mouthful of mead. "I'm a middle-aged widower, Gai. I live in Wimbledon. I invent magic tricks and, occasionally, I perform them.

I have a son and a granddaughter. I'm not going to grow into anything. I'm going to perform less, invent and write more, spend all the time I can with my family and friends, read great books again, listen to music. I'm even going to try to appreciate art because that's one way I can remember Sarah. Once I get out of here, I'm leaving all this behind. I didn't ask for it. A quiet life, Gai, that's all I want."

Gai didn't reply at first, his expression guarded. Then he raised his cup and tapped it against John's. "Then I wish you luck and a quiet life, John. Perhaps you will get what you wish for."

John drank.

"What about you, Gai?"

"What do you mean?"

"If we break her grip and we can leave. What's next for you?"

"Back to Da Luan. Father will be delighted to hear his theory about the crummy zones was right. And I think I know what I want to be when I grow up now, so I'll have some arrangements to make."

"And if we fail?"

"I expect she'll kill me." He re-corked the bottle and replaced it in his knapsack. He was whistling. When he noticed the look on John's face, he stopped. "What? What's wrong?"

"You think she'll kill you?"

Gai shrugged as if it were of no concern to him. "I forget," he said, "you humans have a strange attitude to death. We live, and we die. This is all we know for sure. When we die, we will not be here anymore. Why worry about it?"

John thought of the philosophical and theological edifices erected by humans on the foundation of the fear of death. He wished he could share Gai's casual acceptance of the inevitable.

"But..."

"But nothing. I might die. You might die. Ashtoreth might die, although I'm not sure a god that old *can* die. We'll all do what we have to do. Play our parts. She wants to be a god again, mighty, feared, worshipped by millions. We can't let that happen and, as I'm the only help you have, I'm hardly going to run away, am I?"

"Can't you fetch others?"

"I can't break away from the cage, John. Even if I could, it would take me a moon to return here with reinforcements, and Astarte is moving too quickly."

"Back to square one."

"Yes. So we act tonight. Here's what we'll do."

John interrupted before the noone could speak. "Gai?" The noone looked up. John held out his hand and they shook, the noone's skin as cold as ever. "Thank you."

"Thank me when we've got you out of here. Now sit down and listen."

THIRTY-NINE

Evie, child, I woke up this morning and you had gone. I had no memory of you other than a hazy idea that I had once been passed a baby by John, my son. There are moments when I don't even remember him.

It was only when I saw this letter on my desk and re-read my own words that I was able to piece together the facts. I am an old woman, and I have seen more death than most. The idea of letting go of everything is not frightening to me. But this constant attack on my mind, the blank hours followed by moments when I am aware of what I am losing, well, it's hard to bear at times. When I am gone, and you take my place in the family line, you will know me, and I will know you again. I take comfort in that.

While I have temporarily remembered that you exist, I will tell you how to reach me, if I should die before you need to. Do it as soon as you are ready. Do not hesitate.

My dear, you will have to visit the place where I died. It's most likely I will breathe my last in Fir Trees Care Home, room thirty-eight.

When you persuade your mother and father that a trip

to England is necessary, make sure to do so soon after a visit to the Between. In your sanctum, focus your intent on the art of persuasion, then listen for a call. Follow that call when you hear it. If you succeed, you will find people are extraordinarily amenable for a while. Pliable, even. Again, a warning: don't be tempted to abuse this ability.

Come to England, come to Elstree, find the place where I died, and once you are there, go to the Between. This time, it will be different. When you travel, do so with the thought of me uppermost in your mind. It does not matter that we never truly knew each other, it only matters that you are thinking of your great-grandmother when you go to your sanctum.

Ah yes, the sanctum. I don't need to explain now, there will be time enough when we meet. Yes, you read that correctly. Part of me will be waiting in the Between for you. When you visit the Between from my place of death, your destination will be different. You will arrive at the sanctum constructed by your ancestors, the sanctum of an Adept. I will be there. Not the same person who is writing these letters, not exactly, but a shade, a shadow, an echo. Enough of me to fill in the gaps in your knowledge, to teach you the final steps to becoming an Adept.

And so our correspondence comes to an end, my darling great-granddaughter. I regret not spending more time with you. Life as one of the Three is not easy. You will become accustomed to putting duty before your personal considerations. Yes, that sounds appalling, but the benefits of using magic outweigh the dis-benefits. See? I may be an old lady, but I can still use modern words like 'dis-benefits', even when the very idea of it is an affront to my sensibilities.

Never forget, although very few know the truth, that our world is magical. A never-ending stream of timeless power runs through it at every moment. One day, I believe all human beings will once again use magic. Perhaps, by then, it won't be restricted to females, however outlandish that seems now. I sometimes looked at my son—your grandfather, John—when he was growing up, and thought I saw power there. Augustus said I saw what I wanted to see. I'm sure he's right. Augustus is our Warden, Evie. An old, wise friend to our family. You will meet him after you become an Adept. He's watched over us for a long time.

Now, it's time for me to say goodbye. If this last letter seems disjointed, it's because it has taken me over a week to write. My periods of lucidity are getting shorter and shorter. I wake up to find myself standing by the window, looking out across the grounds of this care home, without knowing how I got there. At such times, I imagine someone is with me, in the room. You, maybe, your father perhaps, or even your grandfather. I want you to know that although you may think the manner of my death is sad, or upsetting, no Adept is ever truly alone.

Do not grieve for me, Evie. Come and find me when you're ready.

Your ever-loving great-grandmother
Mae Frances Aviemore.

PS Burn these letters. Better safe than sorry.

FORTY

As plans go, Gai's was refreshingly uncomplicated. There were easy-to-understand risks and rewards. The rewards were freedom and saving Earth from a return to the wholesale slaughter of ancient mythology. The risk was getting killed.

The mechanics of the plan were also straightforward. John and Gai would enter the cottage together. When Ash appeared, John would cast the holding spell. While she was helpless, Gai would hit her with the most powerful sleep spell he knew.

"And how powerful is that, exactly?"

"Heard of Rip Van Winkle? Same spell."

Twilight arrived about mid-afternoon. John's day had already included what seemed to be days in his sanctum being painfully killed by avatars. A wave of weariness washed over him at the sight of the sinking orange sun.

Gai punched him on the arm. "You can nap later."

Despite the banter, John was aware of the noone's increasing tension as he unlatched the gate at the back of the cottage. They walked in without speaking. John glanced around the room. It looked just as it had the first day he'd arrived. He suspected that if he checked the fridge, the same cheese, butter, and bottle of wine would be in there, unopened, despite the fact he had used them every day.

Gai went to the foot of the stairs and stood aside to let John go first.

The sun sank below the horizon during the few seconds they'd been in the cottage, and the shadows of night reached from the corners to claim the room. John climbed the stairs, his heart rate rising with each step. He paused when he reached the top, looking inside himself for the calm he had found in the dojo. It was elusive now because the woman waiting for him was no avatar. She was no woman either, he reminded himself. She was a god who cared nothing for the suffering of others. Any pain she inflicted on him tonight would not disappear when he stood up. It would be real, lasting pain.

He stood outside the bedroom door. It was half open. All was quiet. John looked back at Gai, whose eyes gleamed in the darkness.

A light came on in the bedroom.

Ash's voice was calm and unafraid. If anything, she sounded amused.

"How sweet, John. You've brought a friend. I've never been averse to threesomes, or foursomes. Or fivesomes. Orgies can be fun, don't get me wrong. And noones are notoriously good lovers. Why do you think so many human women go wandering into the woods in fairy stories? Looking for a ride on a noone, that's why. Came back with a smile on their face and a half-breed in their bellies. Not that your friend is much of a catch. Don't be shy. Let me have a look at him."

Catching Ash by surprise would have been better, but

Gai had allowed for contingencies in the event that she was waiting for them. The already simple plan became simpler still. Attack immediately.

Ash's voice had come from her customary position on the bed. John raised his right hand in readiness.

He held his breath, summoning the detached state he had achieved in the Between, then he stepped into the room and allowed the melody of the spell to unfold, clearing a path for the magic of the realm to flow through him.

When he saw Ash propped against the pillows, he unleashed the full power of the spell. Instantly, he knew something wasn't right. The figure on the bed did nothing to defend herself, her knowing smile remaining in place as the full force of the spell hit her. Her eyes gazed towards the distance, seeing nothing. John was looking at an illusion. Even as the thought struck him, the figure on the bed began to dissolve. The real danger was behind him, in the corner of the bedroom.

He swung around.

Ash stepped out of the shadows. At least, that was what John was prepared for. But the woman he saw, her body painted blue by the moonlight, her hair shaved short for chemotherapy, was Sarah.

John dropped his hands. Only for a second until he recognised the Glamour. It was long enough.

Her hands were raised. John braced himself for the attack, realising too late that it wasn't directed at him.

A light brighter than an arc welder transformed the doorway into a portal to hell. John shadowed his eyes with his hand and was able to make out Gai, his arm thrown in front of his face, his whole body rigid. John watched in horror, seeing blackened flesh peel away from Gai's arm as his defences failed.

John directed the holding spell at Ash. Even as he did it, he knew he was too emotionally invested, there was too much of himself standing in the way. The spell was weakened, the flow of magic stifled. Even so, enough got through to break her attack on Gai and remove the Glamour. The instant her onslaught on the noone faltered, John sang to the wind.

As Ash brought her terrible gaze around to John, the window shattered, and thousands of tiny shards of glass blew into her face and body. She flinched as they struck. John's counter-attack only bought him a few seconds. He ran, scooping up the fallen noone and sprinting down the stairs.

He jumped the last couple of steps and ran for the back door before stopping in confusion.

He was back on the landing. The bedroom door was in front of him, the stairs behind. Without thinking, he ran again. A terrible heat rose from Gai's limp body along with the smell of cooking flesh. John tried not to retch as he reached the bottom of the staircase a second time and, once more, found he was back in front of the bedroom door.

"Let me go!" he roared.

Ash stepped into the doorway, her manner as casual as if they were disagreeing over which television channel to watch. John turned sideways, holding Gai's limp body away from her, trying to protect him.

"How is your pet noone? Is he dead?"

John could feel the shallow rise and fall of the noone's chest. Gai's left arm was horribly burned, and his left leg was damaged. John calmed his breathing the best he could and looked into Ash's green eyes.

"Whatever business you and I have, he's nothing to do with it. Let me take him back to the woods."

"Nothing to do with it? You have been to the Between, John. There is no other way you could know that spell. He has taught you to use your power, and he has encouraged you to use magic to hurt me. You came here to destroy me. I defended myself. Should I have let you kill me?"

John remembered that Gai didn't think Ash could die.

"No one came to kill you. Just to stop you."

"To stop me doing what?"

"Escaping. Gai told me all about you, Ash. The gods' war, the time cage."

Ash had become very still. John knew he could go to the Between, look for a spell to attack her or heal Gai, but two factors stopped him trying. One was that he was so new to all of this. He did not know exactly what he was looking for, he did not know his own limits, let alone the extent of Ash's power. The second factor was his memory of Gai's hands around his throat when he came back from the Between the first time. He would be completely vulnerable for a second or two. He didn't know what Ash might do to him during that time, and he didn't want to find out.

Ash took a step closer. John turned further to prevent her having a clear line of sight towards Gai. She spoke to his back.

"I can be generous, John. I can be merciful. Do not judge me by the stories they tell about me. You can take the noone to the woods. Then you will come back to me."

John headed for the stairs, slowly this time. Ash followed him, then waited at the top of the staircase. He turned at the bottom.

"And if I don't come back?"

She smiled again. It was not the smile the smile of anticipation, or of satisfaction. This was a smile of triumph.

When it became clear she wasn't going to answer, John

crossed the room, unlatched the door, and stepped out into the back garden. Gai weighed almost nothing, so he was able to keep his pace brisk as he walked through the moonlit trees, the night deathly calm around him.

The clearing looked like a painting. Nothing moved. John laid Gai's body on top of the fallen log. The noone's eyes were open, but he saw nothing, staring up at John with no spark of recognition. John remembered the curse that had, eventually, unravelled his mother's mind. If Gai's injuries didn't kill him, he might still be lost.

John sat down and leaned against the trunk, half-closing his eyes. He opened them in the Between.

FORTY-ONE

The comforts of John's sanctum were wasted on him this time. He leapt out of the chair and ran to the library. Logically, John knew that running made no difference. If time didn't exist here, sprinting around his floating house was useless. He still ran.

Inside the vast stone room, he picked up the candle and made himself stop for a moment. He needed to focus on Gai, on his injuries, on how he could help his friend. The terrible physical injuries were bad enough, but he was more worried by the absent stare he had seen on the noone's face. John's lack of knowledge was painfully apparent to him. He didn't know where to look for help. Worse, he didn't understand what, exactly, he was looking for.

He remembered what Gai had told him about sanctums. Each one was unique, constructed from the consciousness of the magician using it, containing all the wisdom, knowledge, and power of the overlapping realms, a limitless repository. But this did not mean everyone who could access the Between could find all that was hidden there. Far from it. John could only hope he would be able to find what he needed without Gai's help.

John pictured his friend, thinking of the horrific injuries to his arm and leg. He walked through the maze of bookshelves, allowing himself to be led by instinct, listening for a call like the one he had heard for the holding spell.

For what seemed like an hour, he turned left and right between the arcane volumes, sensing hints of what they might contain in the same way that he might smell a neighbour's dinner and guess at the ingredients. His thoughts were in turmoil as he searched, going over and over the failed attempt to defeat Ash.

Eventually, even the urgency of his task and the horror of the events that had sent him there lost their hold over his mind, the constant repetition of the same thoughts draining them first of emotion, then of meaning. His mind became tranquil, and as calm returned, he was able to summon his need for a healing spell. A dialogue opened between John and the library, a silent conversation.

He heard a book call to him. It was faint, but it was there. He followed it, the path taking him back to the outer walls of the cathedral of books. The shelf he needed, when he halted in front of it, was almost, but not quite, beyond his reach. He stood on tiptoe and let his fingers trail through the liquid books. Looking up to where the shelves vanished into darkness, skyscrapers of learning, he wondered if anyone, however long-lived, could ever hope to absorb even the tiniest fraction of the knowledge contained in this room.

He found the solid book. This time he didn't flinch when, as his fingertips brushed against the gold lettering on the spine, the words flowed into his hand and arm. The process was quicker than before. A simpler spell, perhaps.

Back in the study, words poured out of his flesh into the

book. It took only a few attempts to master it, his voice rising and falling with the symbols on the page. It was too easy. He doubted a spell he could master so quickly would be powerful enough to reverse the damage done by Ash. He could only hope it would be enough to prevent Gai's death.

The spell now memorised, he prepared to leave.

What made him look out into the slow-motion blizzard outside, John couldn't have said. Perhaps it was an unexpected movement. Something out there didn't belong, something wasn't moving in line with the hypnotic snowfall.

Unsure if he had seen anything at all, or only imagined it, John stood at the edge of the room, staring out into the whiteness beyond, the scene lit by the whirling galaxies above. Out there among the ceaseless descent of feathery snowflakes, a figure—up to its knees in snow—struggled and fell as it tried to make progress. Picking itself up, it managed four jerky steps forward before falling again.

As John stared, the distance between him and the stranger became irrelevant, and he saw as clearly as if they were yards apart.

It was Gai, blindly trudging through the drifts, falling, getting slowly to his feet, then, after a few more steps, falling again, over and over.

John put his hand on the invisible window, feeling the same kind of resistance he had felt when he and Gai had seen the creatures from the Charleston Hotel in Leigh Woods. Like rubber, the invisible barrier pushed back at his palm. He moved right, then left, pushing as he went, looking for an opening. If there was an invisible window, couldn't there be an invisible door?

As he watched, Gai fell again. This time, he was slower getting to his feet, and his next fall came after a single step. He didn't get up.

"Gai! Gai!" John's voice bounced back as if the invisible window were a solid wall. "Shit!"

The locked doors in the corridor.

John ran from the room. The first door on his left was locked, but he knew it was the right one. If this place were built from his subconscious, then his subconscious was telling him this was the exit. He rattled the handle in frustration, then took a run up and crashed into it shoulder first. The door stayed closed.

He stared at the solid wood. If this sanctum was truly his, he must be able to leave it. At the moment the thought occurred to him, a muted click came from the door, and it swung open.

Not quite understanding what had changed, John didn't stop to worry about it. Wooden steps led down a narrow staircase to a heavy, black door at the bottom. Hurrying down, John pulled at the handle. The door opened, and he looked out at the snowy landscape he'd seen from his study.

No wind howled as the snow fell. John expected to feel his face become numb at the change in temperature, but it didn't happen. He looked down at his slippered feet and his pyjamas then stepped over the threshold.

The expected pain of icy snow on bare flesh didn't come. John looked down again. Slippers, pyjamas, a few inches of exposed skin. He lifted one leg and placed his hand on the arch of his foot. It was dry and warm. The snow came up to the middle of his shin as he continued walking, and it took some effort to trudge through it, but he remained dry, unaffected by the snow.

He looked back at his sanctum. The staircase was lit, as was his study, apparently floating in mid-air.

He headed for the spot where he had seen Gai.

The noone was face down, unmoving.

"Gai! Gai! Wake up!"

John shook him by the shoulders. His friend's eyes were open, and he was breathing, but he was unresponsive.

"Shit. What am I supposed to..." John's voice trailed off as he looked around him. The constantly falling snow made it hard to see anything further than a dozen yards away, but, squinting into the whiteness, he could make out dark blocky shapes in the distance. Whether they were buildings or mountains, he couldn't tell. There were no lights, and no other sign of life apart from him and the stricken noone in the snow.

John placed his hand on Gai's forehead and sang the spell he had learned. Immediately, he knew it was wrong. It was like trying to treat kidney failure with antiseptic cream. No, more like trying to give a human medicine designed for an octopus. The part of Gai lost in the Between was untreatable by any spell of healing. John needed to get him back to his body in the Blurred Lands.

Kneeling next to his friend and hugging him to his chest, John half-closed his eyes and pictured the tree just beyond the garden of Sally Cottage, preparing himself to move quickly when he returned.

Nothing happened. However vividly John imagined the starlit woods, he stayed right where he was, up to his knees in snow.

He lifted Gai and put him over his left shoulder in a fireman's lift, then turned and trudged back to his sanctum.

The door was open, just as he'd left it. The first time he tried to cross the threshold, there was a palpable sense of resistance from the house. The way Gai had described it,

John's sanctum was an expression of his soul, as individual as a fingerprint. A sanctum was never shared. John didn't even know if such a thing were possible. He stood in the snow in front of the door, and understood that the sanctum was warning him. For a man who didn't believe in fate, John knew, beyond a doubt, that what he was about to do would forge a permanent link between him and Gai.

He stepped inside and climbed the stairs. The resistance diminished with each step. By the time John reached the corridor, the house had accepted the transgression. John looked at Gai's face as he laid him on the carpet in front of the fire. The noone was still unresponsive. He would remember nothing of this visit, John was sure. If he lived.

John clasped the noone's right hand in his and pictured Leigh Woods again.

This time, the attempt was successful.

The snow was gone, and John was surrounded by trees. He gagged at the stench coming off Gai's scorched arm. The noone wasn't moving.

John sang. The spell was two notes that continued autonomously once John had sung them. The sound echoed as if reflected from the walls of a small room. The spell was connected to Gai's breathing, the notes repeating each time he drew a breath, becoming softer as he inhaled. The noone started murmuring as the spell took hold. His right arm was ruined. If there was magic capable of reversing such damage, the sanctum's library had kept it from John.

John searched the trees on the perimeter of the clearing until he found it: a large oak tree whose sprawling roots had created natural hiding places; some small enough for a squirrel's winter hoard, others large enough for a child to hide in. One of these larger natural holes was further concealed by an ivy curtain across its entrance. John carefully ripped away the leaves on one side, opening the ivy like the flap of a tent before laying his friend inside.

Gai spoke as he was replacing the ivy. His voice was faint, and John could hear the pain in it.

"You have to use the cage, John."

John stooped back inside, placing his hand gently on the noone's uninjured arm. "You need to rest."

Gai grabbed his sleeve to stop him leaving. It took him a few seconds to summon the strength to speak again. "The cage. Send her back when she came from."

That was as much as the injured noone could manage. His head fell back, and his breathing deepened.

"Sleep well, Gai," said John as he replaced the ivy.

John remembered the look of triumph on Ash's face when he had threatened not to return. He tried walking in every direction away from the clearing, and every time, he arrived at the front gate of Sally Cottage.

In the distance, he heard Pan's voice as she called to her creatures. She sounded thrilled, exultant, ready to celebrate.

As well she might, thought John when the black gate rose in front of him once again. He was tired, and he felt much older than his fifty-one years.

Gai couldn't help him any more. No one could help him. He closed his eyes and thought of Sarah. Then he opened the gate and walked up the path to the cottage to confront the god Ashtoreth.

FORTY-TWO

John looked around the living room. Everything was as it always was, down to the sagging sofa, the dead phone, the paint pot he hadn't opened after the bedroom had rejected the first coat he gave it, shedding it like a snake's skin.

At the bottom of the staircase, he put one hand on the bannister, then turned and went back to the kitchen. In the cutlery drawer, he removed the sharpest knife he could find. Blunter than he would have liked, but it was all he had.

As his fingers closed around the wooden handle, the kitchen faded and vanished, replaced by the familiar shuttered window, the fleshy pink walls and the iron-framed bed.

Ash stood by the bedroom window, opening the shutters. The damage from earlier had gone - the glass was unbroken, and the carpet was free of any telltale glittering shards. The moon was waning now, but the stars were bright.

Ash turned to look at him. She was wearing a dark-green gown with flowing sleeves. The gown fell to her ankles, and its demure neckline was high, revealing not even a hint of cleavage. It was a dress that might have been worn by a mediaeval virgin, determined to preserve her chastity by covering up all sources of temptation. On Ash, it looked like the first layer of a professional stripper. The material clung to parts of her body in a way that drew the eye. She took a single step towards John, and even that sinuous movement, the material whispering as her thighs brushed together, suggested the dress would be easy to pull up to her waist, and she would be more than happy to do just that.

Her frank, challenging, predatory gaze fell on the knife in John's hand.

"How tiresomely predictable," she said, lifting the dress a little so she could sit on the edge of the bed. Once seated, she pulled it up a little more and crossed her legs. The extra couple of exposed inches of skin revealed by that movement were as alluring, if not more so, than her usual nakedness.

She smiled. "I would have thought your little noone might have told you about protective charms by now. He's shown you the Between, after all. You don't think you could hurt me with a knife, do you?"

John shook his head. "Self-obsessed to the last, Ash," he said, lifting the blade. He had watched Sarah die. As hard as it had been to witness, as devastating as it had been to know she had gone, it had not been painful. Sarah hadn't fought the inevitable. He had never believed in life after death, but now a desperate hope that he was mistaken took hold of him.

"It's not for you," he said to Ash, then, before she could move or he could have second thoughts, he drew the blade across his own throat with all his strength.

The pain was instant, but not as bad as he had expected. He let the knife drop to the carpet and sank to his knees. The blood loss would soon lead to unconsciousness.

He hadn't thought in much detail about the immediate aftermath of cutting his throat, but he'd seen enough films to expect a lot of blood, spurting across the room. It didn't happen. He brought his hands up to his throat, wincing in anticipation of ragged sliced flesh and warm liquid.

Ash giggled. "I wasn't talking about my protective charms," she said. "I was talking about yours."

The skin of his throat was sore to the touch but unbroken. His head dropped in despair. He and Gai together hadn't been powerful enough, and he couldn't even end his own life to stop her. She spoke as he put his head in his hands.

"The charms that protect you are the work of an Adept, John. Your mother. Ironically, they drew me to you when you turned up a mile and a half away all those years ago. So close! I had to see what manner of creature you were. When I found out you were male, I knew I could use you. Are you not ashamed on her behalf? The first male Adept, and she didn't know it. That's the problem with assumptions. No one thought a man could ever use magic. She protected you with her charms, but I was the one who saw your potential."

He heard her stand up and move closer.

"I will make you a promise, John. When I'm free, when I am once again worshipped by your kind, when I have revenged myself on Da Luan and those that put me here, I will not go after your family. Your mother is dead. As long as no one steps forward to continue the line, I will leave them be."

John raised his head. Ash was opening a drawer of the dresser, removing something small. She held it cupped in her hand. Kneeling in front of him, she showed him what she was carrying. A round grey stone, shot through with darker stripes, nestled in her palm. The sort of stone a child would pick up while walking on a beach.

"Doesn't look like much, does it?" Ash reached for his hand. He didn't resist. His mind was numb. "Magic resides in three places, John. In a realm, which is where we can find it and draw upon it, in a magician, and in an item, stored there for a specific purpose."

She dropped the stone into John's hand. He had expected it to be warm. It was as cold as if it had just come out of the fridge. He had expected it to be light. It was as heavy as a bag full of silver coins. He had expected it, after her little speech, to communicate something of the magic within. It did not, or—if it did—he didn't know how to listen to it.

"It's the time cage," said Ash. John turned it over and over in his hand, but there was nothing to see. "Don't expect it to glow with blinding light, John. It took three Adepts to create it. It would take three to destroy it."

John looked at her then. She was calm, her smile flirtatious. There was no outward sign of anger. It was as if she had forgotten the attack of earlier that evening.

"Three adepts?" he repeated. "But..."

"Yes," she said. "There are only two of us. Your noone is competent, but he's no Adept. You are ignorant, unformed, untaught, but your mother was an Adept, and you are her heir. Or you would be if you were female. I am more powerful than any Adept. I had hoped that our combined power might be enough to break the cage. But I had it all wrong. I need not destroy it at all."

Again expecting anger, but hearing none, John looked wonderingly at Ash. She continued speaking as if she were talking to herself. "I don't know how long I've been in the time cage. Ten thousand years might have passed in your realm, but that has little relevance in here. I came to Earth as a god, but now I have been forgotten."

There was nothing seductive about the look she gave him then. It was the look of someone desperate. John knew that look well - he had seen it in the mirror many times during the past three years.

She stood up and went to the window, speaking with her back turned towards him.

"Stay tonight, John. Tomorrow you can leave if you wish. I will not hold you here any longer."

What? he thought.

"What?" he said.

She half-turned. She wasn't looking at him, her gaze was on the carpet at her feet. Even then, John noticed, she couldn't help holding herself as if she might be about to begin the dance of the seven veils.

"You may leave tomorrow."

He thought of Gai. She anticipated his concern.

"As for your noone, he will be found. The cage traps those who come too close, but the effect is temporary. He will be able to leave soon enough, as will those of my followers who were drawn here expecting my return. John?"

"Yes?"

"Sleep well. I will see you at dawn."

John could trust nothing she said, but he couldn't see the point in her lying. What difference did it make?

"Then I can leave?"

Ash didn't smile, didn't flirt. "If you choose to."

John held up the stone that contained the time cage, but Ash waved it away. "Keep it, put in in a drawer, throw it in the cellar. It cannot leave this place, and it cannot be destroyed. Believe me, I would know if either were possible."

John stood up. It couldn't be this easy. Was she really giving up? What possible advantage could she hope to gain by this?

"Ash," he said, then stopped. Like ears popping at a certain altitude on a flight, the atmosphere in the room altered. The walls were back to their freshly painted inoffensive shade of magnolia, the carpet had vanished. The bed was just a frame, rusting in places.

John stood there for at least a minute until he was convinced that Ash had gone.

There was no sign of her presence. It was just an old, rundown cottage in need of decorating.

He got out of the bedroom, anyway. Just in case.

FORTY-THREE

John made himself a sandwich from the replenished loaf, washing it down with half a glass of wine.

He checked his phone. Still no signal.

There would be mobile reception at the road. Then again, if he could make it to the road, he could keep going, get in his car, drive away from all of this.

John opened the back door, breathed the night air. In the distance, for the first time since he had got lost in Leigh Woods, he heard the muted sound of traffic, and saw a faint glow from the lights of the city to the west.

He stepped outside.

His foot wouldn't cross the threshold. It came back down on the floorboards. He tried twice more. He couldn't leave. Not yet, at least.

The sky was ink-black and starless.

He shut the door, put the stone on the mantelpiece and, draping his sleeping bag over him like a coat, he sat on the old, uncomfortable sofa.

There was no way he was going to be able to sleep.

It was springtime in Wimbledon, six in the morning on the first of May. The rising sun brought a pastel glow to the edges of the blinds. John watched the light insinuate itself into the room, the slats of the blinds evolving from abstraction, through a suggestion of form, to definite, hard-edged rectangles. John knew he was staring stupidly, that he should stand up, make a cup of tea, call someone. Maybe call Harry. What time would it be in Los Angeles? Eight hours behind was... his mind slid away from even so simple a calculation. He was looking at the blinds again. When he looked away, a negative image appeared on the wall, solid, definite and real for a moment before losing coherence as he blinked it away.

Sarah had been dead for an hour.

Birds sang in the garden. They had started at 4:15. Sarah had smiled at the sound, muted by the double-glazing. He had thought about asking her if she wanted the window open so she could hear them clearly, but he said nothing. She had squeezed his fingers. He had squeezed back. Sarah had known what he was going to ask, he had known her answer, and no words had been necessary.

It was inexorable, that light. It was moving across the ceiling as the part of the planet on which southwest London was situated tilted itself towards the unimaginable energy of the nearest star, which was just one among trillions.

The rage made itself known then, just a little. As if a heavy door had been rattled some distance away. John acknowledged this rage, he knew it was there. He imagined a small man in a pinstripe suit handing him a card. "If you should need us, Mr Aviemore. We are always available." There was no number on the card, just a swirling blackness with red sparks igniting and fading, a dull roar coming from within.

Sarah had been dead for one hour and ten minutes.

Smashing every item of furniture, every pane of glass, every piece of crockery was an option. He could start with that chair at the desk. That green leather, never-comfortable, overpriced piece of shit fucking chair. He could start with that, take a knife to it. Get the sledgehammer from the shed and finish the job.

He looked back at the blinds. Perhaps he should open them. That was something he did every morning. This last week, Sarah had smiled every day when he'd let the light in, when she saw the trees again, the buds on the bushes, the ever-changing sky. But if he opened them now, it would be the first time he had done it without her.

Everything would be a first from now on. Like babies. The first step. The first word. Except no one else would understand the significance of these tiny events. The first drink, the first bite of food. The first sunrise. The first sunset.

There was a strange noise in the room. It was barely perceptible at first, but it got louder and louder until it was impossible to ignore. The central heating made a similar sound in winter, but the heating was off, and it was never this loud. The noise wasn't mechanical, either, it was more like an animal, like something trapped and in pain. When John's throat became sore, and he realised the noise was him, he coughed and took a few quick, desperate, breaths.

"Shit." His voice sounded wrong. It was the first word he had spoken. So that was his first word in this new world, the world without Sarah.

If he kept his eyes on the blinds and didn't think about the unstoppable light filling the room, he could lapse into the fugue state, which was almost bearable. But when his awareness drifted out of it, the crying began. John didn't know how to cry. He had no experience of it, no way of knowing how to control it. Sarah was different, she could cry while listening to music, or reading a book, easily, without embarrassment. John's experience was more like being possessed. The crying took hold of him, scraped along his throat, shoved fluid through his eyes and nose, tied his lungs into a knot, punched him in the stomach. The physical intensity of it shocked him, and, when one episode had passed, he would spend a few seconds thinking he had regained control before it would overwhelm him again.

Sarah had been dead for one hour and fifty-five minutes.

John was still holding her hand. After she had taken her last, long breath—the final exhalation more of a sigh—he had watched her face. One moment she was Sarah, the next he was looking at a body that bore some resemblance to the woman he loved. It wasn't her. How twee, that the blandest of cliches should be so accurate.

When it was clear that there would be no more breaths, not now, not ever, he had turned away and looked at the blind, Sarah's fingers gradually losing their warmth as he stroked her palm with his thumb.

He was sitting in a garden chair with a padded cushion. He had tried using the green chair when he had first set up the bed in his office, but it was too high, too heavy, too uncomfortable.

John had been sleeping next to her when her breathing changed. He had become attuned to the tiny sounds and movements she made, knowing when the pain came, when she drifted into sleep, when she moved from unconsciousness into wakefulness. He had gone to get her a glass of water. Her eyes had been open when he came back, her head turned towards the open door. He knew then. She was waiting for him. He had sat down in the chair, taken her hand and smiled at her for the last time.

It was only when he looked away from the blinds and lay Sarah's hand on the bed with all the gentleness of a parent transferring a sleeping baby from their arms to a cot, that John noticed the separation in his own mind.

He was watching himself, from three years in the future. He was in the Leigh Woods cottage, but it was also the day Sarah died. He could change nothing, but he could live through every exquisite moment of pain exactly as he had experienced them the first time.

It was seven o'clock on the first of May. John looked at Sarah's face. He almost said her name, almost told her he loved her, but the room was so full of her absence that, in the end, he did neither.

The final test results had come through, and John and Sarah had been given the last appointment on a dark, Tuesday evening in October.

In a long relationship rich with all the subtleties that arise over decades of growth, misunderstandings, compromises, and hope, John and Sarah had often portrayed themselves to others in terms simpler than the more nuanced truth.

"John's the pessimist, I'm the optimist. We meet somewhere in the middle."

John would grumble about being a realist rather than a pessimist, Sarah would tease him about self-fulfilling prophecies, and friends and acquaintances would happily help them preserve their roles.

Now, when the worst news imaginable might be about to be delivered by a tired, overworked oncologist on the other side of a blue door in a deserted NHS hospital waiting room, Sarah was the one in bleak humour.

"You know what this appointment time means, right?"

John shrugged. "It means it was the first available slot once your results came back."

"Nah. They always keep the last appointment of the day free. That way, if they need to tell someone they're dying, they don't have to keep an eye on the clock, and there's no one in the waiting room to see what kind of state they're in when they leave."

This was a side of Sarah that John had only ever witnessed at home, in the middle of the night, on the rare occasions when she had suffered a bout of existentialist terror. She would make tea, whatever time it was, bring it up to bed and talk about the brevity of life and its utter lack of meaning. John would counter her argument with talk of children, art, love, and the miracle that anyone was aware of anything at all. She would kiss him, turn out the light and go back to sleep, leaving him staring into the darkness, silently agreeing with her.

"No, no," he said, putting down a leaflet on statins and rustling up an unconvincing smile. "You're wrong. That's a bit dark, isn't it? Where did you get that idea from?"

Then the blue door opened, and Doctor Archer beckoned them in. Their names had always appeared on the screen before. Not today.

Suddenly, John didn't want to stand up and take those few steps from the row of chairs to the office. Couldn't they stay here, in the empty waiting room, with the piles of magazines and the posters about free health checks and Macmillan coffee mornings on the wall? It was a waiting room, after all. Couldn't they wait? Waiting was okay. He had thought he didn't like waiting, but now that he was thinking clearly about it, waiting was fine. Waiting implied there was something coming next, something they were waiting for. Couldn't they wait forever? His hand was on Sarah's leg, and it slid away as she stood up and took two steps before turning. And, of course, he stood up and walked towards the blue door because that's what you do when you've been sitting in a waiting room and the waiting is over; when an oncologist with a long list of patients who survived their brush with cancer calls your wife in to tell her she's on the other list.

They were at a wedding in Suffolk. A friend of Sarah's she had kept in touch with after university. Sarah had only recently stopped breast feeding, and Harry was staying with her parents overnight. Desserts had come and gone an hour ago, and the speeches had begun. The father of the bride, having tackled his fear of public speaking with a bottle-and-a-half of merlot, was deep into his fourth anecdote about his daughter's childhood. He'd been speaking for twenty minutes, and the good-natured laughter at his sometimes-intentional jokes was already becoming more sporadic as his audience lost interest. John was mulling over an idea for a prediction routine using wedding invitations when a foot appeared in his lap, the toes sliding along the chair, then flexing upwards to make contact with his testicles.

"Woah!" he said, brought back from his imaginary trick to the real world, where his wife's foot was now massaging his crotch. The other five people at the table turned towards him, so he tried to make the involuntary noise sound like a laugh. Too late, he rewound the speech in his head to the point just before the unexpected appearance of the foot, finding to his horror that the current anecdote was about the death of the bride's mother.

He tried to turn the laugh into a cough, which turned into a genuine fit of choking when he took a gulp of wine, his cheeks red. Most of the guests had turned to look by now, and the bride's father had paused his soliloquy.

"He all right?"

Sarah answered. "He'll be okay. You carry on." John, a napkin held to his mouth, saw the amusement in her eyes, and the arousal. She came round to his side of the table and took his arm to lead him away. John was glad the coughing fit gave him an excuse to bend over as he hobbled away, his erection making it impossible to walk normally.

Sarah pushed him into the disabled toilet and peeled her knickers off from under the obligatory little black dress.

"Trousers off," she ordered. "The way he's going, we might do it twice before he's finished."

FORTY-FOUR

John woke in the early hours. It was dark. He was smiling. His lips, his fingers, his whole body remembered Sarah as if he'd just been in that toilet at the wedding five minutes ago. He sat up, reaching for the glass of water by the sofa.

The knowledge that Sarah was three years dead crawled back into his consciousness, and his smile faded as he remembered where he was, and what was happening. He put the glass down and lay back, closing his eyes. He was terrified he wouldn't be able to get back to sleep, back where Sarah waited for him.

"Please," he whispered, trying to relax, to stop his grief overwhelming him again. "Please..."

Sleep claimed him, and he greedily embraced the dreams it brought.

As near-death experiences go, it wasn't particularly exciting. No injuries were sustained, and although it was dramatic enough to have made a good story to tell at parties, it was soon forgotten. But it was real, and it had happened to Sarah, and it stopped John making a huge mistake.

Human beings, John had always believed, are complex, highly evolved organisms who are capable of rising above their basic animal nature. Therefore, it came as an enormous shock to him when he almost succumbed to a potentially marriage-wrecking surge of lust one Christmas.

The festive season was always busy at the Charleston Hotel, and Marco booked John for an extra two evenings a week. More guests meant temporary staff, and Monique was one of three new faces working in the bar while John amazed his audience. She often paused what she was doing at crucial moments of John's performance, breaking into delighted applause. She loved the moment when a signed card appeared in an impossible new location: a spectator's pocket, rolled up inside the neck of a champagne bottle, or—on one occasion—on the sole of Monique's shoe.

Her shift finished an hour before John was done, so she usually hung around to watch him work. As with any magician, John was a little wary at letting someone see an effect multiple times. But, unlike most magicians, the unique touches he brought to his craft meant Monique never saw what she wasn't supposed to see. She gasped just as loudly each time she saw him spill a drop of blood onto a single leaf, only for it to transform into a rose.

John always gave the rose to a female guest. One night, a few days before Christmas Eve, he threw it to Monique. She held his gaze longer than should have been comfortable. Later, in bed with Sarah, he almost told her but talked himself out of it. Tell her what, exactly? That he had flirted with a bartender at the hotel? Sarah would have said, "So what?" and poked him in the ribs, teasing him that he could barely keep up with her, let alone a young floozy. He could hardly tell her that it had meant more than that, or explain how his stomach had fluttered when, as she left, Monique had blown him a kiss.

She would be gone in a week, once the season was over. And he wasn't going to do anything stupid. That's what he told himself.

So when Monique handed him her phone number the following night, leaning over him as she did so, one hand resting lightly, but deliberately on his thigh, whispering, "Call me," he knew he should throw the number away. Somehow, though, the piece of paper ended up folded into a small square, tucked into the back of his wallet.

When he left the Charleston that night, Sarah was standing on the far side of the street. His immediate reaction was to break into a cold sweat of guilt and think *how does she know?* Then he reminded himself that he hadn't done anything to be ashamed of. Yet.

He waved to Sarah. Occasionally, she would come out to meet him at the end of the show. "One day, we'll have kids, and I'll be stuck at home, fat and miserable, so we should make the most of our freedom while we have it."

She saw him and smiled, waving back. In that instant, he stopped thinking about Monique, although he was very aware of the exact position of his wallet, the angle at which it was tucked into his trouser pocket.

"Bar still open?" she called.

"Yes."

She pressed the button on the pedestrian crossing, waited for a second, then set off anyway. She was almost exactly halfway across when the Ford Fiesta screeched around the corner and accelerated towards her. The driver lost control as it clipped the kerb and the rear twitched, then jackknifed.

There was no way of knowing where the speeding car would end up when it reached the crossing in the next second-and-a-half.

Whatever calculation occurred in Sarah's brain at that point, it was done quickly. Decision made, she raised her head and looked straight at her husband. John looked back, knowing that she had accepted her lack of agency, and chosen to look at the man she loved, just in case it was the last thing she ever saw.

He looked back at her, but—at the precise moment the car entered his field of vision, the rear tyres smoking and screaming as the driver fought for control—his eyes flicked across to it. There was a bang as if a tyre had exploded. As a result, the Fiesta slewed to one side, the rear pivoting around Sarah without touching her. With an explosion of glass and the brief, horrible crunch of metal on metal, it smacked into a lamppost.

The car alarm went off. The driver's door opened, and a scared-looking kid emerged, fell on his backside and swore. His passenger, clutching his arm and moaning, crawled out next, and they were sprinting down the street before Sarah had taken a step.

John ran to her then, and they held each other on the pavement in the cold December air. The car fizzed, creaked and popped as sheets of metal tried to return to their original shape, and fluid from the burst radiator hit the hot engine.

He dropped Monique's number into the fire that night and called in sick the next evening. When he went back, she was gone. John made a mental note. He may be a rational, sophisticated rational, self-aware being with the ability to make his own choices, but when it came to flirtatious

French women, it was as if someone had turned a dial on his trousers back to *caveman*.

Monique, unlike the stolen Fiesta, was an avoidable disaster. He swore to keep clear of any future Moniques. After a few weeks, he told Sarah that he'd fancied one of the Christmas bar staff.

She said, "So what?" and poked him in the ribs.

"It was the best day of my life."

John had read those words in sub-par novels, heard them spoken in Sunday afternoon films, but he had never thought of saying them himself. It was unfair: by nominating one day above others, it declared every twenty-four-hour period in the past to be inferior. It also put too much pressure on future days, preemptively relegating them to second place, at best.

But, as he relived the next memory in perfect detail, those were the words in John's mind. He experienced every single word, thought, and physical sensation of the twenty-second of August 1992. And nothing had ever matched that particular day.

Sarah was five months pregnant. The wedding had been an afterthought. They knew, as only those in their twenties can, that they would spend the rest of their lives together, so the ceremony and party was more for their families and friends than the two of them.

"And I need to take your name, John Aviemore." He had been more than a little surprised at this statement, but he heard her out. "Not that I'm doing it for any other reason than my own surname is a bit crap."

"What's wrong with Cockburn?"

"Ask my brother."

"You're an only child."

"True. But you know what I mean. Don't get me wrong, taking your surname is a bizarre patriarchal tradition that has no place in the modern world."

"We could always combine them, go double-barrelled."

"Aviemore-Cockburn. Sounds like an STD. You haven't thought this through, have you?"

"Fair point. Aviemore it is."

And so, on the first day of their married life, it was as Mr and Mrs Aviemore that they drove to North Wales.

It was a long trip, and they were up just after dawn, leaving Augustus, John's best man, to entertain those who had stayed over after the wedding.

John and Sarah breakfasted on chocolate bars and crisps as they headed along the M40. They found the guesthouse as it was getting dark, at the end of a winding track on the banks of a small lake.

The food was rich, and the view from their room showed snow-capped hills climbing behind the far banks of the lake into the mist. That night, they were too tired to have sex. Instead, they lay propped up on their pillows, hand-in-hand, watching the reflection of the moon on the wind-ruffled water.

There was no one moment of incredible joy or realisation. It was a steady drip, drip of happiness, a sense of everything being in its right place, of the fundamental goodness of life. And, as John lived every moment again, his heart ached with the ephemeral beauty of it, knowing its fragility made it wonderful.

Sarah fell asleep first, and he pulled the eiderdown up to cover her, kissing her on the cheek before closing his own eyes.

Sleep came easily with no thoughts of the past, and no plans for the future. The optimist and the pessimist, man and wife, slept deeply and slept well.

John was woken by a voice calling his name.

"John? John?"

He stopped and looked behind him. A tall girl with blonde hair in a ponytail was hurrying to catch up with him. He frowned and pursed his lips, as if trying to remember, then smiled as she reached him.

"Sarah, right?"

"Yes. How are you? Any more showers of cacti recently?"

"Ah... no, no. Not really."

"Not really?"

"Er, well, a couple of geraniums, um, the odd petunia, but, well, I'm good at dodging now. And there's always, you know, umbrellas and the like."

"Umbrellas and the like? What other devices are you using?"

John hoped he could hold his nerve. He'd been walking this stretch of road every lunchtime for ten days, ever since Sarah had knocked a cactus out of her office window and nearly brained him. Now that she was in front of him again, his tongue was struggling to maintain a connection to his brain.

"Devices? Um..."

"I'm just teasing. Do you fancy joining me for a cup of tea and a sandwich?"

"I, er, well, if it's not, I mean, if you want to, um..."

Sarah smiled. "Unless there's someone else you need to

see? Someone else you've been looking for while you've been walking up and down this street the last few days."

John flushed and stammered. "N-no. No. I haven't, that is, I wasn't, I don't want you to think I'm weird or a stalker, but, well, you know, I was, I was... yes. I was hoping to see you. Again. See you."

"Hmm." Sarah looked him up and down, still smiling. "Luckily for you, I don't mind a bit of weird. Good. Let's go."

She started walking. John followed, then stopped in confusion as she suddenly halted, holding up a hand.

"No. This is no good. Before we go any further, one question."

"Question? Oh, right, yes, fire away."

Sarah's face became serious. "I should warn you that this is a deal-breaker. Wrong answer, and we can't have lunch together. So think carefully."

John blinked, but said nothing.

"Arsenal or Tottenham?"

His eyes flicked up and to the right. He rubbed his chin. Sarah tutted.

"You shouldn't need to think about it. Which one?"

Miserable now, John slumped. "This is something to do with sport, isn't it?" he said. "Is it football?"

In answer, Sarah took his arm, pulled him close, and they walked together.

"Perfect answer," she said. "I may just have to marry you."

FORTY-FIVE

When John next opened his eyes, he spent a few moments trying to establish where he was. Nothing looked familiar. The unswept fireplace, the dirty floorboards, the old sofa and the few pieces of second-hand furniture seemed more of a dream than what he had lived through during the night.

He stood up and stretched, then rubbed his eyes. His state of mind was so heightened that he barely knew what he was doing. His dreams hadn't been dreams. He had spent all night in the company of his wife, something that hadn't happened for three years, and something he had believed could never happen again. Sarah was dead. John had watched her die. He had been the first mourner to throw dirt on her coffin that day in the cemetery. He had shaken hands and hugged a succession of tearful family members and friends, he had paid the undertaker, he had thanked Helen and Fiona for helping with catering and drinks at the house afterwards. He had shut the door behind Harry when he had left to return to America two days after the funeral. He had walked back into an empty house. Sarah was dead, his time with her was over. It was over.

He poured himself a glass of water. It was still dark outside, but an ancient instinct alerted him to the first tiny changes of light that signified the end of the night.

John thought of the bargain he had made with Ash. He could leave at dawn.

For the first time, he noticed a weight in his left hand and looked down in confusion. He was holding the stone that Ash had shown him last night. The stone that contained the time cage.

His bag had a pair of jeans and a T-shirt he hadn't worn yet. He pulled them out along with some clean underwear and went upstairs to the bathroom. He glanced at the bedroom door as he reached the top of the stairs. It was shut.

John cleaned his teeth. He kept his attention on the bristles of the toothbrush as they passed along the enamel of his teeth, pushing up against the gum, moving along, repeating the process.

He couldn't think about last night. He couldn't.

When he washed, he was shocked to find thick, coarse hair on his chin and cheeks. He tilted the mirror and saw the face of a stranger. Gaunt, bearded, hollow-eyed. A little crazy-looking.

His thoughts drifted back to Wales, and the first night of their honeymoon. He could remember it like it was yesterday because—for him—it *was* yesterday.

"No." He bent back over the sink and splashed water onto his face, removing the soap. His beard was full. Yesterday, it had only been stubble. He rubbed the towel over his face, brushed his hair and got dressed. He checked the mirror one more time before leaving the bathroom, angling it to see his whole body. The jeans were hanging off him.

How had he lost so much weight in so short a time? It looked like he was dressed in borrowed clothes.

Despite his lack of belief in predestination, John accepted that certain moments in life were significant, particularly in hindsight. It was tempting to imagine some guiding hand was present, whether for good or ill. The day Sarah had knocked over the cactus was a good example

This was one of those moments. John stood on the landing in front of the bedroom, turning the stone over in his left hand. He pushed open the door and walked in.

The windows were shuttered, and the bedroom was lit by a bare bulb hanging from the ceiling.

Ash was almost unrecognisable. She had pulled her hair back into a ponytail, and was wearing a white blouse with navy blue leggings. As long as he didn't look into those ancient green eyes, John could almost convince himself she was human.

"The time cage doesn't have to be a prison," she said, fastening a watch to her wrist. It was the first time John had ever seen her wearing jewellery. Besides the watch, she had a gold bangle on her right arm and a silver necklace around her throat. "It has become that for me. I won't deny it. But it took millennia before it felt that way. The time cage didn't begin as a burden. At first, it was a source of joy."

She pulled open a drawer on the dresser and removed a half-empty bottle of cheap perfume. The blouse was too big for her, and the jewellery was mismatched. John wondered if Ash was wearing items left behind by previous tenants of the cottage. She was a strikingly beautiful woman, but dressed as she was now, she could walk across Clifton Suspension Bridge into Bristol without stopping traffic.

John turned the stone over in his hand, its smooth

contours brushing warmly across the skin of his palm. It felt comfortable there.

"I can't talk to you about where I come from in terms you could comprehend," she said, picking up a makeup brush and applying foundation to her flawless skin. "But there is one thing you should know. Although my kind are not immortal, we think of decades the same way you think of hours. I was young when I came here. Not to the Blurred Lands. They didn't exist in the same way when I first found your realm. I was young and impetuous. I underestimated my enemies, and I was defeated. The punishment they chose did not seem cruel to them, but those who put me here are long dead. Yet here I am. Did you dream, John?"

She looked smaller and more vulnerable in ordinary clothes.

"Don't play with me, Ash. You know I did." John's mind returned to the memory of Sarah's friend's wedding, and the shocked look on the faces of the other guests when they had finally emerged from the toilet. The intense bubble of happiness produced by the memory burst as he brought himself back to the cottage, the bedroom, and Ash. "Why did you do that? Why did you send me those memories? Even you must have experienced loss. Why torture me with it?"

"Me?" Ash shook her head. "I did nothing last night. You had the stone. You chose the memories. That's how the time cage works. I wanted you to see for yourself."

John sat on the bed. It was just a frame without a mattress again, and the bedroom was uncarpeted.

"I don't understand."

"I think you do. When I was trapped here, I had over a thousand years of memories to explore. I could go back to the greatest moments of my life and relive them as if they were actually happening. Better still, my present self was there, and I could soak in every detail. I found episodes in my life I had forgotten, beautiful moments, conversations, lovers, battles and victories. But, over centuries, it was the small things that drew me back. We are all creatures trapped in time, John, and every moment, before we appreciate it, has already passed. Not here, though. That's what I've been showing you since you arrived. And, last night, that's what you showed yourself. That's what the cage can give you."

Ash opened the shutters. The light outside had morphed from black to dark grey. John looked out. The light seemed wrong for the time of year. Too dark.

"What it can give me?" John knew he was circling around the truth he didn't want to acknowledge. He pictured himself standing up and handing the stone to Ash, but his fingers curled more tightly around it even as he considered the idea.

"Yes, John. Over the millennia, I have exhausted my supply of memories, and my time here has turned from a paradise to Hell. For you, it will be different. Your human life is short. How many more years can you expect? Twenty? Thirty? A few more, perhaps? I am offering you the chance to spend the rest of your life with Sarah."

"No. No." John's voice was so faint, he barely heard it himself, and when he looked up at Ash, he knew he wouldn't walk away from the cottage that day, or any day. Not if he could find Sarah here.

His eyes were full of tears. "What do I have to do?"

FORTY-SIX

"Hold the stone in the palm of your hand," said Ash. John did as instructed, and she placed her palm on top of the stone, their hands closing to cover it. Ash looked into John's eyes. "For you to enter the time cage," she said, "we need to go to the Between."

John looked back at her. She was more beautiful now than she had ever been, but he saw none of that. He only saw Sarah, alive, happy, every moment of their lives together, available to be experienced again and again.

"We go together," said Ash.

"Together."

Ash held John's gaze a moment longer, then nodded and half-closed her eyes. John did the same.

The transition to the Between was instant. John didn't know if this was because he was improving with practice, or because the link with a living god made his abilities more powerful. He was sitting in the Platonic Chair. The stone was missing from his hand. In its place was a strange orb of mist. It was weightless, but when he raised his hand, it followed the movement. When he tried to close his fingers, it became more solid, and he felt some resistance. He stood up and looked out across the featureless plain, the eternal snowfall still continuing its slow descent from the galaxies above to the ground below. A solitary figure was out there, waiting. He moved closer to the invisible window, not understanding what he was looking at.

The figure in the snow could only be Ash, but nobody would mistake her for a human being now. The woman standing outside his sanctum was, if his estimation were anywhere near correct, over twelve feet tall. She was hooded, a dark robe falling from her shoulders to her feet. The face inside the hood was hidden in shadow, but a few strands of copper hair reflected the light of the stars.

She stopped and looked towards John. He walked to the door. His brief career as a real magician, a potential Adept, was over before it had begun. He was giving up a world of fantastic power and ancient secrets to live in a dream. But a dream as real as life.

John headed down the stairs and opened the outside door. Without hesitation, he pulled the cord tight on his dressing gown and stepped out into the snow. He didn't look back.

Astarte, Ashtoreth, the god of love and war, waited for him in the field of snow. As he got closer, John wondered how this might look to an observer. A middle-aged man in pyjamas and dressing gown meeting a giant hooded figure in a snowstorm.

"I have not been here for thousands of years," said the god. There was something different about her voice. Her hidden face turned from left to right to take in the changeless landscape. "Even the gods don't understand this place. We may rule the realms in other skins, but we meet in our true form here, John Aviemore."

A huge hand, its skin tinged a deathly blue, came out of the robe and barred John from walking any further. He looked up. Ashtoreth said nothing but pointed ahead into the snow.

Something was moving. Something big. Something so big, it made the giant figure beside John look like an insect. Whatever it was, it was following a path of its own and didn't appear to have noticed them, judging from its unchanged course.

John watched with a mixture of terror and curiosity as the thing ahead of them came closer. It had no limbs as such, nothing that touched the snowy ground beneath it, and its shape changed as it moved, elongating and contracting like the segments of a millipede. Its skin was rust brown, the colour of dried blood. When it was within fifty yards, John worked out that it was propelling itself through some kind of manipulation and expulsion of the surrounding air, like a flying jellyfish. It was a kind of organic dirigible. Each individual segment, as high as a five-storey building, swelled as it moved before squeezing itself into a smaller shape, the gas within hissing backwards along its body. There was no discernible head, and John could see no way that the thing could perceive the world around it. As each segment ballooned before shrinking, it moved forwards to take the place of the segment in front, which was doing the same. The creature was folding back in on itself so that its motion was circular, each segment having a turn at the front, then making its way down the side, before ending up at the rear and beginning the journey again.

The sound it made was, perhaps, the most frightening aspect of all. There was something horribly musical about its roar. A broken accordion, its bellows rotted and tattered, played by a lunatic. John remembered seeing Concorde take off as a child, clutching his father's hand as the roar of the jet engines grew louder and louder. Just when he had thought his ears would explode, even through the protectors his dad had placed on his head, the roar had increased again in volume before the graceful aircraft accelerated along the runway. The horrendous wheezing he heard now was even louder, and the fact that John knew he was not in his physical body was of little comfort. As the monolithic beast made its way past them, oblivious to their presence, John felt as if his skull and skeleton were vibrating inside his skin.

A minute after the monstrosity had gone, its progress continuing through the whiteness, Ashtoreth withdrew her hand and began to walk again. John hurried to catch up.

"What the hell was that?"

He worked out what was different about her voice in the Between. It wasn't louder, or deeper, it certainly wasn't the voice a Hollywood blockbuster would have assigned to a god, but it was unnerving. The sound no longer came from Ashtoreth's mouth. It was more like a hundred women whispering simultaneously, each of them standing next to John. The voice surrounded him.

"How much did your noone teach you about this place?"

John thought of Gai, injured but hidden, and felt a stab of guilt. He stopped walking.

Ashtoreth's laugh sounded out of place, inappropriate in the hush left after the roar of the giant beast. "He will live, and he is free to go. What did he tell you about the Between?"

They resumed their walk. John could see nothing ahead. He was neither cold nor tired, and he could not tell if they had been walking for minutes or hours.

"He told me my sanctum was safe. But he said there were dangers out here."

Underneath the hood, Ashtoreth nodded. "The Between is the only place every realm has in common." John felt his skin crawl at the unwanted intimacy of the voice. "Unlike the Blurred Lands, where the realms overlap, the Between is no-place and no-time. Those who allow themselves to adapt too closely to the ways of this place may find themselves trapped here. It has happened to some of the most powerful magicians over the eons. That,"—Ashtoreth lifted her hand to point at the retreating monster—"is one such magician. You will find its story in the myths of Shambhala. It has forgotten what it is and where it comes from. Thus it is doomed to wander this landscape forever. You will see more of these creatures if you spend much time here. They are a warning to us all."

She turned towards John again. When he looked up into the darkness of that hood, he could see a glittering where her eyes were and a hint of blue-white skin. "You cannot return here from the time cage. I can only come now because you brought me."

Something in her posture changed. Ashtoreth had seen something. A dozen steps later, and he saw it too; a silvered dome, vast and mysterious, waiting in the snow ahead. It took a while before John worked out the scale of what he was seeing. It wasn't the size of a building, it was more like a small town. Its metallic surface reflected the falling snow, giving the impression that a second, gravity-defying snowfall had begun from the ground, and was meeting the first in mid-air.

When they were closer still, John looked in vain for any kind of entrance. The surface of the dome was unbroken. There was no door, no path leading to it, no sign of any entrance or exit. Ashtoreth's pace did not slow as they came to the mirrored surface. John, half a step behind her, hesitated as he approached it. When he was five paces away, the surface revealed itself to be not metal, but water, held, somehow, in stasis in the shape of a dome.

There was no resistance as they stepped through. A momentary feeling of moisture and cold, and they were inside.

FORTY-SEVEN

John's mind had slowed since making his decision. Once he had chosen a second life with Sarah, he had stopped thinking about anything that might deflect him from his task. He had spent no time wondering what the interior of the dome would look like. But even if he had used all of his imaginative powers, he would not have guessed at what lay within that silvered surface.

John knew, roughly, the size of the space he had walked into, and estimated it would take hours to cross it. But, as he looked around him, he knew only a fool would try. The entire, vast space inside the dome was filled with fog. It had the grey-silver sheen of heavy rain, or of mist from the base of the waterfall when tens of thousands of gallons hit the rocks. Ashtoreth's upper body was hazy and undefined in the silver mist.

The god spoke again, and John flinched at that strange, yet familiar, voice coming at him from every angle.

"Although the dome can't be said to exist in any traditional sense of the word, it can always be found by those who look for it in the Between. The mist is a representation of magic, made physical to enable us to manipulate it. Thousands of magicians are here crafting spells, enchantments, and charms."

John looked around in alarm. He could see and hear nothing, and it unnerved him. In this dense silver fog, the nearest Adept or sorcerer might be within touching distance without him knowing.

As if hearing his thoughts, Ashtoreth answered him. "No one here will encounter any other magician unless they have chosen to do so before entering the dome. We came here with a common purpose, and we will remain until we are finished. The magic we will craft is too volatile for a single magician to handle. Even I would not risk trying it alone."

This was as close as John had ever heard Ash admit to being afraid. Ironic then that it should happen while she was twelve feet tall and intimidatingly powerful.

Ashtoreth turned towards him and lifted her left hand. Floating just above her reflective skin was an identical wisp of material to the one that had appeared in John's hand. It was still there.

"Take my hand." It was a command, not a request.

John thought of Sarah, then placed his hand, as tiny as a child's in comparison with Ashtoreth's, above her fingers. As soon as he did so, whatever they had brought of the stone from the cottage merged and rose above them. There, it separated into strands of darker thread, as if someone was drawing a design on the mist with a fine nib. Within seconds, a pattern had formed, but the lines were still moving. It was a drawing, in three dimensions, of a geometrical shape. John could never have reproduced the shape on Earth - he was sure it couldn't exist there. He suspected he wouldn't even be able to *see* it if he wasn't in the Between.

Here in the dome, his perception was not limited to his human senses.

"It's beautiful," he said, watching the lines move, the whole complicated shape revolving, contorting, twisting, moving in ways John could not comprehend.

"It's the time cage," said Ashtoreth. Her voice held an element of awe. She was looking at a representation of the spell buried in the stone, the spell that had kept her captive for thousands of years.

John thought of Sarah. "What do we do?"

"It is a matter of consent, commitment, and surrender."

"Surrender?"

"When two or more magicians create magic as powerful as this, it is necessary for them to submit to their own creation, each laying aside their will."

John had no idea what that meant in practice, but he had come too far to turn back now. Soon, he knew, he could be back with Sarah, kissing her for the first time, hearing her say she loved him, her voice full of joy and surprise. He could be with her again.

"I'm ready," he said.

Ashtoreth made no arcane gestures, drew no symbols in the air. She did not chant, make any proclamations, or ask if there were any spirits present. She simply looked up at the unfolding spell above them and allowed her mind to merge with it. John felt it happen and heard the invitation inherent in that moment. As he looked up again, the shape was changing, unravelling itself, a thousand pairs of invisible hands undoing a thousand knots. The whole design grew in size, and gaps appeared. At the centre, one such gap, widening and lengthening as he watched, became a doorway.

This was the moment. He knew it. Ashtoreth knew it.

The dome itself seemed to respond with a tension in the silver fog, a hushed expectancy.

A movement to the right drew John's attention. He glanced over, returned to the spell, then froze and turned his body to face the source of the movement.

It was Sarah.

He could only just make out the faintest outline of her face, but those eyes, those grey eyes that had plumbed his depths, found his weakness and his pain, and still loved him, were looking back at him.

"Sarah?" He took half a step towards her. Something was wrong with the perspective Sarah had been only a few inches shorter than him, but now he was looking down at a child. Beside him, Ashtoreth had noticed that something was wrong, and was trying, with difficulty, to wrench her gaze away from the spell unravelling above her.

The eyes, Sarah's eyes, widened, and the face became clearer. John stared in confusion. Then his mind put the pieces together, and he gasped with a mixture of surprise, shock, delight, and sudden, terrible shame at what he had been about to do.

It wasn't Sarah. It was Evie.

FORTY-EIGHT

Later, when John looked back on the events inside the dome, he couldn't remember who, if anyone, had spoken, or precisely what they had said. He knew the confrontation between Evie and Ashtoreth had turned into something dangerous, but in his memory, it all seemed to happen in one elongated second. He had to apply a linear timeline retrospectively to make sense of it.

It must have been Ashtoreth who spoke first. "You cannot be here."

"My grandfather invited me." John felt Evie's hand take his own and squeeze it. "He needs me, so I came."

The fury in Ashtoreth's voice was obvious, and terrifying beyond measure, but she made no move towards John and his granddaughter. Certain things were known in this place, and John was aware that it would be impossible for any being inside the dome to kill another. If Ashtoreth had been free to do so, there was no doubt she would have torn Evie apart with her bare hands, but the power of this place prevented it.

What is that?" Evie pointed at the spell which was still

turning in the mist above them, the threads untying, unravelling, and moving into new patterns.

"It's the spell that kept her in the cottage," said John, wondering how he could explain this to a child. How old was Evie, anyway? He couldn't remember if she was eleven or twelve. He looked at her face again, seeing Sarah in her grey eyes and blonde hair, but also seeing Harry in the line of her chin and her freckled nose.

"The time cage," she said.

John was astonished. Evie grinned, and the uncanny resemblance to her grandmother disappeared for a moment. "I have visited my sanctum, Granddad. Mae taught me how to get there."

John could not begin to understand what was going on, but he knew the danger was far from over. Ashtoreth was chuckling now, the sound of her laughter both chilling and strange.

"Whatever you hoped to achieve, child, you're too late. Your grandfather has already agreed to take my place when the cage is ready for him. Once changed, the spell cannot return to what it was. It must take a new form."

Evie looked up at her grandfather. "She's right," she said. "And the time cage is the most powerful spell ever cast in our realm. It's linked to both of you now, but it's still incomplete. A new spell must be forged here, otherwise the cage might imprison you both. Or kill you both."

Ashtoreth was nodding. "The child is right," she said. "Only you can stop this happening, John. If you break your promise, you will lose your wife forever."

John looked from the dance of dark threads above him to Ashtoreth, then to Evie. His granddaughter spoke with the assurance of a woman. At that moment, she reminded John of his mother.

"There is another way," she said, her voice quiet but strong. "We can change the spell again, adapt it further."

"Change it to what?"

"I don't know yet. I'm thinking. But we can't let it complete its transformation. We have to hold it in place until we find a way to stop her."

Evie looked up, and the threads above responded, changing course, slowing down.

Ashtoreth reached her hands up to her hood and pulled it back. John saw the god's true face for the first time.

Astarte's face was the blue-white colour of stripped bark in moonlight, the green eyes darker than the weed at the bottom of a deep lake. There were no other features, no nose or mouth, and the face was longer and thinner than any human's, suggesting a different bone structure beneath. The copper hair was not hair at all. It was a haze of energy like an aura surrounding that alien visage, sparking and glowing in the silver fog of the dome. When the god spoke again, there was no change to the impassive features. John could hardly bring himself to look at her eyes. "I cannot let you do that, child."

Ashtoreth raised one hand, and the threads moved sluggishly as two opposing wills tried to manipulate them. "I will be free," said the god. "You will not stop me. Not now. Not ever." She pointed her other hand at Evie.

Evie grunted in surprise and pain, doubling over and gasping. She released her hold on the spell, and the threads obeyed Ashtoreth once again. The god was working faster now.

John crouched down and put his hand on his granddaughter's back. "Are you all right?"

Evie coughed and wheezed, then looked up with such an expression of horror and loss that John stepped backwards in consternation. An instant later, and the moment had passed.

"She's trying to distract us. We have to finish this. I don't know what to do, Granddad."

Tears ran down her face. She stood upright, but kept one hand on her belly.

It was at that moment that John remembered what Gai had said to him and realised the noone hadn't misspoken. It was just that John had misunderstood. He turned to Evie. "Can we send her back? Send her back to *when* she came from?"

Evie looked at him, but something else was happening behind those familiar grey eyes. Although it made no sense, John felt as if he wasn't just seeing Evie, but a crowd of wise, powerful women, all considering his words. At the front of the group, her hand on Evie's shoulder, her intelligent face full of sadness and resolve, was his mother. Then Evie spoke, and they all evaporated into the silver mist.

"Yes," she said. She squeezed John's hand more tightly and looked away from him up towards the spell. John did the same, and just as he had been aware of Ashtoreth's mind linking to the threads above him, he and Evie now did the same.

There was no more speaking after that. What happened next passed in silence and in the no-time of the Between. The battle was undramatic, invisible, the combatants staring up as their minds manipulated the spell. As still as three statues, there were no outward signs of the ferocity of the struggle between them.

Evie showed John the shape she wanted the spell to take, faint ghost threads appearing showing what she wanted. John followed her lead. Together, their minds pulled at the threads, re-knotting, unlocking, nudging some in a new direction, forcing others to turn back on themselves.

Ashtoreth reacted to what was happening, undoing their actions, trying to bring the spell back to her design. For a long time, the battle ebbed and flowed. What John and Evie attempted to create, Ashtoreth undid, and a dance of energy chased through the fog above them at incredible speed. But, slowly at first, then picking up momentum, the dance changed, becoming more coordinated as grandfather and granddaughter worked together more effectively, their intention becoming one. Ashtoreth's body hummed with power as she tried to keep up with the speed and grace of their movements. Above them, the spell evolved and morphed.

It was the dome itself that provided the tipping point. All three of them sensed it, a focused attention from the mist, as if some massive creature found a gnat on its skin and was considering crushing it. Ashtoreth's act of aggression towards Evie, although not deadly, had been noticed. A mage breaking the rules of this place had nowhere to hide, even if they were a god elsewhere.

John could not have pinpointed the moment at which the balance of power shifted, but it was clear that Ashtoreth's countermeasures were failing. He and Evie could move faster than she could keep up, and the god was becoming overwhelmed. The sense of incipient violence became stronger as Ashtoreth's fury grew.

A new shape was taking form now. Unlike the impossible geometric representation John had first seen, this was more like a net, or a web, strands of which unfolded and moved towards Ashtoreth, as if to embrace her. Her reaction was swift and decisive. As the nearest strands touched her, she screamed with frustration, spun around, and left the dome the way she had entered it.

The threads of the spell stretched through the silver surface of the dome, but Ashtoreth was gone.

John turned to Evie in dismay. "She's escaped!"

Evie shook her head. "She can't. The cage was built to hold Ashtoreth. Her attempts to reconfigure it would have worked if you had taken her place, but as it is, the cage is still patterned on her." Evie reached up and put her small hand on John's upper arm. "We must finish this."

Without Ashtoreth there to resist them, completing the spell was straightforward. The hard work had already been accomplished, and it was as if the cage worked with them as they eased the final threads of power into their new position. When it was done, energy and life filled the shape above them, and there was tension in its strands as if they were being pulled by something out of sight. John was reminded of the float on a river dipping below the surface as a fish takes the bait.

Evie and John watched the spell tighten, energy building within its myriad threads. Then it moved, flowing through the side of the dome before disappearing. When the last of the threads had gone, John and his granddaughter stepped through the wall of the dome and found themselves in the snowy landscape of the Between, alone.

"Did it work?" said John.

Evie looked at him. "Only one way to find out."

John again felt the power behind those disconcertingly familiar eyes. Evie was more than she appeared to be and was no longer just a child. He felt a sadness at this realisation, and an acceptance. What was done was done, and he and Evie would have much to talk about when they returned to their own realm. If John could return at all, that is. Ashtoreth had gone, the time cage had gone, and he would only know the result of their battle when he left the Between.

Evie took both his hands and stood facing him. "Dad and I are nearby," she said. "Back home, I mean. We're in Bristol."

"You're where?"

"You're quite a celebrity now, Granddad. I'll see you there."

And with that, she was gone, skipping through the snow. He glanced behind him at the vast silver dome, then turned and scanned the whiteness, looking for any sign of his sanctum. He could see nothing familiar, but he felt the faint pull of it, through slowly falling flakes of snow. There was nothing more for him to do here.

He thought of his room, the fire, and the Platonic Chair. *That way.*

John trudged back through the snow and, the moment he had crossed the threshold of his sanctum, he half-closed his eyes and pictured himself in the cottage. He visualised the stone in his left hand, Ash's palm closing on his as the sky brightened behind her.

He left the Between.

In the cottage bedroom, John blinked in confusion. There was no stone in his hand. He dared to hope. Then he looked up, and fear, defeat, and despair replaced that first flicker of optimism.

FORTY-NINE

Ash was holding the stone. Her clenched fist was behind her head, her arm tensed to strike. Her face was contorted with rage, but it wasn't triumph that John saw in her eyes as she threw her punch; it was fear.

He might have dodged the blow, but by the time his muscles responded to his brain's urgent signals, it was too late. The stone in Ashtoreth's hand was inches away from smashing into his forehead.

He closed his eyes.

A tickling sensation as if someone had breathed on his face, then nothing. He waited. Since his skull was still intact, he re-opened his eyes.

The bedroom was empty. Ashtoreth was gone. Not gone in the sense of stepping out, possibly to return, but gone as if she had never been. The entire atmosphere of the cottage had changed, a dark tension lifting, taking with it every last hint of Ash's presence. It was just a rundown cottage in Leigh Woods, near Clifton, a suburb of Bristol. John was convinced that if he followed the path through the gate, and along the narrow lane, he would find people walking dogs, and cars passing on the road.

He put one shaking hand to his face and rubbed the unfamiliar beard. Then he stood up and looked through the window, watching the sunlight breathe warmth into the frosted grass through the trees.

Downstairs, everything was different. The sofa had gone, as had his belongings. In the kitchen, there was no hum from the fridge and, when he opened it, it was empty. He flicked the light switch. Nothing. He tried the living room. No power.

The door was locked, and the key was missing from its nail. John opened the window. A blast of cold air hit him. He half-climbed, half-fell through the gap and rolled onto the hard earth.

He stumbled to the front gate, his legs weak.

John looked through watering eyes at the rotting leaves on the path and the white-tipped blades of grass pushing up between them. The sun didn't warm him as it streamed through the bare branches above. He was cold, his breath coming in puffs of white smoke as he regained his composure. It had been summer when he had arrived at the cottage five days ago.

At the first tree he came to, John stared in astonishment. His own face looked back at him from a poster taped onto the trunk. It was his passport photo from five years ago, a few months before he and Sarah went on their last holiday in the south of France. With trembling fingers, he ripped the picture away from the tree.

Missing. John Aviemore.

There was a phone number to call, a website for more information.

John heard footsteps crunching through dead leaves

somewhere ahead and had to hold on to the tree for support when he recognised the voices that accompanied them.

"Harry," he whispered. The voices came closer.

"Evie, please don't get your hopes up. Yes, I know. But maybe this time it really was just a dream. Honey, we're going home on Tuesday. You have school and I—,"

Harry rounded the corner.

John saw himself through his son's eyes for a moment: a wild-eyed stranger, emaciated, bearded and shaking. Harry came to a halt, glanced over his shoulder for his daughter, then looked back. His voice didn't work the first time he tried to speak, but, finally, he croaked a word out before Evie passed him and threw herself into John's arms.

"Dad?"

An amiable, portly police sergeant visited Harry and Evie's hotel room mid-morning and allowed himself to be plied with generous wedges of cake. He interviewed John, then talked them through the paperwork. It was rare for a missing person case to be so happily resolved, and, more than once, John and Harry had to decline the sergeant's offer of a trip to the pub to celebrate.

A doctor had been called, and—half an hour of checkups and lots of questions later—John was pronounced underweight but, otherwise, fit and good to go.

Harry insisted John stay a night in Bristol before they drove back to Wimbledon. The media would have to be informed and it would be easier to weather the ensuing storm from the familiar comforts of home.

There were explanations to be made. John and Harry talked long into the evening. John had never been much of a liar, so although feigning amnesia was far-fetched, it was the only card he could play. The alternative was telling the truth, and he had no wish to pay the psychiatrist bills that would ensue were he to do that.

It wasn't until the next morning, when Harry went to check out, that grandfather and granddaughter found time to speak alone.

"It worked, Evie." John told her what had happened on his return to Sally Cottage. Evie listened, nodding gravely.

"I pity her, I really do," she said. "The time cage was the kindest punishment under the circumstances, but eventually, I think she lost her grip on reality. Reversing her timeline should mean she won't be aware that she is reliving the whole thing all over again."

"Reversing it?"

"You asked if we could send her back when she came from."

John stroked his chin. Rather than shave, he had borrowed Harry's trimmer, and now sported a neat white and black beard. It made him look like a different person, and that was how he felt.

"What exactly did you do?" he said. "I thought I could follow some of it while we were in the dome, but now it seems confused. I was guided by you, and by my instincts. It was as if the spell itself was trying to help us."

"Exactly," she said. "The best magic, the most effective magic of all, directs the flow of power where it most wants to go. We reversed Ashtoreth's progress through time. She didn't disappear in the cottage, she went backwards from that point."

"And you don't think she'll know what's happening?"

"It's impossible to say for sure, but I think not. She will pass back through her life to the beginning. The earliest record we have of Astarte is of her appearance in our realm, stepping out of a live volcanic crater. Her beginning is now also her end."

Evie turned her head away and reached for another biscuit, but not before John caught a grimace of pain on her young face.

"She hurt you," he said.

"That she did." It was an unusual phrase for a twelve-year-old, but John's mother had used it all the time. Evie had been brought up in America, and her accent and cultural references had reflected this. Now, however, her accent was, occasionally, British.

Evie stood up and moved over to the window, folding her arms and looking down at passing traffic. She looked so much like a smaller version of her great-grandmother at that point, John was half-convinced he would see his mother's face when she turned around.

"Dad and I didn't come straight to Bristol." The timbre of her voice was that of a child, but she spoke like a much older woman. "We drove out to Elstree first, to the care home. I had to stand in the place that Great-Granny died. To complete the process. To become an Adept, one of the Three."

When she faced John, he saw what he had seen in the dome. In the striped-wallpapered room, with the two-bar electric fire, china dogs on the mantelpiece and net curtains hooked back from the bay window, it was even more striking.

His mother stood there, as did his grandmother and great-grandmother. Other women were gathered behind those calm grey eyes so reminiscent of Sarah's. Others were present, too, shades whose existence were barely defined. Evie was still Evie, but she was more.

"Mae wrote to me," she said. "Dad picked up the letters with the rest of her stuff when he came for the funeral. He was so caught up looking for you that he didn't find the letters addressed to me until August. She wrote about our family secret, she taught me our history, and she showed me my future. I was destined to be an Adept. Mae told me how. She would have preferred I wait a few years but, well..."

"I went missing at the same time she died. You connected the dots."

"I did."

John stood up. "You did it for me? But the danger you—"

Evie held up a finger in another gesture identical to one of her great-grandmother's. "I've already lost my nanny. I didn't want to lose my granddad too." She tilted her head. "Blaming yourself for what I've done would be self-indulgent. Mae could have left the letters in a lawyer's office until I was old enough. She didn't. She knew I would act on the information they contained if it was necessary."

John remembered it then, the moment Ashtoreth had turned on Evie, the pain on her face. "You weren't ready, were you? Not really. What did she do to you?"

Evie turned back to the window.

"I'm barren," she said. The statement was so strange coming from the lips of a twelve-year-old girl, even one as unusual as Evie. "That's what Ashtoreth did. She couldn't kill me in the dome, but she thought she could prevent our line continuing. I don't know if she hoped the dome would allow it, or that it would not know what she had done. She was wrong. The dome helped us complete our spell and sent her back. Too late to undo the damage, though."

John moved towards her, then stopped. "Oh, Evie, I'm so sorry. I don't know what to say. I can't imagine..."

"No." Evie's voice was flat. "Neither can I, not really. I

expect it will hurt more when I get to the age where I might want children of my own. I will deal with it then, I suppose. Still..." She turned towards her grandfather. The power in her was as present as if he were standing in front of a massive, humming generator. "... Astarte failed in one regard."

"What do you mean?"

"Grandmother's line will continue. I see our future Adepts."

John thought through the ramifications of that statement. "Your dad had you very young. No reason he couldn't have other children. How do you feel about that?"

"I'd love to have a sister," she said. "But you're forgetting something. Another possibility."

"I don't think so, Evie."

"You may be my grandad, but you're not that old. Who says you won't have any more children?"

FIFTY

SIX WEEKS LATER

Augustus was already standing in front of the grave when John arrived at the cemetery. It was a twenty-five-minute walk from his house in Wimbledon, and the route took him past many of the places he associated with Sarah. He could pass those bookshops, art galleries, cafés and parks with as much happiness as pain these days. John found grief to be unpredictable and had resigned himself to its surprises. Progress was made, certainly, but John knew he would never be entirely free of those crippling moments of agony - the knowledge that she had gone hitting him once again, as fresh as it had been the first time.

Now, two rows away from Sarah's grave, a new headstone, simple and small, marked his mother's final resting place. He walked up and stood beside Augustus, who acknowledged his arrival with a smile and a nod.

There were no flowers on the grave. Mae had never wanted cut flowers in the house, always preferring to see them in situ.

"She'll have flowers in the spring," said Augustus. "I

planted snowdrops, primroses, and daffodils. There will be sunflowers behind the headstone."

"Sunflowers?"

"I'm not a tall person." His old friend said this as if he suspected John had never noticed. "It will give me an easy way to find her when I visit."

John and Augustus were still feeling their way around the new parameters of their relationship. Augustus had not answered to the name Gai for centuries. His full name was Gaius Augustus, but he had dropped the Gaius after his illness and recuperation. He had been found in the Blurred Lands by his father, badly injured. His arm had been beyond any medicine or magic, and his leg could only be partially healed. Augustus's recovery had been slow, and he could not remember how he had sustained his injuries. John's revelations had filled in those gaps for him. The fact that Augustus had chosen life as a Warden, and ended up protecting John's ancestors, had a pleasing symmetry to it.

"It won't be easy," said Augustus. "Not being able to tell anyone what you really are, I mean."

John remembered the moment he agreed to take Ash's place in the time cage. "I'll leave the real magic to Evie. I don't think I have the temperament for it."

"Not tempted to visit the Between at all, then?"

Augustus knew him too well. "Tempted? Yes. Every day."

"You're a good man, John. The realms are safer now Ashtoreth is gone. But Pan is a dangerous enemy, and that's another reason to lie low. She must have her suspicions. A god has been defeated, and you're still here."

"She won't catch me out so easily again." It had been Pan, Glamoured to appear as Helen, who had convinced John to go to the cottage. When Augustus had told him, John had been reluctant to believe it. It was only after he had spoken to Helen that he accepted the truth. She was adamant she would never recommend cognitive behavioural therapy, or do anything so unprofessional as to give John mental health treatment.

"I should think not," said Augustus. "I would expect you to recognise Glamour from now on."

John looked at the headstone which showed his mother's name and nothing else. *Mae Frances Aviemore.* "All these generations," he said. "My mother, my grandmother, all the way back. You knew them all. How old are you exactly?"

Augustus smiled. "Isn't that supposed to be a rude question? I stopped counting after three hundred."

"You help keep the biggest secret in world history. And how do you conceal this secret? You open a magic shop."

"Hiding in plain sight is often the best way, John. And, besides, I love magic. The fake kind, I mean. From what you've said, you started me on that path."

"Yes, I probably did. You were completely fooled by a simple French drop."

Augustus put a hand on his arm. "No one can ever know."

"I didn't even do it very well. You were convinced I'd made a stone disappear."

"We must never speak of this again."

They both chuckled.

"Come on," said John, "let's visit Sarah before we go."

Sarah's grave had her date of birth and date of death as well as her name, but was otherwise as plain as John's mother's. John reached the grave first. When Augustus joined him, they stood in silence for a few minutes before John spoke.

"Ashtoreth nearly won, you know."

"Would you have done it? If Evie hadn't appeared? Would you have willingly imprisoned yourself for the rest of your life?"

John put his hands in his coat pockets. "Honestly? I don't know."

It was dark by the time the two of them made their way along the path that crossed the cemetery, and out to the street beyond. Augustus raised his hand, and a taxi came to a halt in front of him. John realised in all the time he had known Augustus, a taxi had always been there whenever he needed one. If you could use magic, may as well use it for something practical, he supposed.

"Come to the shop John," said Augustus as he slid into the back seat, his eyes twinkling. "There's something I want to show you." The twinkling eyes should have been another hint about Augustus Bonneville's true identity, along with the fact that that he looked like a pixie. He hadn't aged - he had already been ancient forty years earlier when John first met him. John wondered why he had never questioned any of this before. Then the taxi pulled away and headed into the centre of London.

John and Augustus were sitting in the back room at Bonneville's.

It would be Christmas soon, and the magic shop had been busy for weeks with parents buying magic sets. The majority of children receiving them would discover that making magic look real wasn't easy, and give up. But there were always a few who would find their imaginations fired by the effects in the brightly coloured box. Of those few, there would be one or two who wondered if the magic they loved might be a poor imitation of something real. Somewhere, might there be men and women like them who could summon genuine power, and make possible the impossible?

John thought of those few children now. He had been one of their number once, before accepting that magic was only a form of entertainment. He wondered what his younger self would have made of this scene in the tiny back room of the oldest magic shop in London, where a real magician and a mythical creature were drinking gunpowder tea and discussing fate.

Augustus's new favourite tea was even worse than the Lapsang Souchong John had endured last time. He managed a couple of polite sips, then let it go cold.

Harry and Evie had returned to America in mid-November, but the latest news, delivered via a video call from Evie the previous night, was that they were thinking of living in Britain. Evie's mother had agreed to let Harry have custody of their daughter, a decision from which he was still reeling. John detected Evie's hand in her mother's change of heart.

Augustus was scouring the bookshelves and muttering to himself.

"I know it's here somewhere. Hardly likely I would throw it away."

He pulled out a book that looked mediaeval, its cover tattered and faded, the pages within yellow and brittle. Pinching either end of the spine between finger and thumb, Augustus shook it until a folded piece of thick paper fell onto the table.

"Got it." Augustus unfolded the paper and slid it in front of John.

John looked at the paper. The handwriting was fine,

spidery, and so faded as to be almost illegible. It wasn't written in English. It reminded him of the first time he had seen the language of magic in his sanctum. This piece of paper made as little sense to him now as the first spell had done back then.

"I can't read this," said John. "What is it?"

Augustus smiled at his friend, took a notebook from a drawer, uncapped a fountain pen and wrote a few words. He pushed the notebook to John. The language was the same, as was the handwriting.

"What you told me about our time together in the Blurred Lands came as a shock, John. To live this long, yet have part of my life obscured by darkness has been difficult, especially when I have physical reminders of that forgotten time."

Augustus lifted his withered arm a few inches, which was as much as he could manage. "I remember nothing from when I was injured."

The old magician tapped the paper. "However, this survived our first meeting. It does not mention you by name, and it tells me nothing of our adventure together. It's more of a set of instructions. I carried them with me from that time on, but it was only after I became a Warden, choosing exile to protect your family, that I understood what they meant."

He chuckled, and John caught a brief glimpse of the young noone he had met near the time cage, only weeks ago in his own perception of time. Augustus refolded the paper and tucked it back between the pages of the old book.

"The instructions came about from a discussion we must have had. I obviously considered it important enough to write down. The concept it tries to convey made no sense until I had lived among humans. There is no equivalent in

Da Luanish. I believe the human word I was trying to express in my note was 'coincidence'."

John looked at his friend in surprise. "I talked to you about that," he said. "You said the concept was ridiculous, and you asked me for an example. I told you how Sarah and I met. You seemed to think it supported your own belief in fate. I disagreed. I'm sure we would have discussed it more, but circumstances intervened."

Augustus leaned back in his chair and closed his eyes. John had seen him do the same frequently. He was gathering his thoughts. An anecdote was forming.

Sure enough, after a minute or two during which his outrageous eyebrows descended almost to his cheeks, then twitched independently of each other, Augustus began.

"Whether this proves my belief or your own, I cannot say, but I will describe the morning when I carried out the acts detailed in the set of instructions left by my younger self. A city, a date, and a time were prescribed. I closed the shop for the day and set out. I had one stop to make along the way..."

FIFTY-ONE

LONDON 10:30 AM, 3RD JULY 1990

The small figure limped briskly along Waterloo Road. The pavements were busy, but, despite his diminutive stature, no one ever came close to bumping into him, swerving as if he were a lamppost or a telephone box.

It was sunny and warm, but the determined-looking man wore a three-piece suit and a hat. At the doorway of each building he passed, he paused and studied the number before moving on. Even when he stopped in the middle of the pavement, the crowds parted around him.

The figure stopped outside a glass door. He took a piece of paper from his breast pocket. After examining it and rechecking the number of the building, he stepped up and pressed a buzzer. A second later, he pushed on the door, and it swung inwards.

The tiny man, white hair spilling out from underneath his hat, looked at the lift, made a small sound of disgust, and climbed the stairs instead. His progress was swift, despite the fact that he was favouring one leg.

At the top floor of the building, he put his hand on the door, and sang. It was a short song, and would not have won any awards for its musicality, but that wasn't the point. When he had finished, the tiny man had become a tall woman in a flowery summer dress. The woman pushed open the door. Scanning the open-plan office, she made straight for the large window at the far end. When she reached the desk she was looking for, she placed a shopping bag on the chair, removing a terracotta pot. Holding the cactus in both hands, the woman placed it deliberately on the windowsill. It was only prevented from falling to the street outside by the half-open window it was leaning against.

Rubbing her hands in satisfaction, the woman walked out of the office, down the stairs, and out onto the street. A few minutes later, she smiled at a running man, sweaty and flustered, who was bumping into every third person with a flurry of apologies and waving hands. The woman made a small gesture, and the knot in the man's laces loosened.

"Go and get her, John," said the strange young woman, as she shrank, becoming a tiny, happy, old noone.

AUTHOR'S NOTE

Supernatural fantasy mythical multi-dimensional magic novels. If that's not an Amazon category yet, I reckon it should be. There are writers who look at the market, before putting fingers to keyboard, and craft a story aimed squarely at a specific niche. Then there's the other kind of writer, who writes a story they would love to read, and—when they finish—ask *what the hell* is *it?*

No prizes for guessing which kind I am.

I didn't intend to write this book. Not yet. In fact, I started writing a story that's been floating around my brain for over a year. Started it three times, abandoned it three times. For whatever reason, it wasn't ready. And, during that third attempt, a concept I came up with last year, of a place where two or more worlds overlapped, nagged at me. So I wrote The Blurred Lands instead.

Terry Pratchett said, "the first draft is just you telling yourself the story," and that's never been more true for me than it was with this book. It took twenty thousand words before I knew what was going on in that cottage, and why. I cut thirty thousand words from the first draft, because, for much of the opening of the story, I was writing to find out who these characters were, and what they wanted.

At the pre-editing stage, when it was still too long, I sent it to RR Haywood. I'd read his brilliant new book (better not say what it is, because it's not out yet and the title might change) and we chatted about that, as well as about the writer's life, dog-walking, and the difficulty in getting a decent cup of coffee. RRH emailed my draft back with suggestions, comments, and even a fantastic video (!) which cut through the crap and exposed the heart of the story. His input was invaluable. I would beg him to stop writing and be my editor, but I love his books too much.

While I'm thanking people - Phil Quaintrell was a great brainstorming partner, Mrs S and Phil Owens did sterling copy editing and proofreading work, and my select few early readers gave great feedback. Kid Mindfreak (that's Mr Mindfreak to you) came up with a superb cover. Thanks to all.

And now the dilemma. Do I write more stories set in this world? My world-building mind map for The Blurred Lands got bigger and bigger as I wrote. The Between, the seven realms, the remnants and elementals, the Three... so many stories to be told.

I'm going to ask you the question - especially if you're reading this before December 2019, during the first twelve months of publication.

Should I write more Blurred Lands novels? Or should I tell one of the other stories waiting in the notebooks next? Because I'm still not sure...

A word about reviews. For independent authors, reviews are the only way we can compete with books by big publishers. The more readers who review my books, the more Amazon will promote them, and the more likely it is I'll be able to continue writing them. There you go, a big dollop of emotional blackmail. You're welcome. Please review if you can, I really appreciate it.

Here's how you can get in touch:

You can email me - ianwsainsbury@gmail.com

My website is here (and it's brand spanking new as of November 2018, thanks to the brilliant Bodidog Design) https://www.ianwsainsbury.com/

I'm on twitter @IanWSainsbury

Facebook https://www.facebook.com/IanWSainsbury/

I have a mailing list. I email with book news, any promotions I'm running, and I always email when a new book is imminent. If you enjoy my work, please sign up here: http://bit.ly/signupiws

Mrs S is (rightly) insisting I take Christmas off, but I'll be back to the desk in January. Yes, I now make my living doing something that, if left to my own devices, I would do three hundred and sixty-five days a year. I'm a lucky bastard. I know it.

As always, the most important thank you is to you for reading my stories. Not only that but for spreading the word. I made a deal with my readers early on to keep writing if you kept reading. The deal still stands. Thank you for reading, and I can't wait to get cracking on another story for you.

Ian Sainsbury
Norwich
December 6th, 2018

ALSO BY IAN W. SAINSBURY

Children Of The Deterrent (Halfhero 1)
Halfheroes (Halfhero 2)
The Last Of The First (Halfhero 3)
The World Walker (The World Walker 1)
The Unmaking Engine (The World Walker 2)
The Seventeenth Year (The World Walker 3)
The Unnamed Way (The World Walker 4)

Printed in Great Britain
by Amazon